Dial Books
An imprint of Penguin Random House LLC
375 Hudson Street
New York, NY 10014

Printed in the United States of America

Library of Congress Cataloging-in-Publication Data

Names: Taylor, Jessica, date, author.
Title: A map for wrecked girls / by Jessica Taylor.
Description: New York, NY : Dial Books, [2017] | Summary: "Stranded on a
deserted island with a boy they barely know, sisters Emma and Henri have
to find a way to survive together, even after a betrayal back home ruined
their relationship"—Provided by publisher.
Identifiers: LCCN 2016056076| ISBN 9780735228115 (hardback) | ISBN
9780735228139 (epub)
Subjects: | CYAC: Castaways—Fiction. | Sisters—Fiction. |
Survival—Fiction. | Islands—Fiction. | Love—Fiction. | Caribbean
Area—Fiction.
Classification: LCC PZ7.1.T39 Map 2017 | DDC [Fic]—dc23 LC record
available at https://lccn.loc.gov/2016056076

1 3 5 7 9 10 8 6 4 2

Design by Mina Chung
Text set in Kepler

This is a   her
are the pr   any
resembl   es,

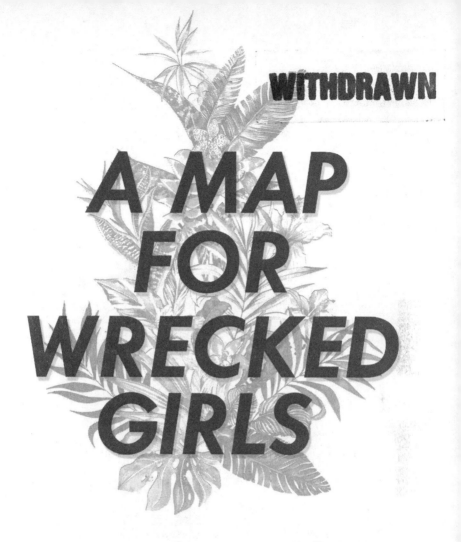

A MAP FOR WRECKED GIRLS

JESSICA TAYLOR

DIAL BOOKS

To all the wrecked girls,
lost in the messiest throes of love and friendship,
and searching for your way

CHAPTER 1

We sat at the edge of the ocean—my sister, Henri, and I—inches apart but not touching at all. The blue horizon was only beginning to swallow the sun and I was already shivering.

We'd been so sure someone would find us by now.

Alex was the first to say help would be coming soon, but I didn't quite believe him. When Henri said it, though—in that moment—I knew it had to be true.

Only months before, I'd trusted Henri more than I trusted myself. Wherever she told me to go, I'd follow. If she said something was true, then it had to be so. With nobody to save us in sight, I tied my hopes to the memory of Henri from before, the older sister with the best advice, the one who never started hating me.

"Rescue crews take time," I said now. My legs wobbled from the life raft bobbing in the ocean all day. I hugged my knees to my chest, forcing them still. "They probably don't even know we're missing yet."

A tear ran fast down Henri's cheek. She wiped it away and with it she took the last of my hope in her. For the first time, I was afraid we'd die on this shore.

Henri shot a glare down the far end of the beach, where Alex stood with his bare feet in the surf. He kept his back to us, like if we didn't see his face, we wouldn't know he was crying. Sobs wracked his shoulders.

"He's a real pillar of strength, Emma," Henri said. "Good job picking him out."

Even though Alex had put at least thirty feet between him and us, in some ways, my sister felt farther away.

The first time I saw Alex gliding down the resort's sidewalk on his rickshaw, arms tanned and legs muscled from seasons of pedaling through sand, I thought he looked strong enough to be my solution. He was broad-shouldered and shaggy-haired but not too pretty—exactly the kind of boy Henri loved to own. Now, as he turned to face the ocean, I felt like I was violating him by watching his tears fall so hard, he gulped at air and gasped for breath.

I wanted to make my way down the beach to comfort him, but I couldn't come up with anything meaningful to say.

Maybe there weren't enough words inside me to tell him, *I'm sorry Casey's dead. I'm sorry you dove down into the blue, blue water over and over again, grasping for a part of him— any part of him—and every single time, your hands came up empty.*

I wished I could say, *I held my breath every time you went under, because all I could think was that I couldn't lose you too.*

This was a secret. I'd only met Alex the day before.

Still, I dusted sand from my damp swimsuit bottoms now and left Henri behind.

The wavy ends of Alex's hair, black and still wet with ocean water, didn't brush his shoulders but sprung beside his ears. I pressed my palm against his bare back, warm, and the moment my skin touched his, he sucked in a breath.

"Are you okay?"

He wiped his eyes with his wrist and pushed back his hair, both hands gripping his head before falling at his sides. "No, Jones, I'm not. Fucking boat."

Alex never called me Emma. Only Jones. It felt sexier being called by my last name. An androgynous name like Henri's. Two days ago, nothing had ever made me feel sexy before. Now I couldn't feel anything but desperate.

"I'm not sure anyone's going to find us tonight. It could take"—I checked the ocean one more time, still empty, infinite, heartbreaking—"days."

"Weeks. Casey didn't tell anyone we were taking off. Nobody knew where we were going. It's a hell of an area to canvass."

Salt from the ocean had crystallized on his face, making the few brown freckles on his cheeks sparkle, the small bump on his nose more prominent. I wondered how he'd broken it. A surfboard, maybe. Or a fistfight. I wanted to know.

His green eyes flicked down the beach toward my sister. "No one would think Casey'd take off this far."

Alex wasn't blaming Henri. Not out loud, at least. But I

remembered her stroking up the inside of Casey's thigh as he stood at the wheel, saying things close to his ear. Things like: *Farther, Casey. Out in the middle of the very blue. I don't want to see land anymore. Take me far, far away.*

"I'm—I'm so sorry."

"You got nothing to be sorry about, Jones."

He was wrong. He didn't know he and his cousin, Casey, had tangled themselves in a web my sister and I couldn't stop weaving, and now, for poor Casey, there couldn't be any escape.

"But I do. For Henri. She . . ."

A shadow stretched onto the sand before us. We turned and Henri stood with her arms looped in the hollow of her back, her head eclipsing the setting sun. She was nearly naked in only her mint-green bikini.

We'd stripped down to the barest of our layers to let our clothes dry. Even though my shirt was sopping wet, when it came down to it, with Henri's eyes on me—and worst of all, Alex's—my fingertips froze at the hem of my shirt. Henri gave me a smug smile when I didn't take it off. As if me standing there in my boy-cut swimsuit bottoms and dolphin T-shirt made her the winner of a contest I refused to enter.

I was glad she interrupted. I'd almost admitted out loud that Henri hadn't said a word when Alex finally reached Casey and turned his ashen face to the sky. That Henri just swam for the life raft and never looked back when we saw Casey's forehead was split open to the bone, a thin trail of blood marbling the water.

Maybe Alex hadn't noticed—he was too busy struggling

to keep Casey's body from being swept under the waves.

Henri held her phone now and frowned, sinking her coral-painted pedicure deeper into the sand. "Well, my phone is trashed."

Our phones—mine was at the bottom of the ocean, but if Henri's survived, then— "Your phone," I said to Alex. "Did it make it?"

"It—it was on the deck." He tensed as I nodded to his back-pack. "This is Casey's—his was on the deck too."

Henri shook her phone and smacked it against her thigh. "Stupid thing won't even turn on."

"Don't." I took it from her, and with the front of my T-shirt, wiped away drops of water that had been trapped under her gold snakeskin case. "Wait till morning. Maybe it'll dry out by then."

"Morning." She sighed. "Okay. Are we going to figure out sleeping arrangements soon or would we rather stumble around in the dark?"

Alex faced the ocean. "Give me a sec."

He was looking for something. Rescue or Casey, I didn't know which. Only that neither would appear any time soon.

"Alex." My hands circled his arm and squeezed above his elbow. "It wasn't your fault."

He shrugged me off and sprung away. "What did you say to me?"

"I said it wasn't your fault."

"Of course it wasn't my fault." He grabbed his clothes off the rocks and yanked the shirt onto his shoulders. Leaving it unbuttoned, he turned to me. "Why the hell would you even say that?"

I opened my mouth to tell him I didn't know, that it was just something people said, but Henri pulled me away and led me back to our end of the beach.

As the sky went from blue to gray, the ocean got choppier and the tide washed debris to our shore. Some items we recognized, some we didn't. A piece of scrap wood here, an empty Coke can there. Nothing that mattered.

The shock lifted and I knew we had to do something to get through the night. My toes squished in the wet sand as I stood. "It's getting dark."

Motionless, Alex watched from down the beach as Henri helped me carry the life raft up the rocky shore. The coarse sand under my feet was nothing like the white sand we'd lounged on for the last three days in Puerto Rico. We wedged the raft between two dry, grassy shrubs, steps from the palm trees dotting the top of the beach and far from the waterline.

Our eyes met, Alex's and mine. We held the stare until something registered in him and he set his body into motion. He fished an old tarp from the surf and shook out the water before he tossed it over the top of the waist-high shrubs. The thin layer of plastic gave me a sense of protection I pretended wasn't fake.

My sister draped herself across the raft first. She stretched her arms over her head as if sinking into the down mattress at the hotel, not inflated orange plastic. As if she didn't care Casey died today. As if we weren't lost.

I waved Alex over, and with my hip, nudged Henri closer to the edge.

"No." He dropped to the sand a few yards away. "You two take it. I'm fine down here."

"Come on. There's plenty of room."

"No," Henri said. "There isn't."

"But you won't be comfortable." I looked from Henri to Alex. "You'll—"

"Jones, stop." The way he said it, all raspy and soft, made me seal my lips. "I've slept in worse places than this."

Before I could say anything, Alex lifted up again from the sand and moved toward the beach. At the water's edge, he dropped to his knees and hugged Casey's backpack to his chest.

"I'm worried about him," I said.

Henri made a face in the moonlight and closed her eyes. "Worry about yourself, Em. Survival of the fittest."

I watched her for the slightest bit of regret before I lost it. "Casey *died* today. Alex's cousin is never coming back. What part of that don't you understand?"

She opened her eyes, but didn't look at me. "Whatever, Emma."

I sighed. My white jacket, scratchy with salt water, was mostly dry, so I bunched it under my head. But the harder I tried to sleep, the more my body ached and swayed with the motion of the waves, my thoughts spinning even though we were now still.

Our mom wouldn't even know we were lost. She would've

come back to our hotel room on Luquillo Beach at the end of her work day, a couple hours ago, and realized we weren't there. She wouldn't worry at first. She always said teenage girls were wild at heart and the only way to make them wilder was to try to cage them.

When we weren't there the next morning, that's when she would call the local police. She'd never make the connection we were on Casey's boat, but someone would notice how it never returned to its slip. Even if they didn't know they were looking for us, someone had to be looking for Casey.

Either way, Mom would be broken. Within the year, she'd lost Dad and now us.

I crossed my arms, and giving her a few inches of space, curled my body in the shape of Henri's. To myself, I said the words I couldn't say aloud. Something I had to say, in case her subconscious might hear and somehow dissolve the barriers between us. *Come back to me, Henri.*

A tear sliced my cheek—the overcast sky and Henri's SPF 8 hadn't protected me from sunburn as much as I'd hoped—and my chest shook from trying to hold it all in.

This trip was supposed to fix everything.

"Em." Henri rolled over to face me. "Please don't cry." Her touch was soft as she pushed a wispy curl from my eyes. "You'll just get dehydrated faster."

The back of Henri's wrist grazed my knee. In the moonlight, her open palm waited. I slipped my hand into hers and managed a small smile.

The abysmal loneliness that had consumed me for months, I felt it ebbing away.

Maybe everything *was* fixed now. Just not in the way I'd planned.

As my eyes closed on their own and my aching limbs relaxed, Henri's voice startled me awake. "This doesn't mean I forgive you. So we're clear."

CHAPTER 2

The Saturday before school started was always an event to Henri Jones—it was the last party of summer. My sister loved summers of kegs and fireworks, romance and flings.

She sat cross-legged on the floor of her bedroom in front of her mirrored closet doors. Her short dress hiked high on her thighs as she spread a sea of cosmetics on the carpet around her.

She ran a streak of foundation under each eye, highlighter down the bridge of her nose, and bronzer beneath each cheekbone—a layer of armor before battle. Because that's what these parties were to her, a war on all the heartbreaking boys in the San Francisco Bay Area.

I stretched across her bed on my stomach as Henri blended the whole thing together. I could have watched her apply makeup for hours. Holding my chin in my hands, I waited for something I could confirm as an invitation to the party. It wasn't so much that I wanted to go, but I wanted to spend Saturday night with Henri.

She rimmed each of her eyes in royal-blue liner and met my stare in her mirror. "Andy asked me about you today."

"What did he want to know?"

"We were hanging out in the Haight, me and him and Ari and Mick—you know Mick, he's got those gorgeous blond dreadlocks—and Andy asked if I'd mind if he took you out sometime."

I rolled onto my back and stared up at her spinning ceiling fan. "I hope you told him there was no way in hell I'd go."

She bit her smiling lips, the way she always did when I slipped in a word like *hell,* and recapped her eyeliner pencil. "What do you think I said?" Knowing Henri, she could have told him anything. "Well, of course I told him you've been dying to get a piece of him forever."

"You didn't!" I sent a throw pillow sailing at her head. Henri ducked and the pillow thudded against the closet doors.

"Of course not. I told him not in a million years did I think you'd say yes." She added another coat of mascara and glanced back at me. "Pass me my purse, will you?"

The top drawer of her dresser was open a crack, enough for me to see what was hidden between her silky thongs and see-through bras: a package of birth control pills.

Henri never had to tell me she was having sex. But I knew.

I'd watched her at a pool party last weekend. With a beach towel wrapped neatly around the waist of my one-piece, I sat in the shade while Henri lounged on the first step of the pool. My wild blond curls were piled on top of my head in a bun she'd styled for me that looked more like an old lady's beehive.

I kind of loved it. In sixty or seventy years, we'd both wear our hair that way every day.

Jake Holt's hand stroked through her silky hair, from root to tip, never once snagging on a tangle or a split end. She curled into Jake, arched her fully inflated breasts against his chest. That was when I knew any semi-state of her virginity was a thing of the past.

I was fifteen, my sister, Henri, sixteen, and I didn't know what could happen in that one year between our ages, but I was just as worried it would happen to me as I was worried it wouldn't.

"Girls!" our mother called up the staircase. "I left some files at the office, so I'm running back downtown for a few hours. The pizza will be here in twenty."

Our mother had been busy keeping up with her work schedule and playing the new role of single mother. Too busy to know Henri spent the weekends with her arms and legs hanging out the windows of moving cars and her lips pressed against the mouths of whatever boy had snagged her attention for the night.

And she didn't know Henri always brought me along to the parties, a silent witness.

My sister didn't acknowledge her, so I said, "Thanks, Mom."

Keys jangled as Mom hesitated. "Oh, and, um, if something happens and you don't feel comfortable driving, I'll have my cell. Henri?"

"You've got it," Henri said. "If anyone at all drinks and drives, you'll be the first to know."

"Henrietta Jones. I mean it!"

Henri cranked up the music after Mom backed down the drive. Within the chaotic walls of my sister's bedroom, there were only two volumes to music: loud and louder.

Laughing, she shouted, "Prepare yourself, Em. This is the year I bring you to the dark side."

She pulled me onto the bed, and never releasing my hands from hers, we half danced, half jumped to a Red Hearts song that vibrated inside my rib cage.

We collapsed on the bed, a jumble of limbs and blankets as the song ended. Christmas tree lights twinkled around us—she'd strung them up three years ago and couldn't bear to take them down. I could have stayed in our own little world forever.

But Henri's attention went elsewhere.

"Who's that?" She untangled her limbs from mine and went to her bay window. I crawled off the bed and stared down below.

A boy unloaded suitcases into the Morenos' driveway. He was tall and lanky, his face shielded by the brim of his orange Giants baseball hat. He looked up to the window Henri and I were leaning out and waved.

Henri pressed closer to the window and, with one hand on her hip, waved back.

The textured wall scraped my back as I slid to the floor and out of his sight. "That's Jesse."

She slipped down to my side. "That's Jesse? Are you sure?"

"I'm sure." Jesse's dad, Eric Moreno, had the same white toothy smile, the same golden complexion. Plastered across billboards around the Bay Area, advertising for his sports recap show on the Latino channel, Eric Moreno's smile was everywhere. I'd seen his face almost daily in the ads on the BART train to school.

Henri crossed her arms and tapped a finger against the smile she was trying to suppress. "You obviously think the years have been kind."

"Year. Only a year."

It had been a year, almost exactly, since Jesse went to live with his mom in Seattle. Rumor at the last block party was that his mom got engaged to a guy with his own pack of kids, so Jesse was moving back in with his dad. Next door again.

Henri pressed our heads together and said in her sexiest noir voice, "Maybe he's been pining for you ever since he left."

I'd always told Henri everything. There weren't many secrets I dared to keep from my sister, from my best friend, except for two. First: I wasn't the Jones sister Jesse had been head over heels for. And second: I really did want him for my very own.

"He's like our brother," I said. "Gross."

Something stopped me from telling her the truth, and I don't know why because me liking Jesse—any warm-bodied boy at all—*that* was something my sister would understand.

Henri had enough making out stories for both of us Jones girls combined. In new cars or BART cars or trolley cars, under historic bridges or rusted-out canopies, inside tents or outside in the rain, Henri had done it all.

She surveyed her appearance in the mirror one last time

and applied a thick ring of red lipstick. "You *are* going to start getting ready soon, aren't you?"

Music pulsated from the white two-story Queen Anne–style house at the end of Balzac Drive as Henri searched for a parking spot.

I'd never been inside before, but I knew the place was Ari Deveroux's. I'd ridden with our mom once or twice when she picked up Henri after a sleepover. Ari was all at once Henri's best friend and greatest enemy.

Henri double-parked Dad's old sedan outside Ari's, blocking two cars in the driveway.

"Really?"

"What? My heels are high," she said. "You wouldn't want me to get blisters, would you?"

"Is Jake going to be here tonight?" I asked as Henri checked her reflection in the rearview mirror.

"Who cares?"

"I thought you were into him."

She flipped the emergency brake on the steep Nob Hill street and flung open her door. "I think he's screwing around with Ari. Good riddance."

Jake Holt had been Henri's weak spot for months. He'd been the only guy who wasn't chasing her, and that blew away her idea of her world. I hated how Henri couldn't be honest that he'd hurt her, even with me.

Henri shouldered through the stream of boys spilling onto the wraparound porch as I followed her up the twisted walkway. She wore a gold top with straps the width of angel hair pasta. It dipped low beneath her scapula and draped there, revealing every bit of her back if the fabric moved just so. You had to look twice to make sure the gold shimmer wasn't hand-painted onto her body.

On her right wrist hung a gold men's watch with a too-big strap that slipped down her forearm with every lift of her hand. It was eye-catching, and so obviously on purpose. To anyone else, it was a fashion statement, but I recognized the watch as our dad's. One of the many things he left behind when he moved out last July.

Henri said Coco Chanel's fashion philosophy was to take off one accessory before you left the house. Henri Jones's philosophy was to add something—something spectacular.

I had borrowed a black cropped leather jacket from Henri. That was my statement piece for the night.

We'd barely graced the threshold when Henri caught Aaron Moser in her net.

Every other party before, Henri would turn to me before she took off with someone and mouth, *Are you okay?* It didn't matter if I was or I wasn't, I always nodded.

That night, with Aaron slipping his hand into her back jeans pocket, she walked on without a single look.

The party wasn't all seniors. There were juniors—my class—there too, but everyone's conversations seemed so solid, so involved, I didn't want to interrupt.

In the dining room, I found a punch bowl with stacks of red Solo cups and filled a cup to the brim.

Someone hovered beside me. "You realize it's spiked. Does Henri let you drink now?"

Without turning, I knew that voice was Jesse's.

The alcohol smelled strong. Watching myself in the mirror above Ari's parents' sideboard, I lifted it to my lips. And I lied. "Henri's not the boss of me." I took a small sip. "How's your mom?"

"Getting married—some prick who wears a fanny pack. I didn't think she needed me much anymore." He dipped a glass of punch for himself. He'd always had these thick eyebrows, and over the last year, the rest of his face had grown into them because somehow they now worked.

When Jesse left, I wasn't that sad because it would be no time before I saw him again for Christmas and spring break. But our parents decided to take us to visit our grandparents in Maine for the week of Christmas vacation, and when spring rolled around, we noticed his dad packing up his SUV. He rented a cabin near Yosemite for the week.

So a whole year went by without seeing Jesse, and over the year that feeling in my chest had started to fade away. Now it spread through me with an intensity that reached my fingers and toes.

"What's been going on with you, Em?"

"Nothing." My reflection swam in the mirror—I should have said something sexy and interesting.

"So your dad moved out, huh? I'm sorry. Really sorry."

"Yeah, last July. We didn't have any idea. About that lady, I mean." We also didn't know we weren't making him happy anymore, our house wasn't good enough, and a loft in the city was the kind of home he was after.

Now our father lived in a world where we didn't belong, with a needy girlfriend who didn't look much older than Henri, a saltwater pool in need of daily skimming, and a flashy Porsche that needed to be raced around the roads of wine country.

Fortunately, we didn't need him either—that's what Henri said.

"How'd you hear?"

"My dad told me when I got back. Your dad's car wasn't in the driveway for a couple days and . . ."

"And what?"

"I sort of asked."

"Why would you ask because my dad's car wasn't there?" I stared at him, into his brown eyes as if they hid the answer. "You knew something, didn't you?"

"People talk." Some of his drink sloshed from his cup onto Ari Deveroux's Oriental rug as he shrugged. He gaped at the punch pooling on the surface of the carpet.

I rubbed my shoe against the stain until it absorbed. "Don't tell Henri any of this."

He nodded. He knew us well enough, I guess, because he didn't ask why.

"So . . ." I didn't know what I was going to say next, but I had to change the subject. "You haven't invited me over for fort building yet. I'm kind of hurt. We used to make some masterful creations with a few sheets and a couple of chairs."

"Oh, man." He smiled into his cup. "I forgot all about our forts, and I forgot how funny you are."

Funny. I was funny. I had his attention, and now I wasn't sure what to do with it.

"I missed you a lot." I lifted my punch and gulped.

"I missed you too." His eyes sparkled—they were focused on me. And then they drifted across the room. "Henri came with you, didn't she?"

He stepped out of the dining room and through the stairway before I could answer. I stayed close to his back as he searched through the house. We passed by Aaron Moser, who Henri had now abandoned, and Jake Holt, at the dark end of the hallway with his thumbs hooked in the belt loops of Ari's jeans.

Like always, Jesse was following Henri, I was following him, and nobody was following me.

Jesse slowed, and before I even saw my sister, I knew he'd found her.

She sat on Ari's parents' snow-white couch in the back of the formal living room, her legs draped over the lap of a guy with a snake tattoo winding up his arm.

While Jesse kept moving, I hung back. He approached and bumped his knee on the coffee table. His lips moved—I couldn't hear what they were saying—and with her hazy half-drunk eyes, Henri glanced up at him. She barely even smiled. The boy said something into her ear and snickered. Henri curled closer to him, and as she laughed, her hair tumbled down her back.

Jesse turned red and strode out the sliding glass door to the wraparound porch. He didn't even cut his eyes my way as I set my cup on the railing beside his hand.

"Nothing's changed," he said.

"What do you mean?"

His throat made a funny sound when he started to speak. "I guess Henri's still trying to destroy herself."

I wondered what chapter of the past he was thinking about.

The childhood we'd shared was full of twisted Jesse-and-Henri memories. The stranger who prowled the wire fence by the jungle gym, the stranger our moms tried to get banned from the playground—Henri loved to rile Jesse up by asking the guy his name. The field trip to the water park when the teachers made Jesse and Henri buddies and she'd disappeared—he'd thrown up his lunch worrying she'd drowned. The time he'd carried her to the nurse's office when she'd fallen from the swing set after accepting a dare from the boys to climb to the very top.

I never thought about Jesse as someone who should have been mine until I saw the way he loved Henri. I wanted to be loved like that, and Henri could never love him back. So it was the perfect solution: Jesse would belong to me.

We would exist in a state of romantic bliss, and because I loved my sister so much, I could live with the fact that he loved her too.

CHAPTER 3

With my cheek glued to the plastic life raft, I opened my eyes to the daylight and reached for Henri. But in the space beside me, there weren't any slim long limbs, no straight blond hair, no biting words waiting for me on the tip of her tongue.

Henri was gone.

I scrambled upright and squinted at the bright sun hitting the sand. On the beach below, I found her. Henri lounged by the ocean with her hair blowing in the breeze, like she was posing for some kind of swimsuit edition.

The life raft's seams stung my thighs as I shifted. I'd been so focused on finding her, setting one thing right in my upside-down world, I didn't even realize my skin was on fire. My already-sunburned arms and legs had totally baked as the sun rose up the other end of the beach.

Wrenching the raft, I freed it from the bushes and dragged it under the shade of the least-sparse palm tree at the top of the sand. Behind the scatters of palms, a jungle of bamboo grew dense and dark.

"I'd move farther in."

Alex stepped from the shadows and watched the surf as he buttoned his shirt.

"Why?" I wheezed. My throat was so dry.

"The sand—it's like a mirror. You'll still get the reflection of the sun." He bent down close to my sunburned arms.

"I guess I slept through that part of *Lost and Alone*."

He laughed, paused, and looked up at me with a weird expression, green eyes flecked with dark brown and yellow. His tan had kept him from burning like I had, but up close, the freckles on his cheeks had darkened.

He stood. "You're fried, Jones. I know it's hot, but you gotta cover yourself up today."

My burn stung as I slipped on my white jacket. "It's fine. It doesn't hurt."

With the back of his hand, he rubbed his eyes, still swollen from crying.

"How, um, how are you today?" I asked.

He straightened his shoulders. "I'll be a hell of a lot better when I get us off this island." He said it with so much certainty. Maybe he was trying to convince me, or maybe he was trying to convince himself. Either way, I appreciated the effort.

He glanced back my way, and his voice went husky. "But thanks for asking."

"Sure."

Alex lifted his chin toward the beach, where Henri'd parked herself in the sand. "And maybe you should talk to Malibu Barbie about staying out of the sun. I tried."

To only myself, I said, "She won't listen."

❖❖❖

The three of us collected driftwood and spelled out *SOS* along the shore. Even though our throats were raw and our empty stomachs in knots, we made that *SOS* first. As simple as it was, it was something. Help would come, and if they didn't see signs of life, they might not hover for long.

With our signal done, we needed water.

Last semester, I'd had the flu so bad, it'd kept me home from school for a week. Fever made me too lazy to find the remote. By the time Henri got home, dug the remote out of the couch cushions, and flipped to Cinemax, I'd caught a six-hour marathon of *Lost and Alone* on the Discovery Channel.

I remembered almost nothing. Except the rule of threes: *Three hours without warmth. Three weeks without food. Three days without water.*

That's how long the human body could survive.

Words shredded my throat as I told Henri and Alex, "We have to find water."

Alex nodded. Henri had spread out on the sand—this time on her stomach—and resumed her impression of driftwood. A sigh escaped her lips. "Someone's coming soon, Em. Do you really want to drink some questionable water before they get here?"

"We don't know when they're coming. It could be weeks, and without water, we'll be dead by then."

"Hey." Alex caught my elbow. "Nobody else is dying."

I looked down at where his fingers curled around my arm.

I liked Alex's hands. Jesse's were as smooth as Henri's. Alex's—they told stories. Of hammering nails into the boats, tugging on taut fishing lines, and shoving off surfboards to ride mile-high waves that carried him right back to where he began.

He cleared his throat and let his hand drop. Then turned to Henri. "Any luck with the phone? Or am I being too tragically optimistic?"

"Still broke," Henri said without opening her eyes.

"Maybe we could bury it in the sand to dry it out," I said. "Like how you can use rice—"

She pushed up onto her elbows. "If we had rice, I'd eat it. I'm starving."

My last meal was wearing thin too—a big stack of banana pancakes with coconut syrup, a freshly sliced papaya drizzled with honey, and a glass of pineapple juice. All at breakfast the morning before. Henri must have been starving. She'd only gotten half a grapefruit, two cups of black coffee, and a waiter's number.

Alex took the phone from Henri and looked it over before handing it back. "Even if it came on, the reception out here would be shit. You're probably not really that hungry, just dehydrated."

"Where are we?" I whispered to myself.

But Alex answered. "An island. There's over a hundred out here. Part of the British Virgin Islands or Puerto Rico. We drifted a lot. I don't know which one."

"But someone will find us?"

He gave me a weak smile. "I'll see what's out there and search for a water source. If there's one to find."

The way Alex walked, like he could leave his body behind

24

if he moved fast enough, made me decide not to follow.

Just before he disappeared around the cliff at the end of the beach, he hoisted Casey's backpack a little higher. It was suddenly strange he'd had the presence of mind to grab it when the accident happened.

The memory hit me like a tidal wave, and I remembered what happened after the explosion, when the boat flooded with water.

Alex's and Casey's feet pounding against the hollow deck, their hands fumbling for the life raft. Me scrambling to find the life vests. Casey saying no, he didn't need one. Throwing one to Henri and one to Alex. We didn't have time to put them on.

A second explosion, and nothing but blue, blue water. The kind of blue that mesmerizes before it swallows you whole.

Alex and I were thrown free from the boat before the ocean started to suck the hull under. We came up from underneath a wall of water and into the light, sputtering salt water.

I couldn't see my sister anymore.

Through the tossing waves, I barreled toward where Henri disappeared. My hands drove down, down, down, and just when I lost hope, her fingers wrapped around mine. And Alex, he was freeing Casey's backpack from the wreckage, slinging it over his shoulder before pulling up Casey, struggling to hold on to him, only to have the waves knock them apart again, for good this time. It didn't matter—Casey's eyes were already glazed over and unblinking against the gray sky.

I don't know how Henri could think straight, but seeing the

way Alex went for the backpack like it was a lifeline made my sister splash across the surface and go for hers too.

Now I moved past Henri, toward the ocean until cool waves lapped between my toes. Seaweed stink drifted up from the rushing and receding water. There wasn't much to do, but I could make a mental map of the area around us.

Miles and miles of blue water stretched out before me. The sun had come up on the right side of the beach, and the day before, it set past the other faraway end. We were facing north—we had to be. Somehow knowing my directions mattered.

I turned to my left, the sandy beach curved until it disappeared into a formation of rocks that jutted out into the water. To my right, where Alex had disappeared, a tall cliff stretched toward the clouds. The tide rolled out, leaving a narrow path of sand before it crashed against the base of the cliff.

With my back to the water, I faced the jungle. Scattered along the top of our beach—it had already become *ours* to me—were flimsy palm trees, and behind them, the sand ended with a thick cluster of bamboo and trees that twisted together in a darkened hush. Somewhere in it, there had to be water.

"Em, what are you doing?"

"Trying to . . ." My throat was too raw to yell. I walked closer and finger-combed the tangles out of my hair as I dropped beside her. Our hair was almost the same color, mine a little more like honey and hers closer to sun-bleached wheat, but Henri's silky strands still looked blowout fresh.

She draped an arm around my shoulders, and for a few

heartbeats, I couldn't worry about being lost, only that she would move away from me again.

I'd never told anyone the future I imagined for my sister and me, dreams that had been part of me as far back as I could remember, so long they'd grown roots and wings. Most girls wanted something different; they wanted to be wives and mothers and architects and Supreme Court justices, but I dreamed of my sister and me as little old ladies living together in a huge, dilapidated house by the ocean. We would spend the beginning of our lives having great romantic adventures. My husband would die before me—because men almost always do—and Henri's lover would perish in some old-fashioned way. He'd get lost at sea or die of Spanish influenza or something. *Lost at sea.* Maybe the damage I'd done had twisted our futures.

Plantation shutters with white, peeling paint would cover all the windows, and we'd leave them open, even while the rain and wind came in and tossed our threadbare curtains against the walls. The wood floors would be pitted from long-ago high-heel marks, but they'd still be perfect for dancing. And that's what Henri and I would do—start dancing at midnight. We wouldn't stop until the rising sun bathed our washed-out wallpaper and our crinkled skin in the light.

When our lives were nearly done, we'd only have each other and all the things Henri and I had talked about—scraggly cats and faded curtains and missing marbles.

"We've been gone for almost twenty-four hours," I said. "I wonder what Mom thinks happened to us."

"She probably thinks we've been sold to a brothel or something. Blondes—they'd pay top dollar for us."

"Not funny."

"It wasn't a joke." Henri trailed a finger through the sand. "You've got to stop worrying. Help will come."

My stomach rumbled. "I'm so, so hungry."

"Shh," she whispered. "Think about something else."

"Like what?" Everywhere my thoughts ran took me to scarier places—the explosion, the hull of the boat shattering, the dropping and drifting farther out on the waves, no food, no water, just an orange speck on all that infinite blue—but they always landed me back on this beach where we would slowly die of either dehydration or exposure. No time for starvation. "Like what?" I repeated.

She lifted her chin to the clumps of branches overhead where some island birds rustled between papery leaves. "Think about last summer when we went to Six Flags."

The day itself, it was perfect, even if those few hours were the beginning of the end.

Our father took us to Six Flags, only Henri and me. We rode the rides until we were dizzy and ate a dinner of funnel cakes and cotton candy. Three weeks later, he confessed the affair to our mom and moved out of our house. He'd never taken us many places before, and Henri said later that guilt made him do it.

That was our last good memory of our dad, the last time we looked at him as a man we could trust, someone planted in our world to actually care about our happiness. Maybe he didn't know that's who he was supposed to be. Or maybe he just didn't care.

All along, throughout the packing of things and the filing of papers, Henri had been by my side.

I hated myself for what I'd done to her.

"Henri, you know how much I love you, don't you?"

She pulled away and propped her backpack under her head like a pillow. Her lips twisted into a smile. A cruel smile that had once been reserved for everyone but me. "I thought you did."

I stood and faced away from her, so she couldn't see the way a few of her well-timed words could damage me. "This place is too green to not grow anything we can eat. I'll be back."

I made it back to the beach after at least an hour of searching the looser-spaced trees at the outskirts of the jungle, but Henri and Alex weren't there. As I walked to the ocean's edge, Henri strode through the sand from the eastern end.

"What's down that way?"

"Pineapples, coconuts, and waterfalls," she said. "Come on. What do you think, Em?"

Even if her attitude was the same, I was relieved she was trying.

Alex moved into sight at the cliff side of the beach hours and hours later. I'd begun to worry. Our eyes connected, but he only shook his head.

No water.

The sun had moved up the beach, relentless, and Henri and I huddled in the shade of a palm tree while Alex wandered around the waterline, staring past the cliffs, a place where the limitless sea bled into the horizon, like he could will a coast guard into existence if he imagined it hard enough.

I left Henri alone and followed the impressions of Alex's feet in the sand.

My shadow stretched toward the cliffs, so even though he never turned, he had to know I was there.

"You were the one who said we should stay out of the sun."

"Maybe I don't want to do what's good for me, Jones."

I took a small step closer. "What's out there? Anything?"

"No power lines. No signs of life. Nothing." He gripped both hands behind his neck, and as his hair fell back down, I noticed he'd left faint red fingerprints. "Go sit with your sister."

I stared at his back, lifted my hand—he didn't turn—and let it fall. The sun scorched the back of my calves on my way back to Henri.

She perched herself on the edge of our raft, her arms squeezing her torso as she shuddered against a breeze I couldn't feel.

"Let's go through your stuff again," I told her. "See if we missed anything."

In the big pocket, there was a sweatshirt, a bikini, the almost-empty bottle of sunscreen, a pair of shorts, a travel sewing kit, and a bottle of Evian that had made my heart explode in my throat—until I'd seen it was empty. And this time, at the very bottom, wedged under the folded seam of the bag: a smashed granola bar.

"Alex! Come over here!"

He jogged through the sand and dropped Casey's backpack onto the driftwood.

I tore the wrapper and divided the bar into three pieces. We shoveled them into our mouths and licked our fingers long after we'd sucked away the last melted chocolate chips.

The wind had whipped all the texture out of Alex's dark hair, so it looked soft and flyaway. He sank his weight into the side of the orange life raft and held a rubber band in his mouth, reaching behind his head and tying his hair into a ponytail.

He rolled his shoulders, winced, and flexed his legs. They were tanned dark and even, all the way from his quads to his long, narrow feet.

His shoes hadn't made it—it hadn't occurred to me until then.

If he'd been in the jungle barefoot, the only place we were likely to find fresh water, his feet would have been destroyed.

"Alex, where did you look for water? Did you just stay on the beach?"

He held up a foot and wiggled his toes. "Can't go into the jungle without shoes, Jones. If I'd stepped on a poisonous snake or whatever, I'd be dead by now."

He eyed my canvas slip-ons and I crossed one foot in front of the other, suddenly relieved and embarrassed my shoes had survived.

"If you couldn't go, you should have let *us*," I said, surprised at the edge in my voice. "We won't survive two more days without water. And now it's too late to search. It'll be dark."

With his chin in his hand, he just looked at me, not saying anything.

Henri's words came back to me. *He's a real pillar of strength, Emma.* And I hated them.

Henri unzipped the front pocket of her backpack, where she had our trip itinerary, her passport, a TSA-approved-size bottle of hand sanitizer, and a pen with the name *Luquillo Beach Resort*—our hotel in Puerto Rico. "Not much we can use here."

She flashed a ziplock bag full of tampons. They were still dry. Henri'd counted out her cycle the month before and she'd been complaining for weeks about the unfairness of PMS in the middle of her beach vacation.

"Except those." I turned to Alex. "What do you have?"

He slid the backpack against his thigh before his hand disappeared into the cargo pocket of his shorts. "Just this." In his outstretched hand was a small pocketknife.

Henri perked up. "So we can slit our wrists?"

Alex's eyes drifted over the surf. "Maybe."

It disturbed me, not so much that Henri joked about it, but that Alex didn't.

"Casey could have had some food too," I said.

Alex tightened his arm around the backpack. "No. There's nothing."

"Should we look?"

A side of his mouth turned up—almost a smile. "Look, Jones, I already checked. Twice. It's only extra clothes and shit. Nothing we can use."

"But maybe—"

"I fucking looked! Okay?"

"Okay. Okay."

"Don't— Just . . . I'm sorry." The whites of his eyes flushed a bright red that only comes from holding back tears, and his irises went a luminous green in contrast.

He got up and walked off between the trees and toward the cliff at the end of the beach.

Henri wiped the surprise off her face and shrugged, as if every harsh word Alex dished out was something I deserved. "Your friend's being an asshole, isn't he?"

"His cousin died," I said. "We're all freaked out."

But Henri was relentless. "Acting like you're the one who did something wrong. Oh, what's the word my therapist uses? *Projecting.*"

She hated therapy and loved to remind me I was the reason she was in it.

"Henri. Help's not coming soon. I hope you know that now."

What I was trying to say was that we were going to have to survive on this island—physically, emotionally—for a while, at least. I needed the old Henri back. We both did.

She pretended not to hear me.

CHAPTER 4

H enri clung to the safety pole in her school uniform and watched the tunnel walls whirring past as we rode BART to school that Monday. This was the first day of her senior year, and whatever emotion she hid beneath her mask of makeup, it wasn't excitement.

If I closed my eyes while the train was soaring under the city, I could almost hear San Francisco moving on above me, and I wondered how I'd make this trip a year later all alone.

At school, we stopped in the B Wing bathroom and Henri gave her navy skirt a roll at the waist, exposing a forbidden extra inch of thigh that was nowhere near as scandalous as half her weekend closet.

Henri hated Baird's uniforms almost as much as our dad hated Baird's tuition. It occurred to me for the first time, I didn't know if he'd keep paying it. The law made us his responsibility until we were eighteen, but a private school like Baird would never count as a necessity.

"Hey, Henri, do you know if Dad's still paying for school?"

Her hands stilled, but only for a second before she went back to tucking in her white button-down. "Fuck him if he won't. We'll go to public."

She knocked her hip into the bathroom door, letting the screech of shoes in the hallway bleed into the bathroom. I moved to follow her outside but she paused and fluffed my hair with her hands. "For body."

Before I could check my reflection, Henri laced her fingers with mine and tugged me into the hall. "Don't worry," she whispered as uniformed bodies moved around us. "This was the summer you got hot."

I didn't believe her.

I was short but sturdy with a stubborn jaw and a long neck, and it wasn't like I had a bad body, but I wasn't Henri. And it wasn't like I didn't have boobs. I mean, they were there. They just didn't brag about their thereness the way Henri's did.

The warning bell rang and we squeezed through the double doors to the MPR, which smelled like a combination of basketball rubber, Axe body spray, and cheap pizza.

Assemblies were always held in the MPR—the multipurpose room. Periods two through four, that's where they taught freshman/sophomore PE. At lunch, they rolled out some tables and called it the cafeteria. For five and six, juniors and seniors exerted the minimum amount of energy required to pass PE.

Henri didn't release my hand as she elbowed us through the crowd, not even when we got in the *H–N* line to retrieve our schedules.

Mrs. Petrakis, the sometimes attendance lady, sometimes school nurse, sat hunched over a file box on the folding table. "Name?"

"Jones," my sister said. "Henrietta and Emmalyn."

Mrs. Petrakis assessed Henri over the top of her bifocals and nodded to me. "You mute or something? Which one are you?"

I shook my hand free from Henri's. "I'm Emma."

There wasn't a good reason for me letting Henri lead me around, only that she was willing and when I felt like I was drowning in high school, having a sister like Henri was a necessary breath of air.

Henri smiled at Mrs. Petrakis and, oozing sarcasm, said, "Have a blessed day."

She collected our schedules and handed me the one with my name: *Emmalyn Jones.*

My mother didn't want to saddle us with names bigger than we were, but our father insisted we have family names. So I was Emmalyn and Henri was Henrietta. We were named after two great-aunts of our dad's who owned a house together in Maine, where my dad used to spend every summer when he was a kid. Someone might have thought Henri got the worse deal with a name like Henrietta. Anyone who thought that didn't know my sister at all.

Beautiful but not too girly, sexy but not too slutty, she was everything every girl at our school aspired to be.

Henri said our names were fitting because we were destined to be together in our old age, like our great-great-aunts.

Two gray old ladies in the bodies of teenage girls. Someday we'd live in a big house with faded curtains, a dozen or so cats, and a handful of our marbles long ago lost.

On all accounts—our destiny, her clairvoyance, and our soon-to-be missing marbles—I believed her.

Henri pointed to the top right bleacher in the MPR, where Ari stood and motioned for Sareena Takhar to join them. Sareena was in my grade—a year younger than everyone else—but Ari was working to recruit her into their circle. The truth was that Sareena, with her velvety black hair and perfect skin, was prettier than Ari. Henri thought it was a friends-close, enemies-closer thing.

"There's Mick and Ari." Henri smiled. "And no Jake. Boo-hoo. I think Ari's already been dumped."

Our shoes clicked against the bleachers as we climbed toward our friends.

"Well, this is fantastic," Ari said without looking up from the inside of her purse. "I left my lip gloss at home."

Henri reached into her book bag. "You can use mine."

Ari held her compact mirror in front of her and smoothed out her asymmetrical haircut. "No, thanks. I'd rather not look like I just sucked on a Popsicle."

My sister's face shifted. This game Ari liked to play, Henri played it better. "As opposed to whoever—I'm sorry *whatever*—you were sucking on last?"

"Ouch." Mick tried not to laugh, which made his blond dreadlocks shake against his shoulders.

Ari looked like she'd been slapped, but she recovered

quickly. Girls like her always did. She pointed to Henri's skirt. "You better unroll that before my mom sees. She said she's not putting up with any shit this year."

Her mom was vice principal, which meant Ari loved to remind everyone of the rules, even if they never applied to Ari.

Only a small space remained between Ari and Mick, not enough room for us both. Henri hiked her skirt a little higher and filled the bleachers between them. "I'll take my chances."

She glared at Mick until he realized there wasn't room for me.

He jumped up, tripping a little. "Oh damn. Sorry, Emma." He sat on the stair beside the bleacher and nodded to his seat.

I wasn't really paying attention, though. I lifted my hand when Sareena smiled and waved at me, but my eyes were already scanning the crowd. Someway, somehow, I'd be able to distinguish the shape of Jesse's head from everyone else's—I knew I could.

My eyes roved over the backs of the heads of the student body. Jake Holt's white-blond buzz cut in the front row, nuzzling a freshman's neck, wasn't hard to spot. No Jesse.

Jesse and I had our moment years ago.

We were thirteen years old in the closet of Kristi Wong's parents' basement, on deck for a not-so-arousing game of seven minutes in heaven.

Other than a ribbon of lamplight filtering beneath the basement door, we were in the dark. Jesse's hands gripped my hips as the warmth of his breath moved closer. I swallowed and closed my eyes. His lips felt wet and slippery. I peeked and watched him kissing me.

His hand slipped under the hem of my shirt, over my navel, my rib cage, reaching the cup of my bra. I jerked away so fast my head slammed into the closet shelf.

"Crap. I'm sorry." He ran his palm over my throbbing skull. "Emma, I thought you wanted to."

"No, I—I do." In a way, I did. I liked Jesse. And I was supposed to like this.

I decided to try again. This time, at least I knew what to expect. I moved my mouth against his, and thought about everything I liked about Jesse.

He had braces and a little bit of acne, but he was funny and when we had to pick softball teams in PE, he made sure I never got picked last.

He pulled away, smiled, and wiped his mouth on the back of his hand. "It's okay. We'll be friends."

Henri studied her schedule, ignoring me still standing there. "Who'd you get, Em?"

I slid into Mick's still-warm seat beside my sister and unfolded mine in my lap. "No surprises. You?"

She leaned over to read. "Ugh. Paxton for trig. You'll be lucky to get a B."

"He gave me a C." Mick rifled through his backpack for his schedule, and an Altoids container dropped out. He fumbled to zip it back inside before his weed and rolling papers fell out, and straightened his tie. "What'd he give you?"

"An A minus," Henri said, squinting at her schedule. "Flynn. Who is Mr. Flynn? And why do I have musical theory for fourth period? I didn't register for this."

"He's new," Ari said. "Mrs. Ostroff checked into rehab in late August. Admin really struggled to find someone . . ."

Even though nobody was listening, Ari kept talking. She got off on letting us know Vice Principal Deveroux had loose lips, so when it came to Baird gossip, Ari heard all, knew all, and repeated all.

The first-period bell rang and the double doors flew open. And there was Jesse, darting through the doors and scanning the crowd. Serendipity must have been on my side, because I could have sworn he looked right at me. Or maybe it was Henri. Maybe for Jesse it had always been Henri.

Dr. Nielsen, our principal, moved to the podium. "Mr. Moreno, please kindly take a seat."

Jesse blushed and took a small bow as he snagged a seat on the bottom row.

Dr. Nielsen cleared his throat into the microphone. "Teachers, faculty, and Baird students, welcome to the first day of classes. Matriculating at Baird is not only a privilege but also a responsibility. I trust you've all refreshed your recollection of the honor code, and if you haven't, might I suggest you do so at your leisure."

As Dr. Nielsen gave his prepared speech, my thoughts went to Jesse. The back of his head, his short and straight dark hair, wasn't so different from any of the other boys at Baird. Whatever it was that was so special about Jesse, I couldn't pinpoint a reason for my fascination.

Something about not knowing made a dark feeling wash over me.

"Em," whispered Henri, picking a stray hair off my navy blazer. "What are you thinking? Are you okay?"

"I'm fine. Everything's fine." I smiled and faced forward.

"This year," Dr. Nielsen continued, "we welcome a talented professional to our stable of educators. Mr. Flynn, would you mind standing?"

A long-legged teacher got to his feet and turned to the bleachers full of students. He wore a pair of dark-wash jeans, even though teachers were only supposed to wear jeans on Fridays, and a rumpled navy blazer over a plaid shirt.

"Mr. Flynn was a Baird student himself just four years ago. Now he'll be teaching various music classes. He also brings with him some interesting hobbies. Let's see . . . Several years ago, when the band's drummer took ill, Mr. Flynn once played the drums for the Red Hearts at the Great American Music Hall on O'Farrell."

The Red Hearts was a San Francisco–based band that broke into the mainstream a couple years ago. They also happened to sing Henri's very favorite song.

A grin spread across my sister's mouth as she leaned forward in her seat and glued her gaze to the new teacher.

Mr. Flynn lifted his hand toward the bleachers, but didn't force a smile. Something about the honesty of it made me think more of him than Dr. Nielsen or Ari's mother or any other teacher at Baird.

When Dr. Nielsen excused the student body for second period, while I was once again searching the crowd for Jesse, Henri snatched my schedule out of my hand and held it side by side with hers. "Meet me outside B Wing at lunch. That's halfway for both of us. We'll walk to that falafel place." She folded my schedule in half and handed it back. "Hey, are you going to be okay?"

"Yeah, you?"

"Absolutely." She smoothed her skirt and shifted her book bag to the other shoulder. "I've suddenly developed an interest in musical theory."

CHAPTER 5

We tasted like salt, our mouths, our fingers. I darted my tongue across my cracked lips and fantasized about cherry ChapStick and cotton-candy-flavored gloss. Two days lost and I almost couldn't remember their taste anymore.

We were no longer flesh and blood. We were dried sweat and salt water.

Henri had sleepily rested her feet against mine. Even though everything was blazing hot, her feet were cold as always.

I shook a little ocean water into Henri's coconut-scented sunscreen to make the bottle last longer and applied some to my peeling arms, trying to work up the will to break away and explore the jungle, look for water.

Alex came trudging down the beach. Even he was sunburned now. He held the bottom of his shirt away from his body and bent low to the raft to let something tumble out. Red, shiny orbs with deep grooves slid across the plastic.

I jumped onto my knees with my stomach growling. "What are they?"

"Breakfast, Jones. Cacao pods."

"Cacao as in chocolate?" It felt light in my hand and smelled more like an orange or a flower than a candy bar.

"Don't get too excited. They don't taste much like chocolate—okay, they taste nothing like chocolate—but they're full of fat, so we'll get full."

We wouldn't starve to death. That was our only consolation. Maybe we'd die of dehydration or typhoid fever, but we wouldn't starve.

I needed to search for water. Three days—that's all we had. But I didn't realize how bad the hours leading up to that point would feel.

Henri picked up a cacao pod and held it out to Alex. "Crack this for me, *s'il vous plait?*" she rasped.

He thumped it against his knee and I did the same. Mine burst into a dozen pieces like a broken pumpkin, but I could still eat the parts not covered in sand. We both popped the pieces of white flesh into our mouths.

They were the texture of lima beans and bitter, but if I closed my eyes, they tasted like plums. I held mine out to Henri, but she gagged and dropped it into the sand.

Tiny worms were twisting through the fruit. My stomach convulsed, and I pressed my hands into my abdomen.

Alex went gray and his shoulders heaved, but he swallowed it back down. He gave us a small, watery smile. "It's just more protein."

Henri inched away from the cacao pod. She dotted runny drops of sunscreen down her nose and across her cheeks, touching her fingers together as if she noticed the thinner consistency. "I'd rather starve."

"Well, Hank." Alex popped another fleshy piece into his

mouth. "If we're here for much longer, you probably will."

"It's Henri, you half-wit."

"Hank is a nickname for Henry." He shrugged. "It suits you."

I kind of loved it that Alex made my name sexier and Henri's less sexy.

My hunger winning out, I tore into my fruit, biting and sucking until what little juice there was slicked down my chin. If I didn't think about the worms, it was delicious.

The pods weren't water, but they were enough to keep my throat from absolute misery. And at least hunger and thirst were a reminder I was still alive.

Henri stood and slipped her shorts down her legs. She kicked them toward Alex and strode toward the water. "I'm going to get wet."

He cupped his hands around his mouth and threw his voice down the beach. "Don't drink any."

Over her shoulder, she batted her eyelashes. "Did you think I was talking about a swim?"

As Henri's body crashed against the surf, Alex moved beside me. "There's something seriously wrong with her."

"No, she's—" She was furious with me, but I didn't know she could carry it this far. Henri at home was bitter and hateful, slinging comebacks and slamming doors, but the tiniest catastrophe—like the Wi-Fi going down—would revive her enough to ask me for the network name and security key, even if her civility didn't last beyond the time it took for the router to reboot. This lost version of Henri—she was relentless. "She'll come around."

Part of his sunburn flaked away as he scratched his cheek. "What about you? Are you okay, Jones?"

"Honestly?"

"No, I want you to lie to me." He smiled. "Yes, honestly."

My whole body felt like it would burst into flames, my heartbeat was a drum in my chest, my temples pounded from dehydration, and it'd only be a matter of time before my mouth felt stuffed with cotton again. "I'm okay."

"No, I mean really okay? This isn't only bad. This is—"

"I know."

"Good. Because I'm not sure I am." From the sand, he grabbed a beer can we'd found—Casey's brand, he'd told us—but Alex's hands trembled as he sliced off the top.

Pieces of the boat had started to wash against our shores. We didn't know how to use everything we found, but we'd drag it all back to the tree line anyway.

"What could have made the boat explode like that?"

"I know. I keep wondering too. Maybe a battery. Or a fuel leak." He picked up another can and cringed when the aluminum cut into his thumb. "So you know, you're right about water—what you said yesterday. We don't find it soon and we're done."

"We're not doing enough. We have to try harder." *I* had to try harder. "Maybe there's water—or help—out there in the jungle."

"We'll use up all our energy doing that. It's a delicate balance." He sucked blood off his thumb and inspected the cut. "Finding food and water burns calories. Makes us sweat."

"But you just said—we can't make it much longer without water. At this point, it's do or—" I thought about Casey just in time to stop myself.

Alex sighed and used his pocketknife to split his sweatshirt up the back. "You're right. If we're going, we go now."

"What are you doing?"

He wrapped and tied the two pieces of sweatshirt around his feet. "They'll get shredded out there. It's the best idea I had." He finished tying them, a hint of a smile on his lips. "What do you think? Good look for me?"

I paused putting on my own shoes and looked him up and down, trying to smile too. "You could start a trend."

Drops of water darkened the white sand as Henri wrung her straight blond hair between her hands. She stood over me, watching me put on my canvas shoes. "Where are you going?"

"Into the jungle. To look for water."

Henri grabbed her own shoes. "No way in hell are you two leaving me here alone."

The air was darker and denser under the tangles of branches. Each time I inhaled, the thickness caught in my lungs. My body didn't know whether to breathe it or drink it.

With a piece of driftwood, Alex hacked through the vines and bamboo ahead. I stayed close to his back while Henri trailed behind. She didn't believe in breaking a sweat unless absolutely necessary. Maybe she finally understood what was at stake.

We passed under trees with cinnamon-colored trunks, and

a spicy citrus breeze hit me. I looked up at the fruit—the cacao trees. As I paused to tie a piece of Alex's sweatshirt around a low branch—markers we might need to find our way back—a vine twisted around the trunk. As it dragged itself onto a high branch, I realized no—it was actually a snake. Henri would have lost it, so I didn't say anything. Just rushed past.

"Alex, what do you think's out here?"

He kicked away the brush at his feet and pressed forward. "We'll find out," he said, "if we're stuck here long enough."

Suffocating heat pressed down as we cut right through the middle of the jungle. Maybe the temperature was truly unbearable or maybe I was feverish from dehydration.

I scanned the areas to the right and left of me as we moved. So many times I thought I saw a trickle of blue. But I'd blink and realize it was only my desperation.

Stings erupted on my bare legs, waves of them. All the island bugs seemed to live in the jungle, and now they were feasting on me.

"How far is it to the other side?" Henri said, sounding bored.

Alex whipped around. "You know, Hank, it wouldn't have hurt my feelings in the slightest if you'd skipped this excursion."

She took a sharp breath. "Alex, you know that cliff down the beach? Why don't you go jump off it?"

"Stop it," I said. "Both of you."

For miles and miles, we pushed our broken bodies over fallen trees, through thick patches of brush, and under draping tangles of growth. I ran out of sweatshirt to mark our way and improvised by crossing stray vines across the path behind us. We walked until the ocean air was masked by the scent of the musky earth. My tongue wasn't dry; it was sandpaper.

"We've been at it almost two hours. Must've covered three miles." Alex had taken off his shirt, and the muscles and tendons on his back shook with each breath. "If I wasn't such a stubborn bastard, I'd say we turn back."

The dry ground crunched beneath my shoes even though the trees were lush with thick, waxy leaves. Those trees could be surviving off the sheer humidity in the air and deep groundwater.

"We're not going to find water, are we?"

The effects of dehydration were etched around Alex's eyes and in the small cracks on his full lips. "I don't think so, Jones."

We moved into a small clearing and Henri plopped down into the dry leaves beneath us. She looked fragile, sitting on the jungle floor, hugging her knees up under her chin. This situation—like so many in the months before—had spun out of my sister's control.

And mine. She wasn't the only one to blame.

The way she'd flirted with Casey, daring him to take us farther from land, had everything to do with the delight she took in watching me cringe.

My hands ached. I wanted to reach out and touch her. But I knew better.

Alex shrugged off Casey's backpack and lay flat on his back. His hip bones jutted over the top of his low-slung cargo shorts.

"Not a spring, a brook, not even a puddle. I can't believe it."

I sat beside them and closed my eyes. Minutes or hours later—it was hard to tell—the dim shadows of the jungle had darkened. "Should we head back before it gets dark?"

Alex's knees cracked as he stood—between the wreck and our dehydration, our bodies had taken beatings. "Give me a minute. I've gotta pee."

Given our worsening dehydration, I wondered how he still could.

"Did one of you touch this?" Alex lifted Casey's backpack by the top handle. He pointed to a spindly tree at the edge of the clearing. "I left it propped here. I just found it on its side. Did you touch it?"

"Of course not. It probably just fell over."

Alex rubbed a hand down his face and focused his blood-shot eyes. "Hello? Hank? Did you?"

"Yeah, I was so glad you left it alone so I could fondle all of your things. I've just been waiting for the opportunity."

"Whatever." He slipped the straps onto his shoulders and pushed through a cluster of trees. "Stay together."

If he felt half as sick or one-tenth as weak as me, he could have collapsed at any minute, and I wouldn't have blamed him for abandoning my sister and me. We were poison. To each other and everyone around us.

Henri watched me staring at the spot where Alex vanished. "If one of us dies, what should we do with the body?"

I looked away. "Don't think like that. And if you do, don't say it."

"It's a legit question. Like if Alex died, I don't know if we could carry him, and we don't have any tools to dig a grave. We'd have to let him rot."

The first time I saw Alex, he glided his rickshaw down the gritty sidewalk separating the beach from the hotel swimming pool. Henri wore black sunglasses that covered half her face as we lounged in the shade of a poolside cabana.

A security guard threw out his hands. "Yo, buddy! This is private property. You can't drive that thing through here!"

Alex parked the rickshaw a few feet ahead of me. "It's on the sand side now, *buddy*. Public beach."

The guard crossed his arms and muttered something about a permit.

"What do you think the boys are like here?" Henri scrutinized a group of guys playing volleyball in the pool. "Emma?"

"Tanned."

"What?" Her voice drifted and I knew she'd noticed Alex.

He pulled off his sunglasses, and for the first time, I saw his eyes—green and rimmed with lashes that would give Henri's falsies a run for their money. He held the temple of the sunglasses in his mouth while he dug a piece of paper from his pocket. Our eyes met over the guard's shoulder, and he took the sunglasses from between his lips. And he smiled. His eyes crinkled at the corners in a way I liked.

He didn't smile at Henri, who was right beside me in a bandeau top and string bottoms. He chose me. Me, wearing a T-shirt and cutoffs, and my hair in a messy ponytail.

Henri swung her legs over the side of her lounge and rested her chin on my shoulder. "Oooh. Emma likes what she sees. I think you should go talk to him. If you have the lady balls. You know I love it when the ballsy side of you comes out."

My cheeks burned with the memory of that night, that party, that mistake.

The security guard took off then on his Segway and left Alex to put away his license.

Henri spread her calves with her coconut-scented sunscreen, and rubbed it in until they were evenly glossy. "I really think you should go talk to him, Em."

"Fine." She would only have more ammunition against me if I didn't.

Alex's attention drifted from the wallet in his hand, and a corner of his mouth lifted as I walked up.

I swallowed. I didn't know what to say. "Nice bike."

"Well, thank you." He ran a hand along the shiny silver handles. "She's all mine." He nodded to the dolphin screen-printed on the front of my shirt. "That is one wicked T-shirt."

It was kitschy and touristy—I'd bought it in the gift shop our first day in Puerto Rico. "Stop it."

"I mean it." He leaned on his handlebars and gave me a wink. "You wanna go for a ride or do you just enjoy breaking the hearts of lesser mortals?"

I pushed a loose curl behind my ear. "A boy with a well-worn line? I should probably stay away from you."

"Well-worn? Fine." He leaned forward more, smiling. "What's your sign?" I laughed and he said, "Seriously, have you seen much of the island? Gone snorkeling or sailing?"

"Mostly just the resort. And some stores. My sister and I shopped."

"Consumers. Excellent." He gave me a sweet, crooked grin. "The more of you, the better."

"My sister did most of the shopping. I watched."

He lifted his chin and looked past me. "Is that your sister?"

Henri wore a smug smile from under the awning. She thought I was going to screw up any minute—I knew how her mind worked.

I nodded.

"By the way she's looking at you, I'd say you're in desperate need of a getaway car."

"You're offering your services?"

His expression didn't change, but something did. There was amusement—in his eyes, his mouth. "Does that mean you're saying yes?"

I climbed into the rickshaw.

We pedaled around the island for hours. I liked him because he talked and talked, yet talked about nothing. There was no pressure to be clever with Alex or be anything at all but myself. When he dropped me off at my hotel at sunset, we didn't know a thing about each other except for our names. His first name. My first and last.

"You're a first-class passenger, Jones." He removed his sunglasses and tapped them against his full bottom lip. "Are you up for an adventure tomorrow?"

"I—" All my boldness vanished, and I looked for any excuse. "My sister—"

"You're both invited. My cousin, Casey, he's got this great boat. He's usually toting tourists around all day, but the boat's free tomorrow. You want to come by? Have a beer or something?"

Memories of San Francisco with Henri flooded my mind—before the chasm opened between us. Boys and beers and adventures that lasted until sunrise. In Alex's cousin's boat, maybe we could have a piece of that back. "When and where?"

He penned some directions on the back of my hand. As I turned toward the mile-high hotels nearly dusting the clouds, he cleared his throat. "I'm going to need payment for the ride."

I patted down my pockets. My wallet was in the backpack I'd left with Henri.

"A kiss'll do."

"Ha," I said. He laughed, and I remembered the ten I'd stuffed in my shorts pocket after buying the dolphin T-shirt the other day. "Here."

"Keep it. You were . . . unexpected."

"No, really. You earned it. That was a lot of pedaling."

He folded the bill in half and tucked it away. "Thank you."

I hesitated, tugging the legs of my shorts down my thighs. Then I caught his chin quickly in my hand and kissed him on his cheek, feeling smooth skin and faint stubble, smelling sea salt, sun-warmth.

Maybe it didn't make sense that I thought—that I knew—he could save our vacation. But attaching myself to Alex would prove something to Henri, make her proud of me for growing up. For being a girl like her.

It wasn't fair to use him, but at the time I didn't care—after all, I'd learned from the very best.

"Stay together," Henri mimicked after Alex had been gone for a few minutes. She got to her feet and brushed off the seat of her shorts. "I'm heading back. Where does he get off telling us what to do?"

"Henri, stop."

She shoved through the tangles of vines and, holding on to a tree, contorted her body through the limbs.

My sister wanted me to go after her. She wanted everyone to always want something from her that she'd never give.

I stayed on the ground, keeping my arms crossed to stop me from pushing up from the dirt and following. Besides, Alex would be back soon. But she could get lost or hurt alone in the jungle. Seconds slipped by and Jesse's words came back to me—Henri was always trying to destroy herself.

At the place where she disappeared, I parted the vines. Trees were tightly spaced, close enough I almost couldn't fit between them. I twisted and ducked under branches.

"Henri!" I yelled. "Henri!"

Sun glowed through the next set of trees—the leaves were translucent as tissue paper. The air felt cooler, not as sticky, almost wet. *Wet.* My hopes so high, they floated to the clouds, I stepped through.

A narrow channel of water twisted through a small clearing. I panted, skidded down a shallow slope, and dropped to my knees in soft brown mud. My fingers skimmed the top of the water and sent ripples cascading. Sulfur wafted up, and I gagged. Stagnant water wasn't drinkable—we'd give ourselves parasites or malaria or worse.

But this water held something else.

Beneath the murky surface was the most unusual pattern of olive green and chocolate brown with the palest beige stripes. I reached into the water.

Yellow eyes opened and glowed up at me.

I shrieked, pulled my hand back. Jaws widened into a padded mouth studded with teeth. I jerked my foot away just as the jaws snapped shut, and in an instant the creature emerged from the mud. A flat, scaled tail—the whole reptile had to be as long as I was tall. An alligator? It barreled closer and my hands flew out before I could think, grabbing at roots, leaves, dirt. I clawed up the bank. It was faster than me. Wild creatures were supposed to be more afraid of us. I opened my mouth and screamed. It kept coming. My fingers locked on a thick, loose branch. The creature reared back with a low, crunching growl, like tires skidding on gravel, and lunged forward. The weight of my body behind my swing, I knocked it across the face. Gasping, I held the branch high—ready to strike again. It sank into the swamp. Camouflage-patterned tail and scaled hind legs. Body with a green diamond spread across its back. Long head. Snout and yellow eyes. It vanished. And I scrambled up the rest of the bank, crashing right into Henri.

I threw my arms around her.

"Em, what happened?"

"We heard you screaming." Alex tugged us apart and raked his eyes over me. "Are you hurt?"

Pointing toward the water, I gasped out something, I don't even know what.

Henri backed farther up the embankment. "What the hell was it?"

"I don't know. An alligator? It was like five feet long."

"Caiman." Alex's hand covered his mouth. "They're not alligators. More like crocodiles. But smaller, more aggressive. And agile. Casey knew a fisherman who lost a hand to one last spring. Mating season. They said she had a nest close."

Ripples fanned over the swampy surface.

"Water's no good anyway," Alex said. "Stagnant. Can we catch a fucking break?" He flicked the water off his hand and froze as he focused on me. "You okay, Jones?"

"We have to get out of here." I almost couldn't breathe. "Now. Right now."

I darted past blurs of ferns and trees and swinging vines, far ahead of Alex and Henri as I followed my markers, all the way back toward the beach. The jungle pressed down on me with each step. As I finally collapsed onto the raft, the weight of Alex's hand spread against my back. He didn't say anything, just sat quiet, watching the ocean.

Wherever Henri had gone, she didn't come back to me.

CHAPTER 6

Henri and I had epic movie dates almost every Sunday afternoon. We'd ride BART to the Cineplex off Haight Street and make it at least a double and sometimes a triple feature before we'd head over to Chinatown for dim sum.

When Mom was working, San Francisco was ours for the taking.

Henri picked the first movie, an adaptation of a book from that author who writes about white people who kiss in the rain. It wasn't really my thing, and it had never been Henri's before, but she dabbed at her eyes when the guy almost couldn't find the girl before she caught her airplane. Our next movie—the one we'd miss for sure if the concession stand line didn't move along—was a musical comedy about two a cappella groups competing for a state championship. The second movie was my choosing.

Henri looped her arm with mine as we stood in line. "Em," she said into my ear. "I know the guy behind the counter. You want free popcorn? Extra butter?"

We'd shared a giant box of Mike and Ikes we brought in from the 7-Eleven to save some cash. The sugar rush left me nauseated and I needed something that wasn't sweet. "Yeah." My hand dove into my pocket. "Mom gave me an extra twenty. I can get it."

"It's not about the money. Don't worry, I got this."

She unwrapped herself from me, and I took a few steps back while she leaned onto the counter and asked for a large popcorn, half butter and half caramel. The boy was helpless. I hated how easy it was for her because it meant I'd have to watch her flirt her way into more free snacks every Sunday.

I'd heard Ari giving Henri a bad time about our Sunday movie dates last year.

What Ari didn't understand was that Henri and I had always been defined by each other. Anyone without a sister couldn't have understood.

Nobody could hold the same place in your heart as your sister. Love or hate her, she was the only person who grew up exactly like you, who knew the secrets of your household— the laughter that only the walls of your house contained or the screaming at a level low enough the neighbors couldn't hear, the passive-aggressive compliments or the little put-downs. Only your sister could know how it felt to grow up in the house that made you *you*.

Lately, though, I'd felt Henri slipping away.

As we waited for our popcorn, I caught a flash of my dad's prematurely gray hair around one of the pillars in the lobby.

"Henri, look."

"Oh, God, it's him. And—" Henri stepped behind a pillar and pulled me to her side.

I peeked around and saw *her* in her Parisian-chic striped top, skinny black pants, and ruby-red flats. *She* didn't have a name in our household—we called her *she* or *her*, and if Henri was talking, *she* was most definitely *it*.

Our dad wore a douchebag Tommy Bahama shirt and I knew she had picked it out.

"He brought *her* here," Henri said. "*Here*."

She blinked her thick lashes fast toward the ceiling, her eyes glossy, wet.

This place, this theater, for the last two years I'd thought of it as ours—just Henri's and mine—and before that, it was just a Jones family Friday night.

Maybe the theater had really been theirs. Everywhere, I saw them—from the high counter where my dad would lift eight-year-old Henri's toes off the purple carpet so she could pay for our tickets to his popcorn order that Henri was still replicating: half butter, half caramel.

"Maybe we should go say something," I said.

She noticed me watching her and waiting for an answer. "What would you say?"

"I don't know? Hi?"

Henri tugged at her collar and crossed her arms, making herself small behind the pillar. "What would be the point of that?"

She was right, like she'd been right the day the divorce was finalized and she said it for the first time: Our connection to him died the day he walked out the door. It was past time I'd tried to accept it too.

"You want this?" said the guy behind the counter.

He had the mega-jumbo bucket of popcorn in his hands. He winked and asked for Henri's number, but she scooped it into her arms so fast some of the popcorn scattered onto the awful purple movie-theater carpet.

"You girls doing anything later?" he said.

Henri spun toward the theater doors. "Everything."

As we rounded the corner, I looked over my shoulder. Our dad was watching us. He knew we were there, and he hadn't crossed that purple carpet.

He lifted his hand, but Henri tugged me inside the dark theater.

The seats were almost entirely empty inside. We loved nothing the way we loved a dark theater. Henri would yell at the screen when the characters didn't do what she wanted or when the writers had the girls do something stupid.

Halfway through the movie, she hadn't spoken a word.

I wished I could kill the nerve that tied me to my dad, like Henri almost had. I focused on his flaws. But that didn't help much, not when those flaws were what made him easy to love. I remembered this day—I must have been nine. Mom took Henri to the dentist and my dad and I went shopping for a new car. It was summer. A bright afternoon. We'd test-driven an SUV, but as Dad talked financing with the sales guy, another car on the showroom floor captured my attention. It was the color of maraschino cherries and had only two seats. It looked like Henri's Barbie car but so much better. I told him that was the car for us, a joke, but he looked to the manager and said, *We'll take it.*

Dad rolled down all the windows on the way home, let me choose the music, and we flew—caught actual air—down the hilly San Francisco streets. That car felt like it had been made for just the two of us. He laughed his big, roaring laugh—the laugh equivalent of a bear hug—and he said, *Wait until your mom sees. She's going to be so surprised.* Mom *was* surprised—but not like we'd hoped. *There are four of us, Steven! What are we supposed to do with a car that seats two?* I hadn't even thought about the impracticality of that car. My mom looked angry, but more than that, she looked hurt, almost helpless. I felt sorry for her, how he always forced her to be the bad guy, but still enamored with my dad for doing something so wild and spontaneous.

Later that year, he took a business trip to Ontario in the middle of winter and came home with a tan.

Now as our hands touched inside the greasy bucket of popcorn, Henri's eyes locked with mine.

"Henri, does it ever scare you how dad left the way he did? I mean, our house was his house. His presence felt so . . . permanent, like he couldn't leave even if he wanted to. But he could and he did."

She handed me the bucket and pulled her feet up into her seat and faced me. "It would. Only if I didn't have you."

I took a handful of popcorn into my palm and noticed her

glancing toward the theater door. "But you do, and you have Mom too."

When Dad left, Henri looked at Mom a little differently. It was almost part sympathy, almost part fear.

She stared at me for a long time before the corners of her glossy mouth curved upward and she turned toward the screen. "I only need you."

I didn't understand my sister, but I'd seen the way she'd latch on to the nearest person when I couldn't be at her side. Every time I'd try to disappear into my room to do homework or read a book, she'd do a belly flop onto my bed and start talking about the summertime outdoor concert lineup or she'd make me take quizzes from the backs of magazines.

Nobody was closer to my sister than me, but even I couldn't figure her out.

We stayed after the movie ended, through the credits, and after the lights came up. There was nothing my sister hated more than an ending. Any kind of ending. *Happy endings are the saddest of all,* she'd say. *Because if everything's happy, then it should never have to end.*

The janitor swept popcorn off the purple carpet as we grabbed our purses and stumbled out the doors and onto Haight.

Sometimes when I walked down Haight with Henri, I liked to pretend we were hippie girls from a movie about the 1960s, soaking up the sun in the Summer of Love. Maybe that's why I'd chosen a tea-length sundress with a swirling pattern of turquoise and fuchsia that almost looked like tie-dye. When I'd emerged from my room wearing it that Sunday, Henri said I was lucky we had to wear uniforms to school. I didn't care.

I'd never shared my daydreams with Henri, but maybe on some level she'd known, because that day she'd worn a pair of light-wash jeans and a boho-chic white trapeze top.

The summer before, we'd been walking down Haight toward Golden Gate Park when a man filled the sidewalk in front of us and said, "Can I interest you girls in some weed or some shrooms? You want to smell colors?"

Henri just laughed and said, *Not today, thanks.* Even though my heart was beating in my eardrums, I bit my lips as she tugged me past him, holding my smile inside, and loving how that encounter made my fantasy a little more real.

I was scanning the street for that man, wondering if he lived nearby, when Henri yelled "Em!" and pushed me up against the brick front of a record store.

Holding my shoulders firm, she looked at me with an excitement and an intensity she felt for nearly nothing. "That's Gavin inside."

"Who?" I rubbed the back of my head.

"Sorry," she said, and then, "Mr. Flynn. He likes his students to call him Gavin. It's so progressive of him. It puts us all on the same level."

"Yeah, until Ari's mom hears about it."

"That woman is all bark, no bite, trust me. But seriously, his name is Gavin. Isn't that unusual and kinda sexy?" She glanced through the window once more. "I'm going to say hi."

"Henri, this is a bad idea."

"Why?"

Her mind was made up, and I knew nothing I could say would reach her.

"Wait here," she said.

The glass door closed and sealed my sister inside.

Through the windows, I watched.

Henri strolled into the store, casually at first, running her fingers along a rack of bumper stickers by the door.

Mr. Flynn's back was to her, so she traveled behind him and perused the records on the other side of the aisle.

Pretending not to see him, pretending not to care, that was Henri at her best.

He pivoted and so did she—she couldn't have timed it better. He had an album in his hands and he passed it to her, gesturing to the song titles. She smiled, and he ran a hand over the stubble on his chin and smiled back. It was a delicate dance.

As they moved toward the entrance, Henri knocked her hip against the rack of bumper stickers and sent them fluttering to the floor. They spread across the tiles and both Henri and Mr. Flynn dropped to their knees, grabbing at them. She lost her balance a little and his hands steadied her shoulders. She met his eyes, and her cheeks flushed.

I'd never seen Henri embarrassed around the opposite sex before.

She glanced away and looked so pretty with her mascara-darkened eyelashes against her cheeks that most boys would die. I realized the game Henri was playing and the appeal of Mr. Flynn.

He wasn't a boy.

Mr. Flynn collected the last of the bumper stickers and Henri shoved them onto the rack without stacking them.

They mumbled a few words and Henri headed toward the exit.

Before she reached the glass door, she looked over her shoulder to make sure Mr. Flynn was watching her walk away.

Henri wasn't disappointed.

We stopped off for a dinner of gelato at a shop on Powell. Our salty popcorn left us craving something sweeter than dim sum and I could tell our brush with our dad left Henri craving anything that could make her forget. Or maybe it was Mr. Flynn that made her want dessert.

The streetlamps flickered to life as we shut the glass doors to the shop behind us.

We walked down the sidewalk toward the BART station, scraping our nearly empty gelato cups with our plastic spoons.

Henri pushed her red sunglasses to the top of her head. "These remind me of birdhouses." She nodded to the pastel-colored houses. "I want to live in one someday."

"They're too far from the ocean. I think we should live right by the sea."

She smiled into the breeze. "I guess we'll need two houses, then. One for summer and one for winter."

I took a few steps before I realized Henri had frozen herself to the sidewalk and wasn't beside me. She held her spoon in her mouth and pointed her gelato cup across the street to cable cars for the Powell-Hyde line.

"Hey, you wanna?" she said with her lips still around the spoon.

I hadn't ridden a cable car since a third-grade field trip. I'd taken a seat on the inside and squeezed my eyes shut while the car bounced down the steep hills. The Powell-Hyde line was the steepest street in the city.

"I thought you said those were for tourists."

"It's getting dark." She tucked the sunglasses into her cleavage and held her hand out to me. "Let's be tourists for the night."

We looked both ways and—even though no cars were coming—we ran too fast across the street to the ticket booth.

Henri paid for our tickets while I held a place in line. Only about a dozen people stood ahead of us, so the next cable car that pulled up was ours.

As I headed toward the innermost section, Henri caught my hand and stopped me. She grabbed on to the side rails and stood on the narrow platform on the side of the cable car. My legs quivered as the line moved ahead of us and tourists filled seats I desperately wanted for myself.

The cable car started off with a slow clank down a steep hill that made me lock my knees around the safety bar. Momentum picked up and sent the cable car gliding down the slanted street.

Henri grasped the bar with one hand.

She leaned far from the car and arched her back toward the speeding asphalt. The wind picked up the hem of her top and beat the cotton against her bare waistline as she faced the sky. She didn't even bother to tug it down.

I almost yelled out for her to stop, but she was cinematic under the glow of the streetlights, with the scenes of the city passing behind her like a film reel and her hair flying. Never had I been so mesmerized by Henri—she was electric. My sister made people flock to her, no one more than me. Henri was a habit I wouldn't kick, a drink I shouldn't have drunk, and a party I couldn't crash.

She opened her eyes and caught me watching her. I looked down at the road passing under my feet. Henri smiled a little and cupped her hands over mine. She squeezed and anchored me to the bar. Wordlessly, she told me to tilt back.

Even though I knew—and she had to know too—that the feeling couldn't last, for just a minute or two, I could be just like her.

My legs shook as I dropped my shoulders and leaned outside the cable car. Still, I kept my eyes shut.

Tightening her grip around my hands, she whispered, "I won't let you fall."

That was when I opened my eyes to the lights of the city soaring around me and the faint stars twinkling above. The city felt too small to hold everything inside me.

Only when the cable car came to a stop at the end of the line did Henri let go of my hands.

CHAPTER 7

Now every little sound from the jungle made me hug my arms and imagine walls stacking, a staircase rising up, a roof clicking into place—all the pieces to a house by the sea. Whatever was beyond those trees, real or imagined, I couldn't turn my back to it for more than a few seconds.

Henri and Alex had gone separate, sluggish ways around the island—Alex determined to search the stagnant water source for something drinkable and Henri changing her bikini. We were surviving, barely, on juice and fruit from cacao pods. Alex and I were. I don't know what Henri was surviving on. Malice maybe.

Humidity mixed with my sweat made my body a sand magnet. My legs, my hands, my forearms were coated in a fine grit. I gathered my hair, ungluing strands from the back of my neck and winding it into one big mass that I didn't have a way to tie back. Alex had made it to the island with a rubber band, but he'd lost it in the ocean. The smallest of luxuries were the ones I missed the most. I kept my eyes on the beach, but even they felt gritty.

Like Alex, I found myself staring at the sea, ready for help to come that never materialized. After three long days, I wasn't sure it ever would.

Something small and red bounced across the ocean waves. Sun glinted off the blinding sand, and I shielded a hand over my eyes.

It was the ice chest we'd had in Casey's boat. My legs trembled as I stood. It *couldn't* be. But maybe it was.

I darted across the sand. It didn't matter that it was a chance in hell—right now that ice chest was our best chance at staying alive. As the sand ended, I took the deepest breath my lungs could hold, and I dove.

The sea sloughed away my dirt and sweat as I glided through the water. I came up for air to hone in on the ice chest. Where the ocean water got colder and darker, I swam out.

My scalp screamed as someone yanked a fistful of my hair. Arms came around my waist and heaved me backward. I grabbed the sturdy wrist—it was Alex's, not Henri's. And I shoved at him, kicking my feet against the water. "What the hell!" I spluttered.

But he was too strong and dragged me toward the shore. He had the advantage being so much taller—he was walking across the ocean floor before my feet found bottom.

Finally, I touched down on slick rocks and scanned the horizon. The ice chest was gone. *"What are you doing?"* I yelled. *"That ice chest—"*

"I don't care!"

"But it had water—"

"Thirsty is better than dead!"

"Thirsty like this is *almost* dead." I shoved him, but he hauled me from the waves and planted our feet in the sand.

"Did you not notice the riptide, Jones?"

My mouth opened, and I stared out at the ocean.

"See the ice chest dragging out to sea?" He pointed to the horizon, where the ice chest bobbed, a faraway dot of red. "You could have been that far out by now. Being caught in a riptide is like . . . it's like— Imagine being trapped on a treadmill you can't turn off. It's like that. If you don't know how to get out, you wear yourself out and you drown."

"I—I've never seen one."

"Now you have." His shoulders slumped as he looked at me, his clothes soaked and dripping. "It's fine—you didn't know. I only know because I was caught once. Learned my lesson."

I pulled myself onto the beach. "What do you do?"

"I was surfing. My leash broke and I lost my board. I swam parallel to the coast until I got out. That's what you do. But damn. You scared the shit out of me, Jones. The surf's been crashing in wild all morning. Then it went calm. Flat as a pane of glass. And I saw you. And the foam on the water pulling away from the beach. You were far enough out—it was just starting to catch you. I was fifty feet away when you went in." He faced the beach, and as he turned his back on me, his voice cracked. "I wasn't sure I could—"

Behind him, I reached up and squeezed his shoulders, but Alex turned and blinked down at me through wet eyes. Slower this time, prepared for him to jerk away, my arms circled his waist. This time, he relaxed and wrapped his arms at the dip of my lower back.

Nobody except my parents had touched me—not with any meaning—in months. With my sunburned cheek against his shoulder, I pressed back.

But the opposite sex led to tragedy for Jones girls.

I wouldn't be shattered like my sister and my mom.

I broke away and headed for the top of the beach.

"Did I do something wrong?" He followed me through the burning sand.

"No, I just need to get out of the sun."

Back in Puerto Rico, when I'd decided Alex would save our vacation, I thought there were only five days to play before we packed up our suitcases and headed home without so much as a good-bye. Out here, he was inescapable.

My hands seemed to leave trails through the air as my sister and I lay on the raft that afternoon. The water source hadn't panned out like we'd hoped—all Alex found was a spring that barely broke the surface and dribbled into the stagnant, caiman-filled water. My eyes wouldn't focus, no matter how hard I blinked. I was almost unconscious when Henri whispered my name.

"I have eyes," she said. Sunlight peeked through the trees but did nothing to warm Henri's icy stare. "I can see the way you look at Alex, and I know what's happening."

"Nothing's happening, Henri." I whispered it. My throat hurt too much. If I was looking at Alex any *way,* it was because of the solitude, and the fact that the only other person stranded with me was trying to crush the leftover pieces of us.

Her fingers were splayed on the raft between us. I wrapped my hand around hers, but her bones stayed stiff, never curling around mine.

"I've been thinking about that day."

"What day?"

Her silence said everything. I looked down at the nail polish I'd had to apply myself the night before we left.

"I wished I was dead," she said. "When I found out what you'd done, for a second, a heartbeat, I wished I was dead. I should have been more specific with my wishing, though. Like if I was going to die, it should be fast. Not like this."

I picked my polish until bits flaked away. "I've told you I was sorry so many times."

She didn't move a muscle except to tap her fingers in a staccato rhythm that was so unlike my cool and collected sister. "*Sorry*'s a childish word, Emma. When you're a kid you think it's a cure-all, but now it doesn't mean a damn thing. Sorry isn't enough."

Not quite sleeping but not quite awake, Henri and I stayed as still as possible in the dark shade of the life raft. A fleeting part of me thought that raft might be our way off the island. Now I couldn't think that far ahead, only breathing shallow to keep my lips from cracking and bleeding more.

"I've got something."

My eyes opened to Alex's voice. He slicked a hand through

his long hair and fumbled with the cargo pocket of his shorts before pulling out a brand-new bottle of water.

Part of me might have thought it was a mirage because I nearly sobbed when he dropped the weight of it in my hands. "Are you for real?"

"You two can split it."

Henri planted her hands at her waist. "Don't be a hero. We'll third it."

Alex sat in the sand and drank first, a little less than the third he was entitled before he passed it to me. "Go ahead, Jones. Drink."

Each swallow was ecstasy and torture. It wasn't much. Only a twelve-ounce bottle. But it was heaven against my sunburned lips, and I drank too fast. A trail dribbled down my chin, and I would have cried over depriving myself of that sip—literally cried—if it wouldn't have meant just losing more water.

The little bit wasn't nearly enough to replenish what we'd lost. But we'd bought ourselves at least a little more time before our bodies started shutting down. We'd need gallons and gallons before help came. If it ever did. I looked out at the vast blue. It was surreal to worry about water when miles of ocean water stretched around us.

Henri wiped the lip of the bottle with the heel of her hand before she finished it off and stared Alex down. "So, where did you get it?"

He paused. "I've had it. I just wanted to wait until we really needed it."

"You asshole." She hurled the bottle at him, but he crossed his arms and it bounced off and down to the sand. "You had this all along and you didn't say anything?"

He clenched his teeth, but then relaxed, almost smiled. "If you knew I had it, you would have drunk the whole thing that first night. I was doing you a favor."

My sister could be terrible, but in this, I was on her side.

"You don't know what we would have done," I said. "Who says you get to decide when we drink and when we don't?"

He stalked down the beach and retrieved the bottle. "Considering the fact that I'm the one who had the water? I'm the one who says. I was waiting for the right time. And this is it—you, Jones, you seem to have reached your breaking point." As he twisted the cap back on, he looked over at me. "Look, I don't want to fight. I just want to get off this island." He glanced at Henri, then back at me. "I think I know how."

"You can't be serious," I said.

"Serious as a shark attack."

"Really," Henri deadpanned. "A shark attack."

Alex ignored her. "Jones, if someone's looking, let's help them find us. We've gotta build a signal fire, something to draw attention. Lots of dry brush and a little green to make it smoke like hell."

I trusted Alex, mostly. Even if his thing with the backpack was weird. "Okay, fine. But you have to promise—you don't make decisions without consulting us. We're not stupid. We deserve a say."

He held out his hand. "Deal." I took it, but he didn't so

much shake it as hold it, brushing his thumb quickly along my knuckles before letting go. He smiled. "And for the record, I never said you were stupid."

Henri turned away. "Unless you've found a working airplane, I'm skeptical of your rescue plan."

"You can be skeptical all you want, Hank. But if you want to go home, I'd suggest working less on your tan and more on finding dry brush."

I eyed the empty bottle sticking out of the cargo pocket on his shorts. "What about finding more water? We'll never make it long enough for a plane to find us."

"We do this first. But then we don't have a choice—we're going back into that jungle." He sighed and plastered on a smile, squinting at us. "What I mean is, I politely suggest we go back into that jungle, and I sincerely hope you both agree."

We went separate ways, canvassing the beach for the driest brush we could find. Tall grass sprouted up from the sand in dry yellow tufts. It sliced my hands as I pulled it up by the roots, but this small stuff would ignite the fastest. I collected piles and piles.

If we made the signal fire big enough, someone might save us before we had to set foot in the jungle again.

Henri was the first one back to the life raft. My arms held almost more than I could carry, and I let it all tumble to the sand beside a small bundle of branches Henri'd found.

"This is all you got?"

She crawled to the edge of the raft and rested her cheek against the plastic. "This is never going to work, Em."

Alex and I used a stone to dig a groove in a large piece of dry wood. With the board propped between our knees, we took turns spinning a stick against the wood to create friction.

After hours of trying, my palms ached and were covered in swollen liquid-filled blisters that would be agony when they burst. Alex flexed his own hands and winced—his calluses hadn't stopped him from hurting too.

"Is driving a rickshaw that hard on your hands?"

He rubbed the skin at the edges of his thumbnails and cracked his knuckles. "Oh, uh, I restore old surfboards."

"For fun?"

"Well, sorta." He picked up a stick and started drawing patterns in the sand. "After I moved down here, I couldn't afford a board. An average one's like five hundred. But this guy said he'd sell me a single-fin for fifty. I should have known it would be torn-up for that price. It was from the seventies, though, a classic." I could picture him—Alex on the water, longish hair and vintage board, a silhouette against the sun and waves. "I sanded it, straightened the fin, filled gaps with resin, and re-glassed it. When I finished, I took it out on the beach and, like, five guys asked who refinished it for me."

"What was it like—out on the waves?"

"I wouldn't know." He flushed through his tan. "I sold it."

"Oh."

"To a guy on the beach, that first day." He laughed in a way that didn't mask the sadness at all. "He didn't even surf. He wanted to use it as a countertop for his bar. But it paid a few

77

months' rent. Now I buy damaged boards, work on them when I can. At night. Or when tourism's slow."

"Do you do it for the money now or is it a hobby?"

"Both," he said. "I'm not as bad off as I was when I first got down here, so I can be pickier about who I sell to—girls and guys who are actually going to use them." And quieter: "Love them."

I straightened up—I didn't realize I'd leaned so close as he talked.

He looked at me, then away fast, but he glanced back, and gave me a smile that changed his face—embarrassed, real. He seemed younger.

From the raft under the trees, Henri's raspy voice cut the silence. "I knew the fire wouldn't work."

"Thanks for the vote of confidence," I said. "It's nice to know we can count on your optimism."

She lifted her hand. "Anytime."

Alex got to his feet, keeping his hands on his knees and breathing deep. His legs steadied and he exhaled, shook out his hair, his smile long gone. "I'm going to look for something better to use for shoes. We can try with the fire again later."

As he stormed off, I called, "If we're all going back into the jungle, we have to do it before dark." But he disappeared into the trees without answering.

Henri fished her phone out of her bag. "It came on."

I crawled close. "Really?"

"No bars, though."

Alex was right—no reception. If we had to save ourselves, Henri's phone wouldn't help.

Henri clawed at her legs. "The bugs are eating me up. Just what I wanted for graduation—West Nile." She gave me a sideways glance as she stood. "Hey, look what *some*one left behind."

Casey's backpack. Alex had left it in the shade.

"You still think we can trust him, Em? After the water?"

"I don't know. Maybe he thought he was doing the right thing."

Henri crossed her arms, and wearing a smirk, took long steps in the direction of the backpack. "He carries it everywhere he goes. Won't let anyone touch it. It's shady."

"It was Casey's. It's got, like, sentimental value."

"He had water, Em—all this time. Water he didn't tell us about. Maybe he's got a whole supply of food and water in that backpack. Maybe he's saving it for after we're dead."

"He wouldn't do that."

"If there's nothing in it, why was he so worried we'd touched it?" She stepped across the sand, her fingers dancing toward the zipper. "Could a little peek really hurt anyone?"

"Don't."

"You're awfully trusting. Survival of the fittest, Em. Survival of the fittest. What harm could it really do?"

At first I'd thought Alex was lazy—comfortable to bum around Puerto Rico on a rickshaw, forget college, forget everything. I wasn't sure anymore. He could have killed himself coming after me in that riptide. But also, if I wasn't lying to myself, I did want to know what secrets he was keeping.

"Fine."

Carefully I unzipped the outer pocket and Henri's hand dove inside.

She lifted out a condom. "Maybe we won't be totally bored on this island after all. Oh, wait, only one."

I felt around inside the pocket and my fingers closed around something. I lifted out two clear ziplock bags, both containing a couple dozen tiny pink pills. "Casey must have some kind of a health condition or something."

"Are you serious?" Henri practically howled with laughter. "If there was something wrong with him, these pills would be in little orange bottles with childproof lids." She opened the bag and spilled a few into her palm. "OC," she said, pointing to the words stamped on the pills. "Em, this is Oxy. OxyContin."

"It's a prescription drug, though."

"Yeah, a prescription drug people buy on the street and take at parties. Sounds like your friend has a problem."

"No," I said. "This was Casey's. Casey's backpack. He must have had the problem."

"Then why does Alex keep disappearing?" Henri waited a beat. Made a *duh* face. "To get high—that's why. It makes sense with all the mood swings. What an asshole too. He didn't even offer to share."

All this time I thought his attachment to the backpack was sentimental. Was he only protecting his drugs? Stuck with Henri was its own kind of torture. If I was also stranded with someone more concerned with fading into oblivion than trying to get us home . . .

I grabbed the bag roughly and shoved the pills back in, zipping the outside pocket. "I can't believe you talked me into this."

"Oh, come on, Em. You didn't even look in the big pocket."

"Henri, don't touch that backpack again. I mean it."

I curled up in the life raft, hating myself for letting Henri get to me. She could plant a seed of doubt in my mind and water it until it sprouted and bloomed and made me grow into someone I didn't want to be. Worst of all was when Henri was right.

Alex bent low, re-tying fragments of his sweatshirt to his bare feet. "Didn't find anything better, but I'm heading back in. Anyone with me?"

The way I could feel my heartbeat in my eyelids at just the mention of the jungle was nothing less than terrifying. "I'm— I'm in."

"You and Alex go," Henri said. "Someone needs to stay on the beach in case someone comes looking for us." She unhooked the neck strap of her bikini top and retied it around her back, the way she would do at home when she didn't want tan lines.

This wasn't the Henri from home, who had the kind of will that would have pushed her across the island three times already, clawing through the jungle and begging—no, *demanding*—that we find a way home and find it now.

Whatever had changed in her head since the accident, Casey's death, I couldn't imagine. Maybe I didn't want to.

Alex and I left without a word.

We forced our way through the bamboo, hacking away the brush and swallowing the ground without talking. I'd taken Henri's backpack in case we found anything to carry back, gripping the straps to steady my hands. To my right, the incline increased toward the cliff. "How high do you think that cliff is?"

Alex glanced back, laboring to breathe. "Maybe two hundred and fifty feet. Give or take."

"If we climbed it," I said, "we'd be able to see more of the island. We might find water. And we'd see if there's any other land close."

He stopped walking, and faced the rising incline. "Jones, I am so clearly seeing the errors of my ways. I should have let you call the shots from day one."

We pressed up toward the cliff, sweat soaking my shirt as we wound upward through heavily perfumed flowers and trees with shiny leaves that smelled like citrus. Our island was a beautiful hell.

Alex grinned, reaching out to a tree for balance. "And now we come to the hiking portion of our island tour."

I barely smiled. "I want a refund."

This Alex, he was different. But the backpack hadn't been in his control for the last few hours. Maybe the drugs were a way to numb the pain of losing Casey. Of being lost here. I almost understood.

We stopped a second to breathe, and Alex asked, "So, who's looking for you, Jones?"

I weighed the effort it would take to keep talking with the need to tell him. "Our mom. She has to be wrecked. And our dad. If there isn't a golf tournament or a wine-tasting at home he and his girlfriend can't miss."

"Sounds like a stand-up guy. And home is?"

"San Francisco."

"Home to Alcatraz," he said. It was an odd thing to say, and I held up my palms and shrugged. He stood straighter. "Oh, I, uh, read a book about those guys who escaped in the sixties."

"Alcatraz, huh? Interesting reading choice."

"I found it in the seat pocket on my flight to Puerto Rico. My earbuds broke. It was either that or the flight safety manual."

"Good call. Have you seen Alcatraz?"

"Nope. I've never even been to California. Someday, though."

The trees rustled above, sending leaves raining as a rat scurried down a branch. I shuddered and started walking again, heaving Henri's backpack higher.

"What kind of things do you do in San Francisco?" he asked, falling in behind me.

After he'd told me about the surfboards, I wanted to say something cool.

Henri's hobby for the last year had been boys. The smoother, the sexier, the more likely to ruin her, the better. Me, I guess all I'd ever had for a hobby was Henri.

"High school," I said. "And stuff."

"Stuff. Yeah, I enjoy *stuff* sometimes myself. When the mood strikes."

I smiled back at him briefly. Kept walking. "Who's looking for you?"

"No one." He said it fast, like he'd been waiting for the question, and the lightness in his voice vanished. "It was just me and Casey. Well, maybe my uncle—Casey's dad. But he lives in West Virginia. He probably has no idea."

Just the two of them. "How old are you?"

"Almost eighteen."

Wind tangled our hair as we reached the top of the cliff. I put my back to the ocean and looked below. Our island was kidney-shaped, with our beach cradled inside the indentation. The whole mass of land couldn't have taken up more than a few square miles. The sand, gravelly and gray when it was under my feet, outlined the island in a pale yellow against the cerulean ocean. Palms and trees with wild twisting trunks and green tops sprouted around the perimeter, growing into the boughs of larger trees across the island's middle. I scanned the jungle, searching for any speckle, any glint of blue, but thickets of bamboo veiled everything beneath them.

"Nothing," said Alex. I turned to him. But he wasn't searching the jungle. He was searching the ocean. The water spread out before us, around us, to the very edges of the world. No boats. No help. And no other land.

"How far can we see from up here?" I asked. "Five miles? Ten?"

"More like twenty, I'd guess. In the ocean, on a surfboard, they say you can see twelve. But we're higher. On a calm, clear day, yeah, we can probably see twenty miles from up here." Alex blinked fast and focused on me before he lowered himself to the dirt. "Sorry, Jones, I gotta rest again. My heartbeat is going wild."

"Mine too." My fingers brushed my pulse point. "Dehydration?"

"Think so." He coughed into the neck of his T-shirt and fanned out the fabric. "I'm so damn thirsty I'm about to drink that ocean dry."

"Let's take a break—for real." I unlooped Henri's backpack from my shoulders and dropped to the ground. "Talk about something—anything other than water."

"Okay. So, your sister's a real charmer."

"She—she feels awful about Casey. She just wants to wait until she has the right words to tell you how sorry she is."

"As endearing as it is that you lie for her, you're not very good at it."

I looked at him quickly. "Well. I'm sorry she's being rude to you." I swallowed. "It's not about you. It's me."

"What'd you do to her?"

"It's—" I couldn't say it. "It's a long story."

His hand grazed his cheek, absentmindedly scraping the dark stubble along his jaw. "We all sell our souls for something." A vein in his neck bounced. "But yeah, I'd rather have less of her attitude. We wouldn't even be here if it wasn't for her."

"You don't know where she's coming from." Or what I did.

Even with the wedge between us, I'd defend Henri till the end. *I* could think what I wanted, but that's because she was my sister. She was mine to love and to hate.

She'd teased Casey about the boat version of the mile-high club as we sped farther from land, and Casey showed her tricks with his lighter, holding a slim Newport in his mouth, its smoke ripped away by the wind as Puerto Rico fell off the horizon.

Every press of her body, lick of her lips—I knew she'd done those things to watch me squirm.

"He wouldn't have taken the boat out to impress her," I said. "If it wasn't for me—"

"Stop. You're definitely not to blame for Casey."

"No, I am. What she was doing to him, playing with him, she was doing it to mess with me and . . . What?"

With his chin in his hand, Alex was looking at me with a weird level of interest. "Do you always blame yourself for your sister? Or is this a new thing? If the roles were reversed, do you think she'd be down on the beach, tearing herself up over something you did because she liked getting a rise out of you?"

I didn't have to answer.

"Hey, I'm sorry. I shouldn't have said that." He scooted across the dry dirt of the cliff. In a second he was so close I could almost hear his rapid heartbeat. He touched two fingers under my chin and made our eyes connect. "We've got to think about surviving only. Nothing but surviving. We need water, food, and shelter if we're going to make it. We don't need to get along, but it'd be easier if we could."

I nodded.

Alex reached behind me and squeezed my shoulder, his thumb working a soothing arc into the sore muscle. "If you could have one thing right now, Jones, what would it be?"

Henri back. That was what I always wanted. "A satellite phone to call for help?"

"Boring. This is a game, Jones. Something from home that's not on this island that would be perfect. What do you want?"

My shorts were stiff from salt water and so uncomfortable with my bikini under them. "I, um, I have this pair of jeans I've had for years. They're a little too short, so I roll them up. They're softer than cashmere and the knees are so thin you can almost see through them."

"They sound very sexy."

"Trust me, they're not—"

A rumble took both of our gazes to the sky. A plane flew over the far side of the island.

"Shit," he said. "It's headed toward the beach."

We jumped to our feet and ran downhill, through the brush and bamboo, not even worrying about snakes or caiman or anything else. As we reached the beach, waving our arms over our heads and jumping up and down, the plane was already far over the water.

My sister stretched out under the shade of the tree line in her string bikini. Asleep. Her tank top and shorts were hung up in a tree.

Alex grabbed on to his knees, panting and glaring at Henri. "Are you trying to die here or did you not see the plane?"

Henri sat up, holding her loose top against her chest, and yawned. "Maybe you should take the next watch."

The tarp overhead shuddered in the breeze as I waited for Henri to fall asleep. Bug bites coated my body like an inflamed second skin. When we were kids—and even now—I couldn't sleep until her breathing leveled off. Like Henri had to go first. Where Henri went, I followed.

As I tried to sleep, I replayed the last four days. I'd lived with an angry Henri for months—she didn't respond to questions, or responded sarcastically, delighted in embarrassing and one-upping me. This Henri on the island was the same, but also someone different. Someone with a secret.

A sound startled me from the space between dreaming and awake.

Soft whistles sifted through the palm trees, almost like the sound of the ocean inside a seashell. The winds picked up, so violently, I shivered and zipped my white jacket.

The night sky darkened from muted gray to charcoal to black. Alex and I both got up and moved closer to the water. On the back of my hand, I felt it—a drop of rain.

I stuck out my tongue to lick it away, but Alex took my hand and touched the drop. He moved it between his fingers and shook the hair from his eyes, looking from it to me. "No way."

The drops multiplied into a steady drizzle. Alex fumbled with his buttons and stripped off his shirt. He stood in the rain with his arms stretched wide and his mouth open to the sky.

Perched on the edge of the life raft, Henri opened her empty water bottle and held it above her head.

"Get up," I said.

Her weight barely lifted off the plastic before I pushed the life raft out from under the trees and into the rainfall.

Rain came down so hard it ricocheted off the life raft and stung my skin, but soon water pooled at the edges. We crowded around, cupping handfuls of it, drinking as much at a time as our hands and mouths would allow.

CHAPTER 8

Our mother picked us up the first Friday in October and drove us to Los Cilantros, our favorite Mexican restaurant in Berkeley.

Henri and I dipped our chips in a side of jalapeno ranch while our mom perused the drink menu.

"I think I'll have a sangria," Mom said.

Henri squeezed my knee under the table and sat up in the booth. She gave the waitress her most mature, don't-even-think-about-carding-me voice. "Make it a pitcher."

"Nice try. Give it five more years." Mom lowered her menu only enough for her eyes to show over the top. "Six for you, Emma."

Like anyone else with the slightest grasp on the girl Henri truly was, our mother never took her attempts too seriously. Others had tried—like our dad—to untangle the delicate strands of Henri only to end up with a ball of grit, fire, and comebacks.

After we decided on two orders of fajitas and a taco salad,

Mom folded up our menus in a neat stack at the edge of the table. "Girls, I'm sorry I haven't been around much the last few months. Work's been a nightmare, but it'll get better."

I had a mouthful of chips and covered my lips to speak. "Why is it going to get better?"

"Your father and I will get the money side of everything settled soon." Now that the actual divorce was set in stone, what my dad seemed to value most came second—the money. "Until his lawyer and my lawyer get it together, I need more cash flowing in to make the mortgage, the car payments, the lawyer bills, half of your father's boat payment that he's saddled me with—" She cut herself off and brought the back of her hand to her lips. "I'm sorry, I shouldn't—"

"It's fine," Henri said. "I think most of the dirty details have made themselves apparent."

"Well, I'm sorry for that."

Mom turned her face toward the sunlight streaming in the restaurant windows. Fine lines etched around her mouth, faint gray hairs peeked out of her roots, and sadness filled her hazel eyes and didn't lessen even when she caught us watching her and forced a smile that made me want to fold in half.

Divorce was hell, and my mother's appearance was proof.

She reached across the table to dip a chip in our jalapeno ranch. "But I do have some news. The company is sending me to the Puerto Rico Investment Summit in February, over your break. It's only for five days."

Henri propped her elbows on the table and leaned forward enough to show her teal panties over the waistband of her uniform's skirt. "You mean, we have the house to ourselves?"

Mom chased down her chips with a long drink of sangria, eyebrows raised at Henri. "No," she said, swallowing. "I have to meet some clients in Puerto Rico, and I'll barely be able to check in. Your dad's been working on a room for you girls to share at his place. He said he and Simone would love to have you."

Henri pressed her lips together. "If *it's* going to be there, then I won't be."

"Please, Henri, you don't need to make this any harder than it has to be. It's only for five days. Besides, it's time we all start healing."

After Mom paid the bill, Henri called shotgun and got the keys. My sister hugged her headrest and frowned into the backseat at me. "Five days of Dad and *it*. Really?"

"At least we have each other."

"There's nobody else in the world I could do it with." She swapped Mom's iPod out for her own. "Oh, gawd. Can you imagine Mom in Puerto Rico all by herself? How sad is that?"

"She said she'll be working while she's there. I guess she'll only have to suffer through the dinners alone."

I hated the image of our mother sitting alone at a table overlooking the beach at night, glass of wine in her hand, and that same sadness flooding her eyes.

Someday she'd be old and there'd be no one by her side. Not even a sister to share a house with by the ocean.

Henri twisted her neck at the restaurant doors. "Shit. Here she comes."

Mom climbed behind the wheel, and Henri cranked up the soundtrack to *Wicked*. Henri always took the role of Elphaba and left the Galinda/Glinda parts for me. As my sister and I were defying gravity at the top of our lungs, Mom dialed down the volume.

"Have you girls done more thinking about next year?"

She shot a look at Henri as she drove, but I knew my sister would never answer.

Henri was graduating in eight months with no plans. She was tired of high school, but not quite ready for anything more. My sister lived for glitter and bubbles and golden tans and boys in fast cars—she was never cut out for institutions.

Finally I piped up from the backseat. "I've been researching colleges. I think I've found seven. Four reaches and three safeties—"

Mom's stare was serious in the rearview mirror. "That's excellent, Emma. I'm glad one of you is applying herself."

"Give it a rest," Henri muttered.

Showing up Henri wasn't my plan, even if that's what she thought. I only wanted to create a distraction to take the heat off my sister.

"Henrietta Katherine Jones." Mom's whisper was always more terrifying than her scream. From the backseat, I held my breath. "You either need to be going to school or you need a J-O-B."

"Jaaaa . . . Jaaaawb." Henri pretended to sound out the word and popped her lips at the end on the *B*. "Can you spell it more slowly? I'm not sure I got it."

My mother removed her sunglasses and stared across the car to where Henri sat tousling her hair in the passenger seat. "Come on, Henri, give it some thought. Right now it's your choice. You don't want it to be mine. There's still time to put a deposit down on NYU. Not much, though—the early-decision deadline to accept is in two weeks. And if it's not NYU, I have no problem enrolling you at BACC myself."

Bay Area Community College—Henri's worst nightmare.

I pressed my temple to the cool backseat window, ready for an explosion. Only, my sister stayed quiet. Henri's reflection filled the side mirror, her lips sealed together as she followed the white line on the side of the road.

Mom always underestimated the strength of Henri's will. That was a mistake I never wanted to make.

Our mother parked the car in front of our house, and Henri threw open the car door and headed inside. While Mom and I collected grocery bags from the trunk, Henri slammed the front door so hard, the front porch vibrated.

Mom shook her head as our house settled. "She's a walking catastrophe."

"She's just having a hard time."

Mom hoisted a reusable grocery bag higher in her arms. "Because of your father?"

"I think so." But I didn't really know what had happened to

Henri in the last few months—if it was our dad walking out or my sister discovering worlds I hadn't yet imagined.

I shut the trunk, and as my mother shouldered past me, I could have sworn she said, "Damn him."

I traveled up the stairs inside, following the noises overhead from Henri's room—drawers sliding open, hangers being flung, the crack of thrown shoes landing on the wood floor—and found Henri on her knees in front of her dresser.

"What are you doing?"

Handfuls of bright lacy bras from the bottom of her underwear drawer spilled onto the floor as she sifted through them. She relaxed with relief when her fingers closed around a green strapless bra. "Ari texted me. I'm going out tonight and so are you."

I used the toe of my boot to scoot some dirty clothes away and make a spot to sit.

She grabbed a bottle of nail polish, slipped my wool-lined boots off my feet, and began to paint my toenails tangerine.

I tried to pull my foot out of her reach, only Henri wouldn't let go.

"You just did them."

"Practice, Em." She touched our foreheads together until my smile matched hers. "What if I paint your nails tangerine and you decide your wardrobe would look better with coral? Or what if we find the perfect shade of turquoise?"

She brought the back of her hand to her forehead in the most dramatic, most Henri-like way before her brightest grin lit up the whole room.

Her act would have been convincing enough for most. Not for me.

As my nail polish dried, Henri draped herself across her bed and opened a magazine. "We're going to pretend *it's* not even there, okay? It's just us—me and you and nobody else."

"At Dad's house."

"Everywhere."

I touched my fingertip to my toenail. The polish was still sticky.

"You're going to ruin them." She licked her finger and flipped a magazine page. "You're the only person I've ever really loved, do you know that, Emma?"

"That's not true. What about Mom and—" I knew what Henri would say if I said *Dad*. "What about Mom?"

She shrugged. Henri's greatest strength and greatest weakness was how easily she could turn on and off her love. I always wondered if she was born that way or if it was a skill she'd learned to keep her safe from a world that might not love her back.

Maybe I'd never know.

"Henri, you love Mom. You're just mad at her over BACC."

"I mean"—she rolled onto her back and hung her head off the bed, staring at me upside down—"I guess I do love Mom. But it's not one-hundredth of how much I love you. Like, you know when we were little and we'd say we loved each other to the moon and back. Well, let's say I love you to the moon and back—because I do. Now take Mom. In comparison, like, maybe I love Mom to Nevada and back. Or to the street corner and back." She flipped around and folded her legs beneath her. "Does that make sense?"

"Sure." I had to fight to keep the horror off my face. "But she just wants you to make some plans. You have to have *something* in mind."

Henri pitched her magazine aside and crawled to the edge of the bed. "Mom thinks I'm really screwing things up. But I'm not. I've got plans. Mom doesn't know about them, but whatever. I was supposed to go to college far, far away. I *did* get accepted into NYU, you know." She held her chin high and laughed.

That acceptance letter had been stuck to our fridge with a magnet for two weeks. Until one day when I went to get some orange juice and it had disappeared. I didn't know how long its absence had gone unnoticed. All I knew was that it was gone and Henri had been the one to take it—for some secret reason nobody else could understand.

She fluffed up her hair, leaving it messy. "I'm not saying this to make you feel bad or anything, but the reason I didn't go is because I didn't want to leave you behind—not with everything that happened with Dad."

I covered my eyes. "Henri."

"No, stop." She peeled my hands away and dropped off the bed right onto me. Her knees pressed under each of my armpits as she forced me to look at her. "This is a good thing. I don't regret anything at all."

"But what are you going to do?"

"I'm going to wait until you've graduated, then we'll use our graduation money to rent a car and we'll spend weeks driving cross-country. That's when we'll go to school together, anywhere you want to go. Okay?"

"Henri—"

"I'll have to find a way to hold off the dragon—Mom, I mean—until you're legal."

"It's a long time away, though."

I couldn't stand the thought of leaving Mom all alone, even though I'd never tell my sister.

"No, it's not. It's going to be Christmas, my birthday, and before we know it, spring break. We'll have my big graduation blowout in the spring. We'll only have one tiny little year before we can run far away from here. Okay?"

"Okay."

"Okay," she repeated, breathing the word and making it into something bigger than it was.

CHAPTER 9

Henri slept too soundly that night while I listened to the noises outside the tarp. Now that our raft held our drinking water, it wasn't easy to sleep on the hard sand.

The air still carried the earthiness of rain, even though the sky had closed up a few hours after it began. In those cool, drenched hours after the storm passed, when my stomach stuck out from being so blissfully full of water, thirsty snakes and rodents twisted through the bushes.

Now the island came alive after dark. Screams and cries of something wild scrabbled at the edges of sleep, chasing it from my tired limbs, and I could hear the crunching gravel of the caiman's roar.

With my eyes closed, I tried to focus on the crashing waves and imagine the long corridors that would connect the house by the sea that I'd someday share with Henri. Our house would have two wings and we'd sleep at separate ends all day. Almost all day—at some point, Henri would throw open my bedroom's French doors, climb into my four-poster bed, and press her icy toes against my heels.

I peeled the tarp back a little. Down the beach, Alex groaned, and reminded me how lost we were. Four days lost.

The night was humid, still, the darkness through the overhead branches speckled and dense, like salt across black granite.

The more I squirmed, the worse my back ached. For hours, I searched the starlit sky for some sign of life. As soon as I thought I would never sleep again, I passed out.

Alex's sobbing woke me up.

My eyes adjusted and I propped up on my elbows. Henri slept beside me, one limp hand draped above her head and the other arm tucked against her side. With the moon shining on her white-blond hair and down the slope of her nose, she could have been a porcelain doll instead of a real-life girl. I didn't know how I looked, but I could feel my filthy waves standing out from my scalp. Catastrophe suited Henri; it didn't suit me.

The full moon illuminated the sand as I made my way down to the water.

Alex cleared his throat where he was lying on his back by the ocean. "Couldn't sleep, Jones?"

I shook my head.

"Yeah, this isn't what you're probably used to, huh?"

"That's not why I couldn't sleep."

"I didn't mean it like that." He rolled onto his side and pulled something from beneath him—a book so waterlogged, the front and back covers rolled around and touched. "Hey, I'm sorry if I've been moody, or quiet . . . or whatever. I keep thinking—and sometimes it's easier if I don't talk."

I thought of the Oxy—what Henri had said about its effects. But I didn't care about the drugs, only the reasons he was sneaking off to take them. "You've been thinking about Casey?"

Alex rubbed his hands down his face. "Yeah."

"I only knew him a few hours. I . . . didn't even know his last name."

"Roth. Same as mine."

Alex Roth. Knowing his full name, a part of him from outside this place, was comforting, a reminder that all we needed was rescue to slip back into the versions of ourselves from before. "What was he like?"

"Uh . . . Kind, I guess. Considerate. Lazy in a way. I was kind of jealous of him—being happy doing so little. But he was good at leading boating tours. We both were. People loved them . . . Present company excluded, of course."

"I was saving my complaints for the comment card."

He laughed. "No doubt."

Something buzzed by my ear, and I swatted at the air. Sleeping in all our clothes only made me hotter and stickier, but it was the only way to protect my arms from bites. "If we had a fire, do you think it would keep the bugs away?"

"If it was smoky enough, probably, yeah. A shelter would help too. But we don't have tools to cut down trees or anything. It'll take weeks collecting whatever washes up before we can start on anything decent."

Weeks. Every time someone said anything at all about making plans for the future, my panic built. I couldn't imagine our four days lost multiplying.

My hand brushed his book. It was too dark to read the title. "What are you reading?"

"A success manual."

"Like, success in what? Getting girls?"

"I rely on my natural talent for that." He smiled, then dog-eared a page and moved it behind him. "Making little bits of money turn into millions. Compound interest. It's called *Finishing Rich in the Modern Age*."

"Finishing rich? That's what you wanted."

I said it like a joke, but a grimness settled over him. "Apparently more than anything."

I hated this shift in him. "Hey, you never answered, when we were on the cliff. What do you want? And please, don't be boring."

"Never." He smoothed the sand between us and scooted closer. "Okay, back home—in West Virginia, not Puerto Rico—I had a Jeep. A Wrangler. With one of those tops that popped off. I left it open-air until it was too freezing cold not to. When I couldn't sleep, I'd drive. The headlights on the road, the wind gusting through, when I got home I was so relaxed I'd just pass out."

"What color was it?"

"An alluring chartreuse."

"Green?"

He smiled. *"An alluring chartreuse."*

"But you couldn't even drive it here."

"It's a Jeep, Jones. Built for rough terrain. I could drive it down the beach, over sand dunes . . . If I still had it. I sold it to get to Puerto Rico."

I leaned back, and opened my eyes wide to the shock of the night sky over the beach. Not salt. Stars like clouds of sugar were frozen across the black atmosphere. They were like nothing I'd ever seen before, even though they were the same stars over San Francisco, shrouded by fog, and the same that had glowed dimly above Puerto Rico.

I lowered my chin slowly until I'd followed them to the end of the horizon. San Francisco was oceans away but Puerto Rico was out there somewhere to the northeast. "How far do you think it is to Puerto Rico?"

"I don't know how much we drifted. A hundred and fifty miles, maybe?"

"A hundred and fifty. So, I guess swimming it is out of the question."

"Only slightly."

"Hey, you read that book." I lifted up, inched closer. "Those prisoners who died swimming out of Alcatraz, how far was that, like two miles?"

"One and a half. Give or take. And don't be such a dream-crusher, Jones." He grinned through his fake outrage. "Some people think they made it. That they're alive and well, eating oysters and playing checkers on some beach in Brazil."

"Is that the camp you're in?"

"Well, obviously . . . I like being right."

In the moonlight, Alex's cargo shorts looked different. They were striped—a dark color like navy and a lighter gray. This had to be the extra set of clothes in his backpack. I focused harder. Alex wore nothing but his boxers.

He smiled before I looked away. "My shorts are stiff from all the dried salt water. I can't really sleep in them. Not that I could sleep anyway. I could, uh—put 'em back on if my immodesty is bothering you."

"No, no. Leave them off."

Alex's teeth flashed in the moonlight and he laughed, face tilted to the sky for a second.

"I mean"—heat burned all the way from my forehead to my kneecaps—"you can, if you—"

"Jones. It's okay. I'm only teasing you." He draped his shirt over his lap. "So, um, is your sister holding up okay?"

"Henri's a survivor. She won't let this or anything get her down for too long."

"What about you? Aren't you a survivor?"

I'd never really thought about it. "I want to be."

He nudged me with his elbow. "You've got a lot on your sister."

"Hm."

"For starters, you're a good person."

"She is too." His words were a knife in my chest.

"No, she isn't. It takes one to know one."

The ache of his voice stopped me from asking more questions.

We sat shoulder to shoulder in the blackness. Before sunset, Alex had dipped in the ocean to keep cool, and I could smell the briny salt on his skin. His shirt—a different shirt, *Casey's*, Alex said when he caught me looking at it yesterday—still carried the powdery scent of detergent, of home.

We were far enough from the waterline that the sound of the waves lapping against the shore was faint, and the quiet filled with our own breaths. We didn't say we were scared— we didn't have to say anything at all.

Maybe something happens to people who are lost, when death isn't some faraway possibility. You reach an understanding about when things need to be voiced and when they don't. Alex and I had reached ours.

As the sky lightened, I yawned into my hand.

"Some sleep would do us both a world of good, Jones."

"I don't know if I can."

He hugged his arm around my stomach and lay down behind me. Into my neck, he said, "Maybe we should try it like this for a while. You know, in the name of surviving and all?"

I didn't argue. It felt safe and good lying beside him. I needed someone and Henri wasn't going to be that person. She wasn't offering anything I could take—at least not at a price. And I didn't feel small for wanting some comfort. Alex needed it too.

I let my eyes close. I could shut them for a moment and listen to Alex's breathing.

Sunlight shone over Alex's shoulder, leaving me in the shade of his sleeping body. His limbs were tangled with mine, but I slipped under his arm and got to my feet.

Up the beach, Henri sat with her arms wrapped around her knees. Her eyes were on me, watching me. Watching us.

Alex and I stood on the highest rocks out in the ocean, on the western end of the beach, with our legs wide and our spears perpendicular to the water. We were starved for anything that wasn't cacao pods, but after hours of standing on the rocks under the afternoon sun, my shoulders itched with sunburn. Henri's sunscreen had gone empty after the first two days, and now there was no choice except to let our skin sizzle. We'd tried all morning to fish with Henri's sewing kit, but the thread wasn't holding and the fish weren't biting the safety pins we used as hooks.

I shielded my eyes and looked for Henri on the beach. She said she'd work on building a fire so we could cook anything we caught, but she must have been under the trees. So far, we hadn't caught a thing.

Algae covered the rocks beneath my feet and it took all my concentration not to slip. I flexed my legs, and hard muscles balled up on the backs of my calves. My arms and legs had grown stronger from pushing through sand. The island made me strong. That was the one thing the island gave me that I loved.

Every time a large fish swam by, Alex would thrust his spear into the water, right over the tops of the fish, and scare all the little minnows into the coral and shadows.

He missed again and groaned before setting his spear aside and taking a break.

My muscles quivered, and I slid down to the rock beside him and dangled my feet in the water. Brightly colored creatures swarmed around our toes.

His thumb traced a healing cut on the bridge of my right foot. "What'd you do here?"

"Sharp coral."

His fingers went higher, to the muscle at the back of my calf—my leg that hadn't been shaved in a week.

"What?"

As much as I thought my unshaven legs didn't bother me, Alex's hands on them were unbearable. "My legs aren't exactly soft to the touch."

"Au natural." He smiled and ran his fingers over his bristly jaw, which was growing in more reddish brown than the rest of his dark hair. "I could be into it."

I pulled out of his reach. "Alex, what do we do if another week goes by? And then another?"

"Jones—I don't know. I mean, if it becomes months—two or three months"—he lifted his shirt and wiped the sweat from his forehead—"we'll die for sure, right? The weather will change. Puerto Rico. Hurricane season. We'll be swept out to sea and we'll die."

"What's the alternative?"

"We get off the island."

That seemed perfect and impossible and everything I dreamed about every night.

A big fish wove around the rock beneath Alex's feet, and he stabbed at it.

"The water bends the light. You're never going to catch anything that way."

"Well, Jones, no offense, but I don't see you doing anything with yours." He gestured at my spear. "At least I'm giving it a go."

He scratched the scruff on his cheeks, and I remembered how his stubble had felt against the back of my neck in the early morning hours, his soft breaths blowing beneath my ear while he slept. I wondered so much about Alex, his dreams of finishing rich, how he got to Puerto Rico.

"Alex, you—" I stopped. He would have mentioned it if he wanted me to know. "Never mind."

"What? Just ask."

"How did you end up down here? In Puerto Rico, I mean."

He rolled his shirtsleeves up to his elbows and splashed a handful of salt water onto his face. "I wanted to go to college. I guess I was saving up."

"*You* wanted to go to college?"

He brought his hand to his chest and grinned. "You wound me."

"It's just that you have that whole surfer vibe going. Not like in a stupid way—I mean, you're smart. But you know, you drove a rickshaw—not exactly college essay material. What's the deal—what were you doing down here? With Casey."

Maybe it was mentioning Casey, but Alex put his back to me. I thought he was going to shut down, and I wished I hadn't asked.

But he inhaled, breathed out, and said, "So, Casey came

down to the islands to escape life for a while, have an adventure. When Casey said I should come meet him, I thought it sounded like a cool way to make some quick cash and get away from my hometown." He spoke carefully, like he was saying everything in his head first. "Because my dad, he'd been pounding on me for years, every day since my mom left. Drugs kinda took over his life, and he wasn't a fun addict." He pushed his hair back with one hand, glanced at me. "I'd moved out, was living with friends. Wanted to pay for college myself, without asking for anyone's help. What Casey was offering sounded like a fresh start."

The bump on Alex's nose—maybe his dad had done it. I hoped I was wrong, that it was from a surfboard or a jealous ex-girlfriend.

He got to his feet and poised his spear above the water. "What's your deal with your dad? You said he left."

"I—I shouldn't have even complained about mine. It's not like he hit me."

"There isn't some, like, limit line. I don't hold the monopoly on shitty dads."

"There weren't any words either, not that Henri and I were supposed to hear—not, like, verbal abuse. Last July, he just told my mom he'd met someone special. But he said it as if she wasn't special, as if Henri and I weren't special. He wasn't being an asshole—I think he thought it would soften the blow." I looked up at Alex, his steady gaze, his parted lips. I wasn't convincing him my dad wasn't terrible. I wasn't even convincing myself. "Maybe he is an asshole."

"Last July," he said. "Emma, that's fresh. I mean, I get that you want to accept it, get past it, but it's not like an overnight thing. Why are you forcing it?"

I hadn't thought about the *why* before right then. All I could see was my mom, zombie-like as she moved through that summer. Henri, changing in dangerous ways.

"Well, for my mom. She begged him to stay, to try couples counseling, to take a vacation. But he was just done. And Henri went off the rails. It was easier on both of them if I pretended to be—if I *was*—I don't know . . . the well-adjusted sister or something."

"I think you had that right the first time." He gave me a sad smile. "The pretending part."

"No," I said. But I remembered nodding along when Henri told me he was dead to us, pushing down the feeling that knifed through me. I'd gotten so good at pretending, I'd almost convinced myself. "Maybe."

A large gray fish rounded Alex's rock and both of us froze as it undulated in my direction. All the little minnows parted as the bigger fish came through.

I didn't breathe as my spear broke the water.

The fish twisted and squirmed on the end of my point.

"Shit!" said Alex. "Shit shit shit! You did it!"

He threw down his spear and grabbed me around the waist. As he spun me around, I tipped my head to the sky. Clouds spiraled above me and the green smell of the mossy rocks wafted up from where Alex was turning, not so carefully, on the slippery rocks. For the first time since landing on the island, I felt this familiar rush. A lightness . . . happy.

He slung me over his shoulder and ran—with me holding my fish on my spear—all the way back to the beach. He plunked me down on the sand, and when he did, he fell over me. The warmth of his sun-soaked skin pressed through my T-shirt and I almost wished I'd dared to wear only my swimsuit, just so I could feel more of him. We toppled over, both trying to keep the fish from touching sand, with our cold feet pressing against each other's calves, laughing and gasping for air.

Henri glared up from her spot on the beach.

I stood and dusted the sand and the feel of Alex from my skin.

Deadpan, she said, "Good job."

Alex bent beside the raft and refilled a water bottle that had washed up after the crash with rainwater. It wasn't totally sanitary to use it to hoard our water. But what other choice did we have?

All around Henri were dozens of tiny seashells. I'd seen them scattered along the shoreline, seashells and sand dollars I'd never seen the point in collecting. She'd strung the tiny shells one by one onto her roll of thread and had already made enough to loop around her wrist five times.

"What are you making?"

She didn't glance up from her shells. "Jewelry." A partially filled strand of only blue shells hung from her wrist. She pushed it higher onto her forearm. "Five shells. Five days we've been on the island."

Five days. Knowing it had been that long somehow made it

worse; if nobody had found us yet, maybe they weren't looking.

I scanned the shoreline for any signs she'd tried to build a fire. "So the fire didn't go well?"

"Nope. I tried."

It wasn't even about the fire. It was about the game. It was about control.

Alex muttered, "You've got to be fucking kidding me."

"She said she tried," I said.

He rushed past me and grabbed Henri by the upper arms. "Let me see your hands, then."

She kept them balled in tight fists, pulling them inside the pockets of her sweatshirt. Alex jerked at her arms until her hands came free.

"Stop!" I pulled at him. "Don't hurt her! *You're going to hurt her.*"

He looked my way as he pinned her to the ground. He wasn't Alex anymore, just rage and desperation. "Why do you care, Jones? Tell me, seriously, why do you care?"

Because anything Henri dished out, I had decided to take.

It was true—I wouldn't fight with her like she wanted. I had to be the bigger person because for one night I decided to be the smallest, most hideous person alive.

Alex didn't understand. And I couldn't tell him. Or anyone. Not even Henri herself.

"What difference would it have made?" She struggled to break his grip. "You and Emma tried and all you have to show for it are blisters. How would it have helped if I ruined my hands too?"

He held her wrist and pried open her right hand. The skin was baby smooth; her palms weren't even red.

"Well." She smiled up at him, relaxing into his arms. "It's good to see you've got a little savage inside you. I do too."

He met her eyes and his face drained of color. In my bones, I felt his shame—I knew what it felt like to let myself become something horrible.

He released her and she backed up in the sand, rubbing a faint red mark on her arm.

Alex tore at his hair. "You know what? Fuck it. We'll eat it raw."

We filleted the fish into bite-size portions on a piece of sheet metal we cleaned in the ocean, and divided our meals among three large waxy leaves.

We sat in a circle cupping our leaves in our hands as the fish jiggled. The pieces were white like albacore, not the deep red of raw tuna or even the pink of raw salmon. Alex stared at his like it might spontaneously cook itself if he concentrated on it hard enough.

"Fine. I'll go first." I popped a chunk into my mouth, chewed twice—not enough to get any flavor—and swallowed. Eating that fast, I only caught the taste after it was on the way to my stomach. It didn't taste good but it tasted like survival. "It's not even fishy. I guess because it's fresh."

Alex took some between his fingers, dropped it on his tongue, and swallowed. "Doesn't get much fresher."

Henri looked at hers like it was a guy who had driven her

to the party and had now served his purpose—she was ready to discard it.

Alex rubbed his forehead and focused on my sister. "Look, it's simple, Hank—if you don't eat, you'll die. Make your choice. I don't care what you do."

She picked up a twig and nudged at the fish. "I think I'd choose death over eating this."

"Come on," I said. "You eat sushi all the time. And you got on board with the cacao pods—you can do this."

She moved her fish around inside her leaf. "That's different. You didn't happen to find any wasabi and soy sauce while you two were trudging through the jungle, did you? And the cacao pods are gross."

Alex and I emptied our own leaves, shoveling every bit of fish onto our tongues. Still starving, we watched Henri play with hers, turning the leaf in her palms.

"Here, Em." She handed me hers and walked a few yards down the beach.

Henri definitely knew she needed to eat, that her body was now cannibalizing itself.

She'd read magazine articles to me back home, as she debated if we were eating enough Omega-3s to keep our skin clear and glowing, about the dangers of crash diets. Before she'd declared we had to eat more salmon, she'd read aloud how fasting and anorexia could make blood pressure drop super low, dangerously low, send vital organs into failure.

She knew all the dangers. Ignored them.

I remembered her telling me she wished she was dead, that

she should have been more specific and wished to die fast. Maybe starving herself was a way to end her suffering sooner.

Could she really be doing that?

Had she really slid from betrayed and sad to suicidal?

I watched Henri move down the shoreline, the fish momentarily forgotten. But my sister turned around.

She put a hand on her hip, right above the line of the bikini bottoms she'd tied low. "Emma, I'm going to rinse out my clothes. Let me wash yours too."

My stomach tightened. "Henri—"

"It's a good time. They'll be dry before night if I put them out now." She stretched out her hand and wiggled her fingers. "Give me your shirt and shorts."

My hands went still at the hem of my shirt. I wished I could go back to that day we boarded Casey's boat, when Henri told me to borrow her cobalt bikini. If only I'd said no, I'd be stranded in a comfortable one-piece.

My body had always just been there. I wasn't embarrassed by the way it looked, not until Henri. There was an expectation then, for my body to be this sexy thing I enjoyed, the way she enjoyed hers. And an object of desire. Something I didn't feel at all.

Henri didn't know all that, only that it was an issue for me. This was my sister hurting me in the best way she knew how.

I tugged my dolphin T-shirt over my head—quickly checked that my boobs were still inside the cups—and not daring to breathe, I stared Henri down.

Alex averted his eyes. I loved him for looking away.

Henri held my gaze for a long moment before her lips turned into a little smirk. "You know—I think I've found a solution to our whole lack of clothing." Still smiling, she reached behind her back. "We've been looking at this whole stranded thing the wrong way. In fact, I'm falling in love with this island. We're free here. There aren't any rules."

With the tug of a string, the weight of her breasts dropped from her top. Alex sucked in a breath, but he did a double take at me, and stalked off into the jungle.

Henri threw the top onto the rocks and strutted toward the ocean wearing only her bottoms.

CHAPTER 10

I was blowing away a chunk of hair that kept falling in my eyes, leaning up against the B Wing stairs where I always met Henri for lunch, when she bounded down the steps.

"Go on without me," she blurted. "I have something I have to do."

"What?"

She glanced back up the stairs leading to the music room. "I'm hanging out with Ari and Mick. I'll see you after school."

Henri hummed a Red Hearts song all the way to the top of the landing.

The halls cleared as everyone found their friends and headed off campus, but I stood in place, weighted down to the tile floor, as I thought about the music room at the top of the stairs where Henri had musical theory with Mr. Flynn.

I wished I could go back in time and find a solid indisputable reason to keep my sister on the sidewalk and out of that record store.

I almost didn't hear Jesse say, "Hey."

He scanned my uniform, from the white button-down I'd ordered a size too big to my navy swing skirt.

The tangerine polish Henri had applied for me had chipped off my right big toe and I moved my left sandal in front of it. "Hey."

He buried his hands deep in his navy trouser pockets and dropped his backpack beside me. "Are you waiting for Henri?"

I followed his gaze to the empty stairs he'd seen Henri run down every day for weeks.

"No, she's having lunch with Ari and some guys. A lot of guys. I don't know what they're doing—it was probably code for something."

"Like what?"

It wasn't true. And if he knew her at all, he'd know that if it was code for something, she would have told me. But I wanted Jesse to think Henri had this huge life that didn't involve him. "You know how she is."

His shoulders slumped, and he turned to the school entrance behind us. He unhooked a Giants baseball hat from the carabiner on his bag. Jesse's dad always brought home sports swag from the station, and Jesse was never without a hat unless he had to be—he wore one every day at lunch, and always got in trouble for forgetting to take it off when classes started back. He pulled it low over his eyes and smiled. "So, you want to have lunch with me? Beach Chalet?"

North Beach was fifteen minutes away, maybe twenty during lunch hour. "We won't have time to make it back."

"Well, if you don't wanna . . ."

With the wind tangling my hair, the rickety cable car bounced beneath my feet just like that day with Henri. This time the sides of my hip kept bumping into Jesse's. Little touches that should have been electric. I wanted to press closer, but I didn't want to cross a line that couldn't be recrossed.

He came back as something more. I saw what I'd known was always there, hiding under that too-wide smile and floppy hair that turned up around the edges of his dress-code-defying baseball cap.

We picked up speed on a downhill slope, and the ocean air slapped us in the face all the way to the Beach Chalet restaurant.

Frescoes decorated the archways inside. I stopped to stare at the paintings of people swimming beachside in old-fashioned, high-waisted swimsuits. I hadn't been to the Beach Chalet since my dad took us out for brunch on Henri's birthday the year before.

The glass front of the restaurant gave a view of the ocean that mesmerized me. Fog didn't block the ocean for a change, only clear sunshine all the way from the building to the faraway horizon.

Henri and I would live in a house with a view like that.

We ordered some Chalet Beignets and coffees and headed onto the beach. The fall air was chilly, but the sun glinting off the sand made us brave the cold.

Jesse paused at the end of the sidewalk to tug off his tennis shoes. He hooked his thumbs into the laces and his bare feet stepped onto the beach. I yanked off my sandals and followed his path through the sand.

It wasn't unusual for Jesse and me to do something alone. He was a senior like Henri, but even though they were the same age, she'd always been more worldly. When we were kids, Henri wouldn't have a thing to do with him—which wasn't so different from now—and I always ended up being Jesse's playmate when Henri wasn't around—which also wasn't so different from now.

If the three of us ever did anything together, Jesse only got invited because I'd done the inviting. That didn't mean he wasn't madly in love with Henri, even back then.

He tore the lid off his macchiato and sipped. "That's a rough break about your dad."

"Yeah. Henri's having a really hard time with it, I think."

Jesse bit into a beignet and scattered powdered sugar down the front of his shirt. He could never eat anything without wearing it. "What about you?"

"It's a good thing in a way. He was making my mom miserable, even though she would have done anything at all to make it work. It was the way it all happened—that woman. I guess there's no good way, huh? No *Hey you, we've spent like twenty years together but I'm gonna move out and love somebody else now.*"

With his mouth full of beignet, he said, "Parents are the absolute worst."

I paused. "That sucks about your mom too."

"She's happy now. I guess that's what counts. I was going

off to college next year anyway. And it was weird being with my mom—Colin, her boyfriend, had one of those no-shoes-in-the-house rules. Does he not realize how much bacteria is on bare feet? What a douche." Jesse sighed and leaned back, resting his forearms against the sand. "So, is Henri dating anyone right now?"

"Did you seriously drag me out here to ask about Henri's love life?"

"It's only a question." Laughing, he socked me in the arm so hard, I was sure I'd bruise. "Is she?"

"Henri is definitely dating someone. In fact, she's dating everyone. Why, are you still into her? I thought that was some weird, hormonal puberty thing."

He peeled the sleeve off his macchiato. "Nah. I'm not into her anymore. I was just asking." He nudged my ankle with his big toe. "I miss our games, though."

The summer before Henri and Jesse started high school, she used to make the three of us play her favorite game: choose a way to die and explain why. Jesse always said there was only one way to die, a gun to the head, quick and over. Henri said that was stupid—she heard about this kid who shot himself in the head and the bullet lodged in his skull or something. He ended up living, sucking the rest of his meals through a straw.

I could never commit to an answer. Henri always said she didn't care how she died—she just didn't want to do it alone.

Jesse and I raced through the empty halls of Baird. We were beyond late.

My feet got ahead of me, and I stumbled. As I lurched forward, Jesse caught my hand and we kept running, his fingers twisting with mine. I wished he'd never let go, that I could keep him forever and ever.

But his hand slipped free.

"My class is in here." Before the D Wing door shut behind him, he grabbed the doorframe. "Hey, Em, sorry I made you late."

My PE class had started ten minutes before and I was a good three-minute walk to the locker rooms outside the MPR and still wearing my uniform. *My gym shoes*—they were still inside my locker.

My sandals slapped down the hall as I broke into a sprint toward my locker in B Wing.

The combination failed three times before the locker squeaked open.

Above me, at the top of the music room stairs, the water fountain turned on. There was Mr. Flynn bent at the waist and drinking from the fountain. I bent low and watched him from between the air vents of my open locker.

The *click-clack* of heels echoed between the floor tiles and the fluorescent overhead lights. Vice Principal Deveroux, Ari's mom, came right at me. I was busted.

"Hall pass, Ms. Jones."

I grabbed my shoes and slammed the locker shut. "I don't have one. I'm sorry."

Henri was always telling me not to say I was sorry. She said it was a sign of weakness and I didn't need to go around apologizing for myself. Our sociology teacher talked about it too, how girls said they were sorry so many more times a day than boys.

My sister would have held her head high and said the perfect thing to get her out of detention. Henri would have never been sorry.

Vice Principal Deveroux folded her arms and tapped her sling-back heel on the tile floor. "You realize that means after-school detention."

"I'm sorry," I said. Again. "I—"

"Hey, what's taking you so long?" came from the top of the stairs.

She glanced up the stairs. "Excuse me?"

"Oh, I wasn't talking to you." Mr. Flynn jumped the last three stairs and landed beside me. "Are you ready?"

He was talking to me. "Oh, um, yeah."

"Sorry," he said to Vice Principal Deveroux. "I was in need of some help with the seating arrangement in my room. I'm writing her a note for—" Behind her back, I held up my tennis shoes. "For PE."

"Mr. Flynn, you have a stack of hall passes. Use them."

The sound of her heels became a soft tap, and I said, "Thanks."

"No problem. Gavin Flynn," he said, as if I didn't already know his name. As if all the girls at Baird didn't already know. "You'll have to call me Mr. Flynn, though. I tried to do the whole *call-me-Gavin* thing, but administration put the kibosh on that."

"Emma."

He held out his hand and I had to switch my gym shoes to my other to shake his. I expected a standard hand pump, but it evolved into some weird, complicated handshake I completely screwed up except for the fist-bump at the end.

"Well, come on." He pointed himself to the stairs and waved me up. "You'll have to wait out fifth period with me."

Those stairs. The place where Henri had run down for a moment an hour and a half before only to run up again as if something dangerously exciting waited at the top. My sandal touched down on the first step as though it might not be solid.

I wasn't afraid of Mr. Flynn. I didn't think he was some perv or anything like that. But something about crossing into this very adult world Henri had created made my steps uncertain.

Henri had a way of bending people, slowly, carefully, and by the time they were breaking, they were so enamored by her charms, they didn't even care. If she'd wanted Mr. Flynn, I had no doubt she could have him.

Mr. Flynn opened the door to the music room and held his arm out in a *ta-da* kind of way, like he was pulling back the wizard's curtain in Emerald City.

I followed him into Oz.

"It's my prep period." He flipped on the lights. "So it's just us."

Rows of chairs all faced a whiteboard he'd filled with names like Carlos Santana and The White Stripes and Ty Segall.

He grabbed two chairs from the bottom row and sat in one backward, straddling the seat and crossing his arms over the back. It was the kind of gesture I'd seen in movies—the "cool" teacher trying to act young and fit in with the students. But Mr. Flynn wasn't trying to be anything. He *was* cool. He *was* young.

"So, what's the story?" His hands clasped together seemed so much larger than Jesse's or any other boy's at Baird, reminding me he was still too old for Henri. I only wished he knew.

"The story?"

"Why you're late." His mouth twitched with a smile and he rolled his eyes. "Oh, there better be a good story. If not, you better make one up because I think I deserve a good story."

Taking the chair across from him, I crossed my legs at the ankles. "Oh, um, just a long lunch. We went to North Beach."

"Cool. Where'd you eat?"

"The Beach Chalet."

"Nice," he said, dragging out the *i* and snapping his fingers. "Okay. The next time you go to the Beach Chalet, I expect a bag of their Chalet Beignets. Okay? Then we'll be even."

He launched into a story about North Beach, about him when he was a Baird student. His friends built a bonfire one night—which you totally weren't supposed to do—but I wasn't really listening. I was thinking about Henri and which chair was hers. She took a seat in the first row for his class, I knew it. I knew everything.

It was watching a car crash, a fraction of a second before it happened, when the cars were moving too fast for anyone to stop them.

The moment I'd heard her humming that Red Hearts song, I knew.

"So is it true?" I said. He squinted, not understanding me. "That you played once for the Red Hearts?"

"Oh, that. Yeah. Once upon a time."

The bell rang and I dragged my chair into place, but I turned back. "So, I don't get it. Why'd you help me?"

"Ugh, I don't know. I went to school here. I know how it is. And you didn't hear this from me, but maybe Deveroux isn't my favorite person. Maybe."

I looped my backpack onto my shoulders. "Well, thanks. I better get to western civ."

"Your sister is Henri Jones, right?"

"Yeah, Henri's my sister. How did you know?"

"Deveroux. She called you Ms. Jones."

"Oh, oh yeah, she did."

"And you look like her. It was a lucky guess."

"Who? Henri?" That was something only my mom's friends would say and only to be polite.

"She's in my musical theory class. Smart girl."

He had no idea.

CHAPTER 11

There comes a point when you're so lost, you realize you might not get found. Nobody said it out loud, but after twelve shipwrecked days, even Henri combed the shores every morning for anything we might use to build a real shelter.

Most mornings brought at least a piece or two of beach trash—water bottles and cans, mostly. They reminded me there was still a world out there, a civilized one. What Henri and I had done to each other wasn't all that civilized—maybe this island was where we truly belonged.

Ribbons of wood fell to the sand as I used Alex's knife to whittle the point of a branch into a spear. Henri watched from the shade, resting a hand against the sharp clavicle now jutting from beneath her skin. Alex stacked my spear with the rest.

The protein from the fish had revived our broken bodies, Alex's and mine. I felt it coursing through my bloodstream. Already our muscles were stronger, our minds sharp enough that we knew one thing for certain—we had to catch more fish.

"You need to eat a little, when we get more," I said to my sister. "I swear it's not bad."

The cacao pods were all she'd try, and even then it would

take hours for her to force herself to consume one, picking the beans from the white pulp, and carrying them with her on long walks down the shore.

In a bikini that bagged around her hips, she would move across the sand with a quiet but unwavering determination that some would have mistaken for acceptance. I knew better. Even though she was managing to keep everything together now, the hinges were sure to come loose, and when they did, I only hoped it was me and not Alex swept into her destruction.

She shook out her saltwater-textured hair. "Thanks. But I'm good with not contracting a tapeworm today."

Alex looked out over the ocean, like he did far too often. I thought I knew what he wished for. A ship to carry us back to civilization or somewhere exotic and far away. Or he fantasized about the rolling waves sending Casey tumbling back to us, breathing and alive. Maybe more pills to swallow down and drag him into oblivion.

I wanted something else from the island, and as the days stretched on, and we lost track of time and our common sense, I hoped someone—or anyone or anything that might be able to help—would give it back to me.

I wanted Henri. I wanted her like she was before, smiling and happy and loving me again the way I still loved her.

Nothing would give her back.

My tongue went dry, and I put down the knife and walked to our raft. I dipped my hands under the surface of the water and drank. I scooped another handful, and as I lifted it to my mouth, I gagged.

Dead mosquitoes floated in a thick layer on top of the water. Acidic chunks of my cacao pods rose from my stomach to my throat. I coughed into the crook of my elbow. Water rushed up my esophagus and into the sand.

"If we keep drinking this"—I wiped my mouth with my sleeve, kicking fresh sand onto the mess—"we're going to get sick."

We knew we were taking a risk, letting the raft stay full with still water, but we were too afraid to dump it out. Even though the rains were fairly steady for now, we couldn't count on anything to stay constant.

Alex rubbed my back and focused on me, chapped lips parted. The way he looked at me with such focused intensity—like not even a rescue ship careening into the shore could distract him. I wasn't used to it. But I liked it. And that scared me.

He cleared his throat and knotted his fingers together. "Somehow, we have to find a way to build a fire. We've gotta boil out the impurities."

The intermittent rain showers gave us water, but with drizzles keeping the brush damp and green, we'd given up hope of creating a fire.

"We could fill those water bottles that keep washing up. Wedge them in the sand to catch rain. I mean, we'd still have to drink some raft water, but it wouldn't be as bad as"—I lifted my chin to the raft—"that."

"Yeah, that would help," Alex said. "And if it starts raining, we could dump the raft and let it refill. Really makes you wish you hadn't taken plumbing for granted at home, huh?"

Home, I missed it, and not just food and cold water from the tap. Things like a sweatshirt still warm from the dryer, the pulse of a familiar song coming on the radio at the right time, running through the BART station and darting through the doors a second before they shut.

My visions of Alex at home were hazy.

"Where was home?" I asked him. "In Puerto Rico, I mean."

He glanced to Henri. Turned his back to her. "Casey had this little one-bedroom. No air-conditioning," he said quietly, "usually hot as hell. No cable. I had to go to an Internet café just to check e-mail. When he told me to come live with him, I didn't expect much. But after, maybe, uh, a month or so, I felt really solid." He furrowed his eyebrows and concentrated on something I didn't understand. "It was soulful, being shut off in a new place. Kind of beautiful. Does that sound stupid?"

"No," I said simply.

Henri got up from the shade and sank into the sand right in front of Alex. "Well, then, this should be paradise."

Alex cringed. There was no hiding anything on this island.

"So, a plane flew over today," she added.

I perked up.

Henri shook her head. "It wasn't looking for us. It was a big commercial thing, and even if it had been, it was entirely too high to spot us. I thought about all the people up there, their bags in cargo and magazines in their laps. Where were they going? I was wondering about it. And then I realized, wherever it was, I didn't want to go. I don't want to go home."

"Henri," I whispered.

"I don't want to go home and I don't want to stay here. This island is purgatory." She got to her feet, working her hands through her hair and letting the mess of it tumble down her back. She shot us a cold look and headed toward the far end of the beach.

Alex sighed. "Where are you going, Hank?"

She spun around and took a few wobbling steps, walking backward. "Away."

Once she was out of earshot, he said, "I swore I'd never lay a hand on anyone, not after years of my dad beating the shit out of me. A week ago, on the beach—I almost hit her."

"She can bring out the worst in people." I hesitated, then brought my fingers to the bridge of my nose. "Did your dad . . . ?"

Alex mirrored me, touching the bump. "Yeah, a few times." His cheeks flushed and he kept his hand held over it. "I never got it set right."

In the two weeks since I'd met him, he'd never seemed self-conscious about his looks before—and now I hated that I'd made him feel that way. I knew what it was like to be uncomfortable in my skin.

"I like it," I blurted.

He looked at me doubtfully. "Jones, you don't have to—"

"No, I do. A lot. I don't like how it happened. But it's part of you." I had to stop talking. "It gives you character."

"Thanks." He dropped his hand away and smiled. "I guess we've all got things."

I nodded, and he inched close enough for me to feel the warmth radiating off his skin.

He traced a fingertip along the place where my shorts met my thigh. I felt suddenly dizzy, hot, my breath quick and the beat of my heart too. "But if I'm being honest," he said, "I don't understand why you're afraid to take off your shirt and shorts." He moved higher, to the neckline of my shirt, where my swimsuit peeked out, and he hooked his finger under the blue neck strap. "I'd be lying if I told you a good part of my day wasn't spent thinking about this bikini."

I exhaled a shaky breath as his fingers grazed the nape of my neck and settled there, a good weight.

Our hair flew in my eyes as the breeze picked up. He leaned close.

"Don't," I breathed. I grabbed his wrist and moved his hand from my neck.

My sister materialized at the edge of the jungle, and Alex nodded. He thought she was the reason. He didn't know that Henri ran from one boy to the next hoping they could save her. I wanted to save myself.

Late in the morning, I pushed onto my elbows after an uneasy rest and dusted away the sand the breeze had flown against my arms and legs and face.

The palm trees danced back and forth, like always. Everything on the island was constant. The sand, the sun, the ocean, our desperation.

I rubbed the sleep out of my eyes as I tried to pinpoint the day. Thirteen. Or fourteen. I'd lost track of time—the one thing gone that I could have kept within my reach.

Alex wasn't around, but Henri's arms were scissoring through the waves. Her bare shoulders twisting in the water reminded me of how she'd stripped off her top in front of Alex that afternoon. I could survive the island, but I didn't know how to survive a naked Henri strutting around like a giraffe with breasts.

She emerged from under the surface, letting the water lap against her neck, her shoulders, her clavicles, and finally, the mint-green of her bikini top. She wasn't naked—she'd tied it into a strapless.

Wherever her energy came from, I didn't know. But I worried. The way she loathed me—and Alex too—maybe burning up calories and letting her body feast on itself was the quickest way for her to leave us behind. That or drown.

Stop it.

But I couldn't avoid the thoughts any more than I could extinguish the sun.

Henri plopped down beside me and a few drops of ocean landed on my arm.

"Where's Alex?" I asked.

She pointed at the jungle. "He's looking for something."

The jungle was silent behind me. I felt its eyes, yellow and slit-pupiled like a caiman's. It was all I could do not to turn around.

Henri stretched out her legs to examine them in the sunlight. "I've never been this dark. And you've never been even close."

The wind overhead swayed the trees and moved the shadow lines up our tanned legs.

My sister and I spent most summers the color of caramel, but she was right, we'd never been this tanned. Our mother swore we'd be covered in melanoma by our thirtieth birthdays.

I never believed her. In our big house by the ocean, our skin would match our crinkling wallpaper. We'd mourn our long-dead lovers and stay up all night playing Italian music and dancing through our empty halls. Even with gray hair and folds of skin draping her thin arms, Henri would still be beautiful.

I scooted backward until every inch of my skin was in the shadows.

She flinched. "I meant it's pretty, Em."

"Oh." It had been so long, I didn't know how to take my sister being kind to me. I wished she'd be kinder to Alex.

"Henri, when the boat went under, what were you doing? Why did you leave us behind like that? Did you see Casey? Did you see his head—"

"Of course I saw," she snapped. "But he was gone and Alex was falling apart and excuse me if instead of wasting my time on a lost cause, I decided to get my *still-breathing* sister into a life raft." She blinked fast, surprised or regretful she'd said it—I couldn't tell. Her stomach made a loud growl. "I'll be back."

She adjusted her swimsuit bottoms as she moved around

the rocky side of the beach, her hip bones protruding from her skin. If Henri really was trying to starve herself to death, she had to know I'd stop her. She had to know she would eat some of the fish, even if I had to pin her to the sand and shove it down her throat.

With the wind at my face, I moved until I reached the place where she'd disappeared half a mile down the sand. The beach curved sharply there, and when I made it around the curve, Henri wasn't there. She'd vanished.

A tall boulder stood between the beach and the jungle, and I climbed it to get to a higher vantage point. As I reached, something sharp stuck my palm. I pulled myself up, cautiously, and into a grove of yellow flowers shaped almost like pineapples, with thick, rubbery petals narrowing into sharp-as-glass tips.

Filtered by brush and flowers, in a small depression inside the jungle concealed by the boulder, I caught a glimpse of Henri's bright swimsuit as she carried a large rock against her stomach and dropped it in the shade of a tree.

She propped it between her knees, and picked up something else—a coconut. She brought it down over the rock, and it exploded into five pieces, sending coconut water splashing all over her chest and hair. She swore as she tried to catch the spill.

I looked up at the cluster of coconut trees shading my sister. All around her were broken shells.

Everything about my sister became too much and too little in that moment.

I emerged from the trees. "Are you serious?" I almost screamed it, my chest tight, my face hot beyond sunburn.

With a mouth full of coconut, Henri squeezed her eyes shut.

"When did you find this?"

She chewed and swallowed. "That day we separated. The second day."

"*The second day.* We're out here eating rancid fruit and spearing fish to eat raw, and you have—you have *this*?"

"Em, you just said it—you and Alex have fish and cacao things—and I tried, but I just couldn't bring myself to eat them. You really don't need coconuts too. Aren't you happy I'm not starving?"

"You can't rationalize this, Henri. Not to me and not to yourself. If you don't tell Alex, I will."

"Em?" Henri said as I walked away. "Em? Emma, stop."

I whipped around. "What?"

"There's blood on your shorts."

"Here." Henri held out my damp shorts. "I scrubbed them with wet sand. The blood came out but so did the color."

I slipped the shorts—still soaking wet with ocean water— up my legs.

On top of dehydration, the sleeplessness, the bug bites, the hunger, and the searing sun, I now had my period to deal with. I wondered what Henri had done about hers.

"Why didn't you tell me when you got your period?"

She shrugged. "I did what girls do. I suffered through it

and pretended the lining of my uterus wasn't shedding and giving me agonizing cramps. Sometimes it sucks. Being a girl."

She didn't mean it. Henri loved everything girlish, everything that made her a girl, every bit of power she could exert over the opposite sex.

I didn't hate being a girl, but I didn't love it either.

The sun dried my shorts to my body within the hour. I flexed my legs to break the stiffness of the fabric.

Spots were lighter blue denim than the rest, but all I cared about were the eleven tampons left in Henri's bag. And the humiliating realization we might run out long before we got off the island.

Alex came back at sunset with his arms empty except for Casey's backpack cradled to his chest.

"We're only making it harder on ourselves," he said as I marched over to him. He slapped a sand flea on his neck. "We gotta start acting like we're not getting off this thing any time soon."

"Where were you all day?"

He cocked his head at me. "Just looking. Thinking."

"You can't just disappear on us, Alex. Anything could happen to you alone. It's reckless. Besides, we have to make decisions together—you agreed."

"I'm sorry. I'm trying. I'll try harder. But this—I mean it. We've got enough for a shelter, if we're creative. We can build it."

Alex focused on something behind me and his jaw went slack.

Henri dropped three coconuts between us. "There's more too."

My sister cracked open the first coconut on a sharp rock. She held it up fast, letting the water trickle into her mouth, then she broke it again to get at the smooth white interior. The second was my turn, and I busted it into jagged pieces. The third cracked almost perfectly down the middle once I had the motion and pressure down. I slurped the sweet water.

We drank what we could and used sticks to dig out the white meat. It wasn't sweet like the coconut candy our parents would buy in bulk for the holidays, but it was a welcome change from fish and cacao pods. Everything is a delicacy when you're on the verge of starvation.

Alex popped the last piece in his mouth and smiled at me. "What do you want, Jones?"

Henri snapped her head toward him. She didn't understand our game.

I thought for a second and smiled. "My ceiling fan." The sweltering, unmoving island air was strangling. "It ticks when you turn it on high, but I stop noticing after a few minutes. It's right under a vent, so the air it turns out is almost icy." I twirled my fingers through the sand.

Alex smiled wistfully, the setting sun slanting through palm fronds and highlighting the few dark freckles across his cheeks. "A triple cheeseburger with bacon and avocado. And a side salad—for balance."

"Very healthy of you. I'd have probably gone for fries."

Henri smacked her bag down on the sand and took out her sewing kit. "You know what I want? Silence."

"These tasted like sunshine, Hank." Alex tossed his coconut shell down the beach. "Plenty of energy for shelter building tomorrow. You did good."

"And what did you do," she asked, "all day?"

He ignored her and stared at the raft holding what was left of our water. We'd actually dumped it recently, sure showers would fall and refill it. But the rain stopped and we had to go without water for a panicked day and a half. "Hopefully it'll rain hard enough too and we can dump this again and catch fresh."

I wiped my sticky mouth. "So, where should we build it?"

"The jungle."

The jungle. I felt its eyes on my back. Its rustles, creaks, clicks amplified in the silence. I could hide my fear from Alex and Henri but not from myself. "I vote for the beach. Fewer bugs."

He stared into the bamboo. "We've been here for like two weeks . . ."

Henri spun the blue shell necklace she'd wound around her wrist. "Fourteen days exactly."

"Jones, the beach is exposing us to the elements— mosquitoes, sand fleas, the pouring rain, the blistering sun—"

"But how will help find us?"

"Our SOS." I knew he'd say it. But I was grasping for something—some logic or reason to stay on the beach.

"We'll be farther from the ocean. How will we cool off?"

"We'll walk." Alex pressed his fingers over his eyes and sighed. "We're desperate for a shelter. Look around. What on this beach are we gonna make it out of?" He swept his arm over our collection of scrap metal, fiberglass chunks of the boat, and driftwood—small pieces that wouldn't provide any structure. When I didn't answer, his voice softened. "We need a sturdy tree for a base." He wrapped his fists around the trunk of a skinny palm tree and it wavered. "Not this."

I nodded toward the jungle. "There are way more bugs in there."

"Come on, Jones. There's only one choice to make."

CHAPTER 12

After sixth period on Friday, I grabbed the last of my books from my locker and spun right into Sareena Takhar.

"Emma." She threaded a piece of hair behind her ear. "Do you happen to have the notes from civics yesterday?"

I slid my binder from my book bag. "Yesterday?"

"Ari made me late and with the test next Friday you would kind of be saving my life."

"Sure." I popped them out of my binder and cringed at the handwriting. "Sorry if some of that is hard to make out. Mr. Kaysen wrote a bunch on the whiteboard, told us to write it down, but stood right in front of it. We were scrambling at the end."

"Typical Kaysen," she said. "But these look great. Thank you. For real. Next time you need notes—"

"No prob." I glanced at the time on my phone. "Hey, I gotta meet Henri. See you later." I took off down the hall toward the school entrance where we always met.

Footsteps struck the tile floor beside me as I passed by a booth selling tickets to the winter banquet.

"Wait up." Henri matched her pace to mine in her chestnut-colored knee-high boots.

"Why aren't you coming from PE?"

"I skipped PE to do an extra-credit thing."

I shouldn't have asked. Henri, right there by my locker at the bottom of the music room stairs, told me everything I needed to know.

Jake Holt swung his arm over Henri's shoulders. "Well, Henri Jones, it's your lucky day. Where're you headed, because I'd love to offer my services as your escort."

She picked up the hand stroking the shoulder of her blazer and dropped his arm. "Um, no thanks."

"Well, which parties will we be crashing, then? I haven't seen you around lately. I'd love to be the one spiking your Diet Cokes tomorrow night."

"You'll have to spike the Coke of some eager freshman. But if I get bored, I do believe I still have your number."

He froze in the hallway. "Henri," he yelled, grinning with his arms spread wide as we kept walking. "You have got to be kidding me."

As I started to look back, Henri pressed her fingers to my elbow and guided me on.

"You've been into Jake Holt forever," I whispered.

"Well, maybe I'm through with boys."

Half the lights were blown out in our train car as we rode

BART home from school. Shadows ran across Henri's cheeks as she stared out the window.

Only once the train burst into the sunlight did I see the smile twisting her lips.

With my arms crossed in the seat facing hers, I thought about Mr. Flynn in the music room. He was an adult and even though a part of me knew it was his place to say no, the rest of me knew that when it was over, he was the one whose face would be on the evening news.

With my thumbnail, I scratched the nail polish off my pinkie and watched fuchsia flakes fall against my navy skirt. "Would you tell me if you were doing something dangerous?"

Henri relaxed into her seat and closed her eyes as if she were so unaffected by my question, she was falling asleep. "Stop being so intense, Em."

"Would you, though?"

"If you're asking what I think you're asking, don't worry."

"It's Mr. Flynn's life that will be ruined if you get caught."

She scooted forward in her seat until our knees touched, and dropped her voice. "Hey, he's twenty-two. I'll be eighteen in six months. There are less than five years between us. If I was a little older, it wouldn't even matter."

"But you're not a little older. And he's a teacher."

"There are seven years between Mom and Dad—"

"And look how well that worked out."

"Stop." She dug her fingers into each side of her scalp. "You're probably wondering, *Why him?* And I don't know. It's hard to explain. Gavin went to Baird and his parents split too.

He knows how it is to be nothing like anyone else you know."

I died a little when she said that. I felt she was the only person like me in the whole world.

"And Em, you should hear him play the guitar. It's the kind of music you can lose yourself in."

I didn't want Henri to lose herself in anything this risky. "You better be careful. What if Ari found out? She'd destroy you."

"Nobody knows but you. I know this is hard for you. You're different—and I love you for it—but this isn't your thing. I get it. You've never been into someone before."

That showed how well Henri knew me. She didn't know about my feelings for Jesse, who'd been a part of our lives since his parents bought their house next door when I was in first grade. With Henri, in just weeks, I saw right through to her feelings for a brand-new teacher. There weren't many ways I could compete with Henri, but in this contest, I was the clear victor.

The train came to a stop, and as I stepped onto the platform, I tried so hard to feel satisfaction in knowing her better than she knew me, but I didn't feel like I'd won.

Henri swayed onto the foggy sidewalk, the intro to a Red Hearts song humming between her lips. It occurred to me: In any game involving my sister, we were all destined to be losers—even Henri.

CHAPTER 13

Sixteen days of collecting everything the sea washed up meant we had enough to build a shelter. Henri wanted three small shelters, but we only had enough for one medium-sized.

The next problem became where to build it. None of our debris was that big. We'd have to rely on some existing structure for our base.

Alex and I hacked our way inland, through the humid air, deeper into the darkness. A caiman roared in the distance and I went stiff. But I took a deep breath, dried my soaking-wet palms against my shorts, and moved farther.

"What about over here?" Alex stood in the middle of a clearing, between two tall trees not too far apart. "We'll prop something between the forks in the trees and add branches to fill in the roof."

The thinner tree on the right seemed flimsy. "Do you think it's strong enough to support all that weight?"

He shook the trunk, and the treetop wobbled back and forth. "If it breaks down, we'll move."

"What if it happens when we're inside?"

"Point taken." Alex passed me his water bottle—it had

caught fresh rain—and I took a sip. He drifted away from me, through the thick brush of the jungle. I moved the opposite direction, stopping in a smaller clearing, maybe fifteen feet wide, at the base of a steep hillside.

A tree with a solid trunk had fallen with one end propped between the branches of a squatter, fatter tree. The triangle it formed made a perfect frame for our shelter. Its highest point was a couple feet directly over my head.

"Alex! How about this one?"

He ducked into the little clearing, looked around at the protective ring of trees, at the hill rising steeply on one side, at where I stood beneath the frame. His eyes stayed on me, and mine stayed on him. Spots of sunlight slipped between leaves, casting patterns across his face as he smiled up to the canopy of trees. "Jones, you're a genius."

Dragging all of our supplies from the beach to the shady alcove of the shelter site, about ten yards deep into the trees, took three days. Five more and we'd stripped the bamboo down into cordage—that's what Alex called it—for lashing the roof together. We needed at least another week to finish that part.

The space between the two trees formed the frame of our shelter, so we built our walls outward from the trunks until we had a solid oval-shaped enclosure. Even though the shelter's ceiling wouldn't be done any time soon, we layered soft leaves and palm fronds on the floor to create some cushion and keep us out of the dirt and sand.

Hidden away inside the glowing green pocket of jungle trees and mesh of vines and branches, I didn't think about the caimans as much. I almost felt safe.

When the afternoon sun moved overhead and soaked through the leaf awning at the hottest part of the day, we cooled off in the ocean or lounged in the shade.

Stretched out on our stomachs in the sand, Alex and I faced each other while Henri strung ropes of seashells.

Propping his head in his hands, his lashes dark with ocean water, he watched me. The corners of his mouth turned up. There was a slight line down the center of his full bottom lip. I wanted to touch it. "Tell me what you want, Jones."

I blinked, my eyelids heavy. The heat of the beach was thick against my skin, even under the canopy of palm trees, so I said, "A Thai iced tea. Super cold with extra milk. The kind with so much caffeine, my eyelids twitch for hours."

He opened his mouth to speak, but Henri's whisper interrupted. "Honey lavender gelato."

Sand clung to Alex's chest as he rolled onto his side to face her. "What?"

She rested her teeth against her lips, staring down at her shells. A little louder, she repeated, "Honey lavender gelato. From the shop on Powell."

My throat tightening, I nodded. "After a movie in the Haight."

Alex glanced to me, the tears shining in my eyes, and he smiled at her. "I'm more of a mint chip guy." Even though this game was ours, Alex would let her play. "What else, Hank?"

Getting to her feet, she said, "It's not my turn," and headed toward the water.

Henri made herself scarce once it was time to build the shelter. She claimed she was out scouring the jungle and searching for pieces to layer onto the roof, but twice I found her with handfuls of tiny seashells she'd collected.

Alex scowled when he saw her, but I didn't say a word. At least Henri had something to do.

"You have to stop babying her," he said, once we were out of earshot.

"She's my sister."

"But she's—"

"Don't." If there was one thing worse than Henri hating me, it was Alex hating Henri. He didn't know Henri before I'd ruined her.

Something was wrong with my sister, wrong in worse ways than I'd first imagined—she didn't want to go home. My sister, whose entire existence was live bands, expensive clothes, loud engines, strong liquor, and dangerous boys—she was willing to never have any of that again. Or what was beyond it.

Whatever secret she was hiding from me, I might never know.

Alex's eyes drifted down my body—to me in my bikini top and shorts. My dolphin T-shirt hung from a tree while I worked. We were covered in scratches and scrapes from carrying and cutting down sharp fronds. Keeping it on would have protected me some, but I was hot and afraid I'd rip it stripping vines and not have a shirt at all.

"Hey, Jones, I've been wanting to say . . . to tell you—you've got nothing to be ashamed about."

Heat moved from my chest to my collarbone. This feeling . . . it was new, confusing. I crossed my arms, but I wasn't embarrassed he'd been looking, only that he might realize my body had responded in a way I couldn't control.

He dropped his gaze to my flushed skin and tore his stare away. "Not that I was looking."

"I don't— I don't mind you looking," I said to the dirt, to the sky, to the achingly green trees around us. "I'm just"—I couldn't tell him I'd been living underwater and had just been pulled into a sunlit world—"surprised."

"You're surprised?" He stepped closer and bent his head and searched my face until I met his gaze. His eyes were greener under the leaves, his freckles vivid in the gloom. I could feel his nearness like the wavy haze of heat off the sand. "Jones, I've wanted to touch you since the first time I saw you."

The warmth in me intensified, pulsing through me until now, alone with Alex in this deeper part of the island, I knew I'd been lying to myself.

I wasn't broken. I wasn't above it. I'd just never felt this—struggling to breathe, catching on fire—nothing like this.

"You don't think you look bad or something, do you?"

"It's not like that—" I cleared my throat and stared at the vines I'd stripped. "It's . . . I guess I've spent too much time watching people stare at Henri."

Alex reached for me. I went still as his hand brushed my

face and moved to the soft spot under my earlobe. He dragged his thumb across my lower lip. "You're wrong. Henri's looks are so obvious. You—you're subtler. Much"—he leaned in, not quite touching me, letting only the prickle of his facial hair graze my skin—"sexier." I felt the brush of his eyelashes across my cheek, smelled salt and sawdust and sun and rain. Then his teeth, a gentle tug on my lip. And I kissed him.

We laid thick palm leaves at the sides of the shelter. I focused on the palm leaves. The roof was too high to reach, and we weren't sure if the trees could hold Alex's weight, so I climbed up and he handed me pieces of thatch to weave together. I focused on the weaving.

The kiss. We hadn't mentioned it. But I wanted to take it back. All of it. My hands wrapped at his neck. The soft sound I made against his mouth. The way we pressed close as if we could put our hearts inside each other and keep them safe until we needed them back.

I skidded down off the lowest branch, steadying my hands against Alex's shoulder blades. Heat radiated through the cotton of his shirt and onto my hands. His skin was on fire.

"Alex."

Little beads of perspiration stuck to the skin around his hairline and his breathing was ragged as he stared up the tall, spindly trunks. "What?"

"You don't look so hot."

I pressed my hands to his cheeks, then his forehead. The temperature of his face was even warmer.

His lips slipped into a crooked smile. "Out of everything we have to worry about, my sunburn isn't one of them."

"I don't think it's a sunburn." I'd seen Mick and Ari high out of their minds once, sweat pouring. "Did you, um, take anything?"

"Take anything?" His eyes snapped wide and he laughed. "What the hell would I have taken?"

"Never mind." I walked a few steps away, hating what a good liar he was.

His feet slipped out from under him as he tried to sit on a wet bed of leaves.

"It couldn't be anything you ate," I said. "We've eaten the same things."

My stomach constricted as I thought of the last fish we'd eaten, even though it had tasted fine. Contracting some deadly food-borne illness on the island was unimaginable.

"So, I ate something else." He looked up, rubbing the back of his neck. "Before the coconuts, I found some mushrooms in the jungle."

Leaves crunched as I moved closer. "You didn't."

"Look, I put a piece in my mouth, just to see, but my tongue went numb almost immediately."

"You can't take risks like that, Alex! We all need each other. I need . . ." I glanced away.

"That was yesterday, Jones. It's been almost twenty-four hours. Poisoning like that hits hard and fast, right? Not like this. It must be heatstroke or sunburn or . . . or infection."

"Infection? What hurts?"

He clenched his teeth and brought his head between his knees. "My head, my arms and legs, these fucking cuts."

Scrapes and cuts—we were covered in them. The palm fronds were sharp enough, but cutting them down meant stretching across the blade-like edges of the pineapple-shaped flowers. "Do any of them look infected?"

"Can't tell. I think I messed up my back really bad carrying piles of palm fronds on it."

"Take off your shirt. Let me look at you."

His long fingers trembled, fumbled with the buttons. I moved close, undoing the bottom button and the next four up before he managed the first. He shrugged free of the shirt, and his skin was covered in a solid sheen of sweat.

A short piece of rope that had washed onto the beach held up his sagging cargo shorts. Now that he'd thinned so much, his muscles were more prominent under his skin. He wasn't super built when we'd washed up here, broadest and most developed in his arms and shoulders and legs, probably from fighting waves on his surfboard and driving the rickshaw. He was almost rangy now, narrowing like a triangle from his armpits down to his waist.

I moved behind him. Thin scrapes marked his back, some as tiny and thin as paper cuts, and some long lines of dried blood.

I traced each cut with my eyes, from his neck down to his waist. The skin around each was smooth and still flesh-toned. My hands moved over the tendons on his arms as I stepped around to face him. Only a few cuts ran across his upper torso. I placed my left hand against his chest to steady myself until I realized what I was doing and let go. I worked my way from his shoulders down. As my fingertips brushed a cut above the waistband of his shorts, his pulse raced under my other hand.

I glanced up, met his gaze. "Did that hurt?"

With bloodshot eyes, he gave me a half smile and whispered, "No."

I took a step back. "You're fine," I said. "I mean, as far as I can tell. The cuts aren't infected. It must be something else."

I backed up again and he bounced onto his feet. But as he moved into a sunlit patch of underbrush, his skin took on a gray cast. "I'm not sick. It's a sunburn. I'll be fine, Jones."

As he ducked under a low swinging branch, he stumbled.

Rustling woke me up on our first night sleeping in the jungle. Whatever tossed through the palm fronds was large. Something had made its way inside our shelter.

I pulled my knees to my chest and made myself as small as possible, until Alex groaned.

He'd insisted on sleeping at the edge of the shelter floor, even though he'd taken the spot where the fronds were the sparsest, beyond where the ground sloped downhill and flattened.

Now he tossed and turned through the leaves lining the ground.

I went over and whispered, "Get up."

"No."

I wrapped my arm around his back and felt fever blazing

off him. "You don't need to be down here alone. Sleep next to me and Henri."

As I let go, he lost his balance. I heaved him to his feet and led him to our pallet of leaves.

"You shouldn't," he mumbled. "What if I'm contagious?"

I brought a bottle of water close to his lips and made him drink. "Stop being a stubborn asshole."

Choking on water, he dug his fists into his forehead. "It hurts so bad behind my eyes, Jones. Fuck." He said it like he was angry at himself, as if being sick was something he shouldn't have let happen. "I don't want to die a miserable death out here."

"You're not going to die."

"You don't know—"

"I promise you, you won't."

"You can't promise that."

Adrenaline coursed down to my fingertips. I stood up again, ready to do anything. Everything. Something.

There was nothing left to do. We didn't have medicine or soup or blankets. All we had was time and each other.

I perched on the edge of the pallet, rubbing his back, rocking back and forth to burn off some energy, until Alex's shaking limbs relaxed and he fell asleep.

If there was one thing that scared me more than not knowing my sister's secret, it was something happening to Alex or Henri. They'd become two parts of me I couldn't live without.

I curled in close to them and waited for dawn.

CHAPTER 14

Henri hadn't invited me to any parties that Saturday night, and it was nearly ten o'clock. Never before had I asked if I could go with her, but that night I was worried about my sister and excited to see Jesse, so I decided to swallow my pride and just ask.

The lights were low as I swung open the door. "Henri, can—"

Her phone's flash went off as she snapped a selfie. I flipped the switch by the door, and as light flooded the room, I realized Henri only wore a skimpy pair of lace turquoise panties.

She grabbed a tank top from the floor and held it over her bare chest. "Shit, Em. I thought you were Mom."

"Tell me you weren't doing what I think you were doing."

She tugged on her top and smiled into her phone as she typed with her thumbs. "Really, Em, don't be such a prude."

As she shadowed her eyes in black and painted on enough dark gloss to make her pass for twenty-five, we both pretended I hadn't just caught my sister sending naked pictures to a teacher.

I sank into her bed while she jumped up and down into her tightest jeans, tied the laces of her high-heeled booties, and shrugged on her cropped leather jacket. After she filled a studded clutch with money, an ID, and a lip gloss, she turned to me and said, "Movies tomorrow?" before she headed out her door.

Mom was downstairs on the phone, whisper-screaming at my dad, so I shut myself in my room after Henri was gone.

Hours later, I was deep into an Internet search of Gavin Flynn and his time with the Red Hearts when Henri's door creaked shut. Her soft sobbing bled through the thin wall separating our rooms.

"Henri." I twisted the knob and opened the door a crack. "Henri, can I come in?"

She didn't answer, so I pushed inside.

Her computer screen cast a glow on the bed. She was curled up on her side into a smaller version of my sister, who had always seemed larger than life.

My bare feet dodged dirty clothes and bottles of nail polish as I padded across her carpet. "Are you okay?"

Henri would usually rather die than let anyone see her crying, so I expected her to tell me to leave her alone. She didn't say anything at all.

I arranged myself around her and brushed tear-soaked strands of hair off her cheeks. "What happened?"

"It's over."

I threw an arm around her waist and squeezed. She smelled like leather; she was still wearing her jacket. "What do you mean, it's over? Were you with who I think you were?"

"He said it would've been different if I'd just been a little older."

The weight of Henri's relationship with Mr. Flynn hadn't quite hit me until then, but now that it was over, I couldn't be anything but happy my sister and Mr. Flynn came out of it whole.

I swallowed. I didn't want to make anything worse by agreeing or disagreeing.

"I'm so sorry he hurt you." Those were the truest words I could give her.

She pulled her knees to her chest, sitting up, and rubbed black streaks of Maybelline from her cheeks.

"Tell me what happened."

"We were at his place." My poker face must have failed me, because she said, "I've only been there a couple times."

I dropped myself onto the floor of her room and looked at everything but Henri—her walls, her shoes, her dirty clothes. "Um, what do you do at his place? The kind of thing you used to do with Jake Holt?"

"No." As soon as relief washed over me, she said, "What we do—what we *did*—was nothing like with Jake Holt."

I sighed. "Henri."

Out Henri's bay window, Jesse stared in from his room. She saw me notice and said, "Ugh, creep much? I know he's your friend, Em, but there is something seriously missing there."

Jesse left the window when he saw us watching, but I crossed the room and lowered the blinds anyway.

"I don't think I can go back to the same old bullshit now."

"You don't have to."

Henri broke down, letting tears stream down her face and not holding back. She reached for me and let me lay beside her as she cried.

Later, after she quieted down and we both started to drift off, I whispered, "Did you love him?"

She didn't speak for a long time. "I don't think I'm capable of loving anyone but you."

As Henri combed her hands through my hair, I was thankful the darkness hid my smile.

CHAPTER 15

Dappled morning light streamed between the overhead leaves and into the open roof of the shelter, washing us in a green gloom. Beads of sweat clung to Alex's forehead as he thrashed on the ground. I took his face in my hands—his skin was boiling hot.

I shook Henri. "There's something really wrong with Alex."

Combing her fingers through her bed-head, Henri blinked herself awake. She focused on Alex, then backed up against the tree at the edge of the shelter.

"Henri, please. We have to cool him down."

I'd never seen her so uncollected, so un-Henri-like, but finally, she nodded.

"Do you think he's having withdrawal or a reaction or something?" I asked.

"I don't know." She got behind him and lifted him to a sitting position so I could strip off his shirt.

His eyelids fluttered open. "Don't."

I combed wet strands of hair from his face. Gave him some water. "We have to." His shirt was damp as I ripped it off his shoulders. "You're too hot."

He shivered like he might shake free of his skin. "I need it!"

Over Alex's shoulder, I looked at Henri.

"I think he's delirious," she said.

I put his shirt in his hands, but he threw it into the palm fronds. That wasn't what he wanted. "Alex, what do you need?"

He fisted a handful of fabric at the neckline of my shirt, tugging me close, nearly choking me. This wasn't Alex.

"Alex, you are hurting me." I grabbed his wrist to break free. His grip wouldn't let up. "Henri!"

She pried each of his fingers loose and we both took a step back.

Breathing hard, I kept my distance. "I don't know what he wants."

She scanned the fronds. Her eyebrows lifted as she settled on his backpack.

"It's worth a try," I said.

She tossed it into his arms, and I think I expected Alex to rip into the plastic bag, scattering pills across the dirt as he shoved a few into his mouth. But he just wrapped himself around the whole backpack and relaxed onto the shelter floor.

Henri and I took turns running back and forth to the ocean and collecting cool salt water. By afternoon my calves throbbed from running through sand.

As I ducked inside the shelter, Henri stood over Alex, who had fallen asleep with his arm stretched above his head. "What could have made him so sick so fast?"

"I—I don't know. He put a wild mushroom on his tongue, but he swears he didn't eat it. The fish had to be fine—we both ate it. He thought maybe an infection, but I checked all of his cuts, and they were fine." I glanced to her. "Maybe I should look at you."

She stripped off and brushed her hair over her shoulder. She did a slow twirl as I scanned up and down her bare torso. Only her legs had a couple of cuts—but it wasn't like she'd put in much effort on the shelter.

"You're fine."

"Good," she said. "Let me look at you."

I didn't move.

Henri took a step closer. "It's only me."

I dropped my shorts to the ground and pulled my dolphin T-shirt over my head. Not breathing as she examined my cuts, I waited for her to speak.

"You're fine. All clear. Oh, thank God."

"We've got to do a better job of taking care of ourselves." I stared up at the unfinished shelter as I yanked on my clothes. "Henri, can you help me finish this?"

"Whatever you need."

And for the briefest of moments, I allowed myself to think my sister and I might be okay.

We cut palm fronds and dragged them back to the shelter all day. With a heap of them trailing behind me, I trudged through the forest. My arms were weaker and the palm fronds thicker as we ran out of small trees. But a weight was pressing down on me that had nothing to do with what I was carrying.

Alex had obviously been delirious, but there was something painfully real about the intensity of his attachment to that backpack.

The branches grew heavier—they'd lodged in the underbrush. Henri stepped into sight and bent low to free them.

"Thanks."

"Don't mention it."

I stood and gathered the branches. "Henri, what do you think the deal is with the backpack? Can it really be just about the Oxy? And if it's not, then what is it?"

"You should go through it. You clearly want to know." The smile threatening to spread across her face made me nervous— it worried me for myself that Henri and I were in agreement on this.

"I do. But—"

"Em." Henri grabbed my upper arms. "Don't turn around. Don't move."

"That's not funny."

"No. Really. It's—it's one of those things. A caiman. Ten feet away."

I felt the island tip under my feet, the world plummeting toward an endless bottom.

The brush rustled.

Behind Henri was a tree with branches split low.

"The tree," I said.

Henri whipped around, kicked off her shoes, and hoisted herself up. All I could think as I grabbed on to the lowest branch was that I didn't want to die without Henri's forgiveness, and I didn't want to leave Alex alone.

She let out a long breath as I climbed up beside her. "There—see it? It's leaving."

The underbrush rattled again and I looked down. The caiman's tail slapped the ground before a bush completely engulfed it. I pressed my cheek against the rough bark of a branch, suddenly so tired, I barely had the energy to climb down.

We finished the shelter early the next morning—my sister and I—while Alex slept beneath the trees. We even used our last piece of tarp to make a door so we could seal ourselves inside and everything else out. Or at least feel like it.

Alex had hoped we'd only find the caiman near water. Maybe it was just to manage my anxiety, but I'd taken that hope for fact. Now that we knew better, we used rocks to weight the bottom of the tarp. If a caiman really wanted in, the tarp wouldn't do much, but at least one wouldn't just wander inside.

The shelter wasn't the house by the sea I'd dreamed of. But it would keep us dry.

Henri stood back and inspected the shelter. Her hands were on her hips, but she wore a little half smile that I knew meant she approved.

Back within my reach was the sister I'd grow old beside.

My arms shook with fatigue as I lifted my bottle of water to my mouth and chugged. Then, with the old Henri so close,

I took a chance. "It'll get us by until we can get home. Then things can be like we always wanted—we'll grow old together, like we said we would."

Her smile went flat. "Maybe we're not supposed to grow old together, Em." She glanced at me. "Why don't you check on the patient. I'm going to look for another blue shell. Day twenty-two."

I wondered, not for the first time, if the only thing keeping Henri going was anticipating the moment she'd get to search the sand for another blue shell, find it, and thread it onto her necklace.

Of course, I wished it was me. I wished I was the thing.

"Henri, thank you for everything you did."

Over her shoulder, she waved. "Don't mention it."

I watched her walk away. Henri didn't do anything without a purpose, and if she didn't want to go home, she certainly had a reason.

"Alex." I brushed my fingertips across his freckles until his eyelids fluttered open. "We finished the shelter. Why don't you get inside?"

He coughed and forced himself halfway up, but slumped to the ground again. "Yeah. Okay."

"Put your arm around me and try to stand."

Alex slipped and wrenched me down, but he pushed himself away so he fell against a tree and scraped his arm instead of crashing into me. He hung Casey's backpack in the tree and lurched into the dark, cool shelter on his own.

With a piece of the lining from Henri's bag, I pressed the wound on Alex's arm until it stopped bleeding. After twenty-seven days without soap and running water, Alex still didn't smell bad to me. Even though the detergent had dissipated from his clothes, I liked his smell—a mix of salt, sawdust, and water, like the air after a first rain.

"You did one hell of a job, Jones." Alex shifted, groaned. "Hank helped you, right—you didn't have to do this all on your own?"

"She helped. A lot, actually."

Even though his lips were peeling and his cheeks dark red, he gave me a small smile. "Whatever I have, I'm just—I'm being a burden. You should drag me out to the middle of the jungle and let me die."

"And by *let me die,* I know you mean, *Thank you for trying to save my sorry life. I'm eternally grateful, Emma.*"

His eyes were closed, but his lips twitched.

"But you wouldn't say that, would you? You wouldn't call me Emma."

"Jones suits you better. But I'll call you Emma if that's what you want."

"I like Jones." He grimaced and touched his head, so I said, "Tell me what you want."

He was quiet for a moment, but then he smiled a little. "When I was a kid, I had a tree house. It had a wood ladder and a bucket with a pulley for lowering things up and down. The roof was shingled—not like this—rain- and windproof. I kept every bit of loose change I could find in a jar up there and a couple of *Playboys* too—I was ten. When my dad found the *Playboys*, he tore it down along with the tree. I'd kinda like that treehouse back." He opened an eye. "I'd even let you live in it with me."

I balled Henri's empty backpack under his head as a pillow. "How's your head?"

"It hurts."

"I'm sorry." I stroked his forehead until he closed his eyes. I watched him closely for a reaction as I said, "I wish I could give you a painkiller or something."

He just said, "Hell of a place to die, isn't it, Jones?"

"You're not going to die. You're already getting better. What do I have to do to convince you you're just going to have to stick around?"

"Maybe, uh, you could give me something to live for."

He lifted up but I pushed down on his chest. "I don't know if I should slap you for being a horny asshole or forgive you because the fever has cooked your brain."

"I'm perfectly lucid, Jones."

"You're clearly feeling better."

His grin faded and he focused on my lips. "I thought we had something going on. On the beach that day, and when we were building this thing."

"Alex—"

"Come here." His hands closed around my hips, and he pulled me toward him. Pure want, no thought, I slipped one leg over his chest and let him guide me on top of him.

"You're delirious."

"Am I?" He tangled one hand in my hair, and with the other, skimmed his thumb over my lower lip, the way he'd done before. "I made a mistake the other day, and now I'm making it again," he said. "I didn't ask if I could kiss you. I should have asked."

I didn't answer. He had asked. Not with words, but he'd opened the door for me. Now he opened it wider.

"Are you asking?" I whispered.

"Do you want me to?"

I remembered the taste and smell of him, remembered what it was like to stand on the edge of a world only Henri had dared enter. Remembered the thrill, the terror.

When I didn't say anything, he relaxed into the palm fronds. "Do you think you'll ever want to kiss me again?"

"I—" I pictured that backpack hanging in the tree outside, one of the many pieces of Alex that was still a mystery to me.

"I'm in desperate need of an answer, Jones. Don't leave a dying man hanging, not on a deserted island."

The tarp covering the shelter door flapped behind us.

I leaped off Alex as Henri ducked in with a crown of flowers woven through her hair. Fashion flowed through the blood in her veins, and even here, even with Alex sick, she wouldn't accept a less-than-stellar appearance.

She brought three coconuts and a cacao pod for both Alex and me. Living on coconuts alone had to be unpleasant—but that only showed the strength of Henri's will.

We ate quietly with Henri's clear blue eyes boring into me. She could tell a secret twisted in my mind. I thought back to when she swore she was clairvoyant. Maybe she was telepathic instead.

Alex ate half a cacao pod before he lurched to his feet and threw up outside the shelter in the brush. Henri tossed the rest of her coconut up through the trees as I rubbed Alex's back.

He crawled back inside the shelter and tucked his knees to his chest, offering me a weak smile.

Late into the night, I was awake on my mat of palm fronds.

Alex's breaths went from even and soft to ragged coughs that sounded like they were tearing through his lungs. Maybe he was relapsing, or maybe he'd moved on to another stage of the illness. Either way, I was terrified I'd lose him before I ever really knew him. Terrified I was making the wrong decision at every turn.

Always I'd believed in privacy, even with my sister. I didn't snoop through her drawers without asking, even though I had a standing invitation to borrow anything of hers I liked. But if Alex was stowing away a secret . . .

I lay still until I could be sure Henri's breathing was level and she was in a deep sleep. Carefully, I crept outside the shelter and slipped on my shoes.

I had to stretch high above my head to reach the straps and pull the backpack down from the tree. It wasn't as heavy as I'd imagined. I peeled the zipper back and reached inside. All my touch could identify was paper.

With a loose handful crumpling in my palm, I held some

out to the moonlight. Between my fingers were notes and notes of American dollars.

I turned the backpack inside out and shook it hard. Wads of bills tumbled in every direction, loose ones carried slightly on the breeze. Sentimental value and the drugs weren't what Alex guarded so closely—the backpack was full of money.

How and why would Casey have this much cash?

Something solid hit the ground.

I combed through the leaves in the dark and locked my fingers around something small. The shape was familiar.

The boat that day—I remembered Casey taking long drags off a Newport. Ashes scattering in the wind and drifting into the sea below.

Sitting in the palm of my hand was something we desperately needed—now more than ever. A lighter.

CHAPTER 16

The rooftop party was alive with the sound of Ambisextrous, that month's name for our friend Mick's emo band.

Jesse coined the phrase *ambisextrous* after Mick announced he could jerk off with both hands. Next thing we knew, Ambisextrous was headlining at the best Bay Area spots—most of them gay bars.

The music already pounded against my breastbone, and we were still at the bottom of the stairway, ready to climb three stories up to the roof.

"Hey, I've got a missed call." Henri leaned against the banister to check out her phone. "Oh. Never mind."

"Who was it?"

She made a face I couldn't quite read, looped her fingers around mine, and pointed her leopard-print heels upstairs. Under her breath, she said, "Dad."

I froze and leaned against the metal wall of the stairwell. "Are you okay?"

"Are you kidding?" She batted her eyelashes at me over her shoulder. "I'm fucking fabulous."

We stepped into the crowd, and at the very moment I squeezed her fingertips, I felt Henri's hand let go.

The wake she left filled in with bodies. I spun around and stood on the tips of my toes—the crowd had already swallowed her.

"Someone looks lost."

Mick snatched me into a bear hug.

"Nice party," I said.

It was true. Mick always threw the most amazing parties. As soon as the fog lifted from the city and school let out, Mick had everyone on his rooftop.

"You know it, Little Jones." He shook out his blond dreadlocks and pointed to Jesse, who stood beside the DJ station. "Your boy's over there."

The bass thrummed through my rib cage as I moved through the crowd. Jesse grinned and opened his arms wide. I would have swooned as I fell into his hug if his gesture hadn't seemed so brotherly.

He pulled back from me and left an arm draped over my shoulder. "Why are you drifting through the party all on your lonesome?"

"Oh, Henri's here somewhere."

He lifted his chin and scanned the party. "I don't see her."

"She'll turn up," I muttered.

We went to the booze table, where Jesse poured us two

foamy keg beers. The music drowned all of our words as we sat on the roof ledge.

"Hey, Em, isn't that Henri over there?"

I couldn't see over the thick grouping of bodies. "Purple sequin skirt?"

"Yeah. Who are those guys she's with?"

I craned my neck and finally caught Henri's profile. A boy had his arm around her and one of his hands was splayed across the back of her purple sequin skirt, cupping her ass. He caught Jesse staring and glared back at us with hollow eyes that scared me.

"Hey, Mick," said Jesse.

Mick abandoned the DJ stand and came to Jesse's side.

"You know those guys with Henri?"

Mick squinted across the dark rooftop. "No, they're totally crashing. You think I should kick them out?"

In unison, Jesse and I said, "Yes."

We watched Mick disappear into the crowd before popping out beside Henri. The boys grabbed their plastic cups and headed down the stairs as Mick parted the dance floor back to us.

"They're selling something. They offered me a cut if I let them stay." Holding up his palms, Mick said, "Don't need none of that, you know?"

"Hey, Em." Jesse squinted against the strobe lights. "Is Henri leaving with them?"

I dodged Mick's shoulder in time to see the back of Henri's head disappearing down the stairs.

Jesse set his cup on the railing. "Shit."

I followed him down the metal stairs all the way to street level. It was almost eleven p.m. and the city streets were deserted except for those guys and a few of our friends from the party.

Henri had perched herself on the trunk of an old drop-top car with racing stripes spray-painted down the sides. Someone revved the engine, and Jesse and I bolted to the sidewalk.

"Henri!" I yelled.

She lost her balance, let herself slip down the angle of the car and into the arms of the boy sitting beside her. He kept her steady—I wished I could have done the same.

My sister never got drunk at parties. She liked to stay tipsy enough to lose some inhibitions but sober enough to keep her hair and makeup picture-perfect.

I wrapped my jacket tight around me, and moved to her side. "What are you doing?"

"We're having fun," she slurred. "Come with me, Em. That guy there's got a friend who'll be totally into you."

"*That guy there.* Do you even know them?"

"No, but I'd like to."

Jesse stepped between us and helped Henri down from the back of the car. "Do you really think that's safe? You don't even know them, and you'd take your little sister?"

She laughed and dragged her hand across Jesse's chest. She lifted her chin to me. "Get in."

Jesse grabbed on to her elbows and hauled her against him. She tried to wrench away, but he held tight.

I didn't breathe. If there was one thing Henri couldn't stand, it was someone holding her still.

With her chin at her chest, she stared up at Jesse through her false eyelashes. "You should loosen up, Jess. Get yourself laid. Virginity doesn't look good on you."

He flinched. His feet traveled backward, away from Henri, and he paused and stood so motionless, I imagined him wishing the cracks in the sidewalk would separate and swallow him.

"Fuck this." He threw up his hands, shouldered through the people spilling out of the stairway entrance, and jogged the distance back to the steps and the party.

Henri crawled onto her knees in the passenger seat. Over the sound of the driver revving the engine, I could see her lips moving and her hands waving me closer, but I could barely make out the words.

Finally, I heard her.

Come with me. Come with me. Come with me.

Those words were a song, a prayer, and an invitation into a world I was too afraid to know.

She smiled and kept motioning with her hands as the driver reached across Henri and shut her door. Still, I shook my head.

I couldn't go with Henri. She'd already traveled to a place where I couldn't follow.

Her forehead crinkled, but that loser punched the accelerator and sped down the road.

After the car disappeared around the corner with my sister's hair tangling in the wind, I headed up the stairs to find Jesse.

Through a sea of red plastic cups and Christmas lights, I shoved through the crowd, all the way to the corner of the roof, where Jesse stretched out on a blue-and-white-striped beach blanket.

I lowered beside him, tucking my legs up under me. "I couldn't go with her."

"So she's all alone with them?" He rolled onto his elbow. "You should have gone too."

That reached down deep inside me and pulled my heart out through my throat. I was worth the risk to him, if it meant saving her.

"Don't worry about Henri. She's resourceful. She always lands on her feet."

"Always trying to destroy herself, that's our Henri." His words were garbled. Only then did I notice the half-empty bottle of Bacardi. He tipped his cup toward me. "You want some?"

"Sure." I sipped at the spiked Coke in his hand. It only made me queasy, and I pushed it back to him.

He downed the rest before unscrewing the Bacardi and pouring straight booze.

The cold ocean breeze picked up, stinging my face and neck. I shivered. He yanked the beach blanket from under us and swung it over both of our shoulders.

"I don't know why Henri does anything she does anymore," I said.

"I miss the way things used to be." He lifted a chunk of my hair and played with my wild curls.

"Maybe you should have some water, Jesse."

His palm moved under my chin, and I went still. "You look so much like her now."

The distance between our mouths disappeared, and he kissed me.

His tongue tasted like rum and moved in directions I didn't think tongues were supposed to go. Everything I'd wanted, his mouth on mine. Never had I imagined it would be like this. No, this was what I wanted for as long as I could remember. I wouldn't ruin it.

I draped my arms over his shoulders and arched against him. The beach blanket tightened around my shoulders as Jesse tugged me closer.

When my eyes closed, his lips disconnected.

"Oh, fuck, Em, what am I doing? I'm so sorry."

"No, no. Don't be sorry. It was fine. It was . . . nice."

He lifted the hem of his shirt and wiped his mouth. "I feel like a child molester or something."

The beach blanket tangled with my arms as I stood and shook it and myself away from him. I wanted to punch him in the jaw.

"No, I don't mean it like that." He caught my hands and blew a warm breath into them. "I, like, took advantage of you. Forced myself on you or something."

He got to his feet and held me against him, and as I rested my cheek against his shoulder, I sighed. "It's fine."

We took a cab up to North Beach. Late into the night, he confessed he'd been close to telling Henri how he felt, how nobody could love her like him. When I asked him why he hadn't said it sooner, he wiped his tears away, smiled, and said some mountains were so majestic, even the bravest of men dared not climb them.

It was overblown. But I didn't laugh. Henri made us something bigger than we were, bigger than life itself, and now that she had moved on, we were two broken pieces with one thing in common—we remembered what it felt like to be whole.

I unlocked the front door of my house, which was dark except for the light shining through Henri's curtains.

She'd made it home. My heart almost burst from relief. I didn't want to see her, though—I couldn't forget the image of her driving off into the night with those strangers.

I tiptoed up the stairs and changed into a sleep shirt without turning on a light.

My sheets were cold against my bare legs. I rolled to my side with a pillow hugged against my chest.

My windows didn't provide as good of a view into Jesse's room as Henri's did, but when his lights were on, they cast a glow onto my walls that always kept me awake. The lights themselves weren't the problem, but imagining him a few walls away always kept me stirring.

My room went dark as Jesse flicked off his lights. As I drifted into a dream about swimming in the ocean across from our seaside home, our gray hair tucked into swim caps, the doorknob turned.

My eyes fluttered open.

Henri's weight sank into my mattress. "I know you're not asleep, Em. You stayed out late. Later than me. You're learning all of my bad habits, aren't you?"

"Were you worried about me?"

"No. I knew Jesse would take care of you." She threw her arm around my waist while her chin dug into my shoulder. "You're not mad at me, are you? I couldn't stand it if you were."

"That was a real bitch thing to do to him. To me."

Her breath smelled like tequila and Colgate Whitening. "To you? Em, I knew Jesse would get you home safe."

"But what about Jesse?"

Her fingers glided through my hair. "I know. You're right."

"Then why'd you do it?"

"Everyone was watching."

"That made it so much worse."

She groaned before she let out a little sigh. "I'll find a way to say I'm sorry tomorrow."

I rolled over, facing her. "You can't say you're sorry and make everything right again."

She snapped the sheets and scooted closer beside me. "Someday you'll need someone to forgive you, Emma. All you'll have to offer is a sorry—you better hope they'll take it."

Her feet were ice cubes against my calves and I shrieked. "Just get your feet off me."

She tugged the blanket around both of our shoulders and

pressed our noses together. "You love my cold feet and you know it."

Henri's bed was empty the next morning. Only sheets cast this way, blankets cast another, the makings of at least a dozen full outfits piled on top. Henri never could wear the first thing she put on.

Today was Sunday—our movie day. And she'd left.

Our movie dates weren't a standing occasion; sometimes things came up, but she always told me when she wouldn't be able to make it. She'd never completely ditched me before. I wondered if it was possible to still love someone while you hated everything they'd become.

On the kitchen counter was a big plate of cookies wrapped in cellophane with a note: *Didn't want to wake you up—you looked so sweet sleeping. Take these to Jesse. Tell him sorry for me. xoxo H*

Henri's gifts didn't end with her ability to turn boys into putty. Even though she seemed like the dial-it-in type, she'd always been a wizard with a mixer and a hot oven. My cookies usually ran together into one big cookie that was too crisp on the edges and doughy in the middle. "Old ladies," she'd told me once, "they always bake."

She'd left me alone to take the cookies to Jesse. I wondered if the universe was giving me a sign to make my move.

I changed into a pair of my nicest jeans and a long-sleeved blue sweater with cool leather elbow patches and a big orange bird on the front. I could have gone in Henri's closet and borrowed any scintillating number I wanted—Henri wouldn't have cared. But I liked quirky things. Weird things. I always had.

Jesse stood outside washing his dad's car, the cascading water hose arching above him and forming a rainbow in the spray.

He shut off the water. "Guess she made it home before us, huh?"

I nodded.

Jesse tented his damp sweatshirt from his body and shook the fabric until it didn't cling as closely. "Do you know what happened with those vagrants she took off with?"

"Nope."

He thought I was lying, I could tell. Everyone knew Henri and I told each other everything. She would have given me every little dirty detail of her night if only I'd asked, but I was too afraid the details would be things I didn't want living inside my head.

"I thought Sundays were movie days for you and Henri."

"I thought so too."

"I saw her take off with that piece-of-shit Jake Holt earlier this morning."

She was back with Jake Holt—and back to leaving me for Jake Holt. Maybe he was enough to drag her out of her depression. I knew he wasn't, but still I hoped he could be.

Jesse motioned for me to sit beside him on the steps leading up to his porch. "So what are you doing today?"

"I *was* going to hang out with Henri."

"You want to hang here with me? We can binge-watch something on Netflix and order Thai or something?"

"Yeah, that sounds cool."

He pointed to the plate of cookies I'd set on the step between us. "Hey, those are for me, right?"

Before I could answer, he peeled back the cellophane and snatched a cookie off the plate. He bit into a chocolate crinkle and held up his hand to catch the crumbs. With his mouth full and powdered sugar glued to his chin, his eyes rolled back in his head. "Oh my God, Em. These are so good. Did you make these?"

I hesitated, a moment that ping-ponged in my chest, beating away my sense of right and wrong. "Yeah. I'm glad you like them."

All day, I tried to rebuild the path leading to our kiss the night before. I could get the kiss perfect this time, if I had another chance. Whatever it took to make Jesse see I wasn't the girl next door anymore, that I was more than Henri's little sister, I'd do it.

The opportunity never came.

Jesse walked me to the door after his dad got home from reporting the game. He leaned out onto the porch and glanced toward my yard. Looking for Henri was his permanent state now, as ingrained as breathing.

He'd always be looking for Henri, and I'd always be hoping he didn't find her.

CHAPTER 17

Smoke billowed up from the jungle clearing in warm, gray gusts that filled me with more excitement than Christmas morning.

Henri warmed her hands and face, feeding little bits of dry wood and green leaves into the fire.

We built it only about eight feet from the shelter door, at the center of the clearing, where the branches above were spaced loosest for ventilation. Flames danced around the small pile of wood and dried the humidity from the air. I inhaled, pulling deep inside the scent of the musky smoke and fresh, wet earth. It had been so long since I'd breathed anything like it.

The island wasn't cold—it was never cold—but something about those flames drew us in.

The heels of my hands were blistered and burning. The rock I'd been using as a hammer to beat a piece of scrap metal into a bowl had ripped my skin to shreds. My bowl was wide and shallow and wouldn't catch much water, but we could boil small amounts at a time.

Henri pressed her hand over mine. "You should take a break, Em. That looks pretty good."

We'd been listening for hours to the sound of Alex's ragged

breathing. I'd already speared us a fish, cooked it just beside the fire in a wet leaf. The bowl was something else to keep me busy. "Not yet."

Henri followed my gaze back to the shelter for the hundredth time. "Hey, Em, if he's not okay—"

"He'll be okay."

I knew she didn't believe that. Henri hadn't said much about the lighter, about what it meant—it wasn't like her to give someone grace. Dying, I supposed, meant he got a reprieve.

"Well, if he's not okay, then, well, you and I will be fine. We'll have each other. I— Emma, everything back home . . ."

I looked at her. "What?" I thought she might say something important, something that would let the weight of my guilt float away.

"Never mind. I'm sure he'll be fine."

I didn't know what shifted the balance between us, if it was Alex being sick or the two of us working on the shelter or her sensing something was happening between him and me, but I started to see a side to Henri I hadn't seen since long before Puerto Rico. I wanted her back more than anything. But now that she was within reach, I couldn't be happy.

All I could think about was Alex dying on this island.

Henri threaded another blue shell onto her string. Forty days. I was finally breaking through her icy exterior. It should have thrilled me. But I felt only tired, jittery.

She opened her hand and let a palmful of seashells spill onto the wet ground she'd cleared in front of her. She separated them by color, piles of light pink, seafoam green, beige, and baby blue.

"Why do you care about those so much?"

"They're something to do, I guess. If exposure and hunger won't kill you, the boredom will." She set down the strand she'd been weaving. "I never thought too much about what I might want to do someday. I didn't really think college was for me, but you were going and I would have gone with you. I always thought I'd be better off finding a way to backpack around Europe for a few years or something."

"That wouldn't have been too hard. I'm sure you could have found some stupid boy to pay your way."

"Ouch." Her eyes widened, and she laughed. "I like this bitchy side you've picked up." She placed her seashells in neat rows for stringing, alternating the pinks and the beiges. "I thought it would be cool to make something. I would have been good at making things, like clothes or jewelry. If FIDM wasn't so close to home, I might have liked it there."

A couple Baird girls a few years older than Henri enrolled in the Fashion Institute of Design and Merchandising. Now one of them—Faizah—designs costumes for the San Francisco theater scene. The other girl, Penelope, transferred to FIDM's Los Angeles campus and dropped most of her name. Now *Lo* dresses Hollywood's fashion do's.

"You could go to the L.A. campus. When we get home."

She dragged her fingertips through the shells, pushing the tiniest ones to the left and the larger ones to the right. "There's no home anymore, Em."

"Why do you keep saying that? Why don't you want to get home? What back home could possibly be worse than this island?"

"Let me work on this." She took the rock and metal from my hands without answering, then paused. "Em, do you hear that?"

"I don't hear anything."

"Exactly."

Silence. Alex's painful breathing had been constant. I ran into the shelter, falling into a crouch at his side.

His chest moved up and down at an even rate as I pressed my hands to his face. His skin wasn't burning. His fever had broken. He was just sleeping.

I dropped my head low, my hands still on his face, and looked up when I felt his hand curl around mine.

His eyes fluttered open, and as they did, I remembered the backpack.

I moved to the opposite end of the shelter. "How are you feeling?"

His neck cracked as he stretched his arms high over his head, winced, and let them fall to his sides. "Not too bad. Maybe the worst of it's over."

I handed him a bottle of water. "You want this?"

He drank a few inches and lifted himself onto his elbows.

"Some food? There's fish."

"Nah. I'm not hungry." The skin around his eyes crinkled a little as he assessed me. I could practically see him measuring the distance I'd put between us. "Jones, did something happen?"

He smelled the air and concentrated on the space behind

me, forgetting his question. Smoke trickled inside the open door flap and tickled my throat.

Alex slipped his arms into his shirt but didn't button it. I followed him outside, where Henri sat beside the fire.

"You did it?" He grabbed on to his knees and laughed at the cooked bits of fish I saved for him. "And you cooked. We can *cook*. Holy shit. But how?" He turned to me, face open, incredulous.

Henri gave me a look and disappeared into the jungle. I knew how her mind worked—this was my fight for the fighting.

"We found a lighter."

"You've got to be shitting me." His eyes lit up, and he grinned, still clutching his knees. "Where in the world did you find a lighter?"

Casey's backpack hung in the trees a few inches above me, where I'd put it back. If Alex didn't know the lighter had been in there, if he'd never checked it properly, he'd risked our lives over a bag of money. If he did know, then my sister wasn't the only one with a hidden agenda.

I yanked the backpack free and hurled it at him, a little too hard because he groaned as it slammed into his stomach.

"Where did I get it? At the bottom. Under all the cash."

He looked at me. "You went through this?" I expected him to explode—I had violated him, his privacy, Casey's privacy, the unspoken laws of our island—but he only put out a hand and lowered himself to the ground. "I swear I didn't know about the lighter. I searched the backpack for anything

186

that could help us, but the—but the money—you know about that—"

"I don't care about the money, Alex. All I care about is that you were so worried about Henri and me getting our hands on it that you let a lighter sit in the bottom of that bag for weeks while we ate raw fish and drank who knows what kind of parasites that *probably made you sick*. Ironic, no?"

"That wasn't why."

"What?"

"That wasn't why I did it!"

"Then why?"

His voice rasped in his throat and the whites of his eyes flushed red. "I . . ."

I felt my nose sting, my own eyes fill, and I dropped my voice low enough that my sister couldn't hear me—she was undoubtedly listening. "So you know, I did want you to ask if you could kiss me again. But I'm glad you didn't. I might have said yes."

That night, I used our metal bowl to catch a crab for dinner. My mouth watered the whole time it cooked. We boiled it in salt water, smashed its body with rocks, and sucked on the empty claws.

Our food situation improved in every way once we had fire. Henri and I heated rocks in the flames for a couple of hours and dug a hole in the sand. When the rocks were flaming red, we dropped them into the hole. We wrapped fish in leaves and placed the bundles onto the flaming hot rocks before covering the fish with sand. An hour later, we had moist packets of flaky fish.

Henri and I dragged three driftwood logs from the beach, one at a time, down the path our feet had beat into the jungle, all the way to the clearing. Warmth, food, and heat meant we could now focus on luxuries like seating.

After dinner, we watched the flames flicker for hours. It kept the bugs away, sort of, and other things too, I hoped. We didn't know how precious something like fire could be until we didn't have it.

Most importantly, we could boil our drinking water.

Maybe we'd never know what made Alex get so sick so fast, but more than I could feel the fear of illness, I could see it in Henri's eyes. We knew now how to find food, boil water, and make shelter—survive without rescue—but the one thing sure to do us in was ourselves.

I found Alex, the next day, sitting at the top of the cliff holding something that looked like netting. He'd kept his distance from me since he'd gotten well. And even if he hadn't, I'd have kept mine from him. Still, his absence was a dull ache.

Wind beat my jacket against my waist now and I zipped it up. "What's that for, to catch fish?"

"Oh, it's so much better than that. This is a hammock—or it's going to be. It was all tangled up in the rocks under the high tide—I think it's from our boat."

In the trees behind us, he'd again hung Casey's backpack by its straps. All that money and he couldn't buy a thing on our island. He hadn't even told me what it was for—what Casey had been planning to do with it.

"But I've got some bad news for you," he said. "I—uh. Fuck. There's no good way to say it. I tore a hole in the raft this morning. It was swarming with bugs and I tried to dump the water, and when I did, I dragged it over a rock. Ripped a hole clean through it. I really fucked up—I'm sorry."

The raft water wasn't even gross to us, not now when we could scoop it out and boil it. The raft itself was also there, a chance, a hope of getting off this island if we could figure out how to do it and survive.

"You're sure it was an accident? Or were you looking for another way to sabotage us?"

He stilled, squinted at me, the wind beating his hair around his face. "Tell me you don't really believe that."

I didn't know if I was serious or taking a cue from Henri. I sounded just like her. "What would you expect me to believe? You haven't even mentioned that money, Alex! Or what it was for!"

"You want to know what the money's for? You want to know? Who the hell deals in cash like that, Emma? You're too smart not to know what it was. You looked through the backpack, you saw the Oxy."

I stared at him. I'd wanted him to restore my faith. Maybe not knowing was better.

"It was too easy. Casey, he thought I was good with numbers. That's why I was down here. It's not like driving that rickshaw was paying the big bucks. Or moonlighting in surfboard restoration. So we'd take a bag of Oxy or coke or whatever here. Pick up some money there. Casey and I split a small cut each time. Over and over again. I thought I'd just run drugs for a few years, get enough to put it in something—college or an investment—and make it come out clean the other side. But the truth is that I'm the scum of the fucking earth, Jones."

The hem of my dolphin T-shirt was coming loose and I tugged at the stray threads. "I thought you were just getting high. I looked in the front flap right after we got here and I saw the Oxy. I thought that's why you kept disappearing with the backpack."

He glanced up at me. "I wouldn't have done that," he said quietly. "After the accident—what I did—I *wanted* to be numb. But I wouldn't have put myself in a state where I couldn't think clearly. Not here. Not on this island."

"No," I said. "You just almost killed my sister and me, yourself, all because you were so worried we'd touch the stupid money."

"I didn't protect the money because I was worried you and your sister would get it."

"Then why?"

Tears pooled in his eyes and he fisted handfuls of his hair. "If you saw it, Emma, you'd know what I'd done." I didn't think he was going to tell me until he gave me the weariest, most defeated look. "When the explosion happened, I went for the backpack first, before Casey, before you, before your sister. I didn't even think about it until it was already done."

All those times he pulled away, all the hours spent staring at the ocean . . .

Alex did blame himself for Casey's death.

We weren't so different, Alex and me.

"It's a lot of money," I said. I couldn't see his face. He wouldn't look at me. "Most people would have done the same thing." I didn't really believe it, but I wanted to. I didn't *want* to believe I was the kind of person who could destroy Henri like I did, but I had to. "You could have done worse."

The wind blew his hair across his face and he shook it back. "Maybe with the drugs and all. But not that day. When the explosion happened, I knew the boat was going down and I went for the backpack because I couldn't let the money go with it."

"Casey might have gone for the money if you hadn't."

"Casey, oh God." Alex wrapped his arms around his knees and rocked forward.

I wanted to touch him, comfort him, but I slipped my hands into my pockets.

"I didn't think about him or you or your sister, Emma. I knew that, no matter what, I had to get that money. It didn't even occur to me he could've been hurt. At first, I told myself I went for the money because it's what Casey would have wanted—but that wasn't it."

"What was it, then?" I asked after a long silence.

"Me, Jones. Me. I did it for me."

I looked out over the choppy ocean waves. I couldn't give Alex absolution. Not from this guilt. No one could. I knew this.

I continued to stare out at the end of the ocean, and I imagined something there that couldn't be true.

It couldn't be.

It had to be some kind of mirage or a dream.

I shut my eyes hard and opened them. My blurred vision cleared. It was still there.

A ship.

"Alex." I walked over to him, still looking out at the horizon. "Alex, is that what I think it is?" I started pulling at him to stand before he could answer and waved my arms above my head. "It's help!"

He stood and laid a hand on my shoulder. "Hey, they can't see you. They're too far away. They're right at the edge of the horizon."

I kept waving frantically. "Maybe they'll come closer."

"Maybe," he said. "Don't get your hopes up. See how big that ship looks to us? We're ants to them. Less than ants. They're twenty miles away. More maybe. We're invisible."

They weren't even looking for us. Maybe nobody was.

If anyone noticed Casey and Alex were gone, they would have assumed they'd sailed off to another island. Nobody knew Henri and I were ever aboard Casey's boat—and if they didn't make the connection, then there never was any search-and-rescue mission and there never would be.

Help wasn't coming—maybe I'd always known, a quiet place inside me, growing louder and louder. Now it screamed.

"Then we don't have a choice," I said. "We have to make them see."

CHAPTER 18

Henri came into my room with a pair of too-high strappy heels dangling from her fingers. "It's not too late to change your mind."

With Mom's business trip, we were on our own. We had three twenties for pizzas, a gas card, and a list of emergency numbers, but not the one thing Henri needed the most—an adult to tell her no.

I dragged the toes of my slippers through the carpet as I spun my desk chair around to face her. "Why don't you stay home with me?"

There was nothing I wanted more than a lazy December night on the couch with Henri. She'd do away with all her sequined fabrics and trade them in for worn-in sweatshirts and flannels. I'd make peanut butter popcorn and we'd curl up under a blanket and watch movies about girls who ran up the stairs when they should have been running down them.

"But you said you have to write a paper." She perched on

the edge of my unmade bed and fed the tiny straps of her sandals through the buckles.

"Well, I wouldn't, like, have to."

"Then come with me! What better night than tonight? No curfew!"

I couldn't go to any more parties with Henri.

I couldn't stand in the corner with a red Solo cup full of warm keg beer while she smiled her glossy, lipsticked smile and pressed her fingertips to the overdeveloped biceps of boys who only wanted to carry her upstairs and violate her. I couldn't watch Jesse try to play it cool with whoever was on the popularity B-list while his eyes scanned crowded rooms until he found Henri.

I could, but I wouldn't.

"Hey"—she collected my hands in hers, frowning at the chips in my green nail polish—"I know what this is about. It's because I've been ditching you. I don't mean to, Emma, you know that. It's just that when we get there, you always disappear into some corner. You could talk to anyone you wanted, but you always end up talking to Jesse."

"I like Jesse."

"I do too. But he's . . . boring. He's like"—she tapped her index finger to her yet-to-be painted lips—"worn-in jeans. Why would anyone wear worn-in jeans when they could wear gold lamé?"

I adored worn-in jeans.

She scooped her hair in her hand and swept it over one shoulder. "And, I don't want to say this, but I get the impression he's into me."

"Why don't you want to say that?" Who was she kidding? She loved any kind of male attention.

"Because"—she looked down at my carpet as she buckled her straps—"I'm kind of worried you're into him."

I'd regret the next moment every day after. Because I laughed. "Jesse? He's like our brother."

"I know, right? Okay. Cool." Her warm smile fell away. She looked at me and every bit of Henri's intensity reflected back. "I'd never want anything like that to come between us."

"You don't have anything to worry about."

She walked to the mirror above my dresser and checked her outfit, tugging the shiny pieces into cleavage-baring place. "So, you're sure you don't want to come?"

My paper wasn't due until the end of the semester, so I drifted around the house all evening.

I wasn't some overachiever either. If a teacher would give me a B for a paper I could write the night before, that was good enough for me.

It was strange being alone in my house at night. I couldn't remember the last time it happened. I'd only stayed alone when I was sick and Henri went to school while my parents were at work—when Dad lived at home.

The pictures lining our hallway didn't feel like they were taken of our family. Our smiles were all hollow, which maybe should have foreshadowed our family's demise.

Slipping into my parents' bedroom, I went to the small section of their closet where a few of my dad's shirts remained.

I buttoned a plaid shirt over my tank top and leggings and rolled the cuffs to my elbows—I couldn't snatch one of his shirts while Henri was home and risk her glare, and not when my mom was around and she might turn on the waterworks.

I lowered all the lights and buried myself between three blankets on the couch while I watched all the DVR'd shows Henri wouldn't mind me seeing without her.

I must have fallen asleep, because I woke up hours later to the front door swinging open and someone flicking on all the lights.

"Emma. Emma. Shit. Help me with her."

Jesse's voice. Henri crying.

I blinked until I focused on Jesse—he had Henri slung over his shoulder.

He tried to put her down on her feet, but her heels slipped out from beneath her. We both lunged to get our arms around her waist, and Jesse caught her. All night long I wished I'd done the catching.

I wrapped my arm around Henri's back and helped Jesse get her on the couch.

With the sleeve of my dad's plaid shirt, I wiped mascara streaks off her cheeks. "What happened?"

That only made her sobbing come harder and faster.

"Get those ridiculous shoes off her!" Jesse rushed past the couch and into the kitchen.

Water surged into the sink as I tugged her skirt to cover her thighs. I lifted my chin above the couch and focused on Jesse. "What happened?" He didn't answer. "Henri, come on.

Talk to me." I fumbled with those tiny little straps until I got them loose.

Jesse strode past me and dropped to his knees in front of her.

I latched on to his arm. "You better tell me what's going on with her."

"She's just wasted."

"She'd never drink this much." Henri would have never drunk to the point where she couldn't tell if all her hairs were in place. That night at Mick's was the exception.

"Well, she did tonight." He thrust a glass of water past me and up to Henri's mouth. He held it while she drank, keeping his hand under her chin and catching the dribbles in his palm. "They were passing drinks to her and mixing them strong. She thought it was mostly Coke, you know, but it was mostly rum."

"Who?"

"Drink up." He held the water for her until she drank the glass almost dry. "Jake Holt and his crew. Bunch of assholes."

Henri's throat made a horrible gurgle. Jesse hoisted her to her feet and rushed her into the downstairs bathroom. At first, all I heard was gagging and then the unmistakable sound of vomiting.

"Let me do this."

I pushed Jesse into the hallway and slammed the door, sealing Henri and me inside the bathroom together. I rubbed my hand up and down her back as she emptied her stomach.

In a small voice, she asked, "Did I get it in my hair?"

That's when I knew she was going to be all right.

"Your hair's perfect."

Jesse helped me get her back to the couch and brought her another glass of water.

"She's going to be okay now that she got some of it out of her," he said. "She'll sober up fast."

She was shivering in her miniskirt and bare legs, so he grabbed one of my blankets off the floor and wrapped it around her. Jesse rubbed at his knuckles—they were purple. He unclenched his fist and his whole hand shook with effort.

As Henri came around, he tucked her hair behind her ear. His whisper was barely loud enough for me to hear. "Do you want me to call the police?"

I jumped up so fast, my feet stung against the hardwood floor. "Okay! Tell me what happened and tell me right now!"

"Nothing happened," she mumbled.

"Those guys, the ones mixing those drinks—" Jesse combed through his hair with his hands. "They took her upstairs."

She'd be so mad at him if he'd caused a scene and embarrassed her. "But was she . . . willing?"

"There were three of them. She said no. If she'd been cool with it, it would have been different. She's a big girl—she can do what she wants. But I heard her say no, Em, and they heard her too, and they didn't stop."

My breaths shook free from my chest. "I'll get the phone."

Henri put up her hands. "No."

"Jesse, tell her we have to."

He crossed the room and bent close to my ear. "Look, I was

watching her all night. She's okay. I saw what was happening and I got upstairs as soon as they . . ." He rubbed his swollen hand. "I think I broke Jake Holt's nose."

"Em," Henri said. "Would you grab some ice for his hand?"

We were all out of ziplock bags, so I grabbed a bag of frozen peas from the freezer. I could hear them whispering out in the family room. I couldn't tell what they were saying, but I did hear my sister's words: "Thank you."

She had her forehead pressed in the curve of Jesse's neck as I dropped the peas into his lap. With his good hand, he rubbed her arm over the blanket.

I'd become invisible—I stood in front of the couch for several seconds before they even looked up.

The ticking of the clock on the mantel was the only sound for a long time. Henri and Jesse were touching each other, little tiny touches that would have looked innocent to most people. Her fingertips circling his purple knuckles. His socked feet brushing against her bare toes.

An hour went by.

I thought about Jake Holt and those other guys, what they'd done. It wasn't rape—not yet—but still a crime. I didn't even know the details. Maybe assault? Calling the cops was what I needed to do. But it was Henri's story. If I tried to make her tell anyone what happened, she'd lie.

We ordered a pizza from Crusty Charlie's in the city, and while we waited on the delivery guy, Henri went upstairs and changed into a pair of yoga pants and an oversized sweater with toothpaste stains down the front.

As I paid the delivery guy, Henri said something into Jesse's ear. They'd never kept secrets from me.

Henri ate a small piece of Canadian bacon and pineapple, I ate three, and Jesse ate almost all of the rest. She kept glancing between me and the staircase—she wanted me to go upstairs. I wouldn't dare leave them alone.

Finally, Henri yawned.

I shot daggers through Jesse. "She looks tired. You should probably let me put her to bed."

She worked a hand into the underside of her hair and leaned into the sofa cushions. "I'd actually rather not be alone."

"Well, you won't be alone," I said. "I'll be here."

Henri stood and wiggled her fingers at Jesse. "Would you come lie down with me? For a while?"

He took her hand, and I followed them both up the stairs. I wanted to scream at him that she was drunk. Accuse him of the same thing as those boys at the party. But Henri wasn't drunk at all anymore. Hours had passed and she was stone-cold sober enough to know what she wanted.

I was terrified of what that was.

Before Jesse shut the door to Henri's room and locked them both inside, he stared right at me.

I stood in the doorway of my room. I didn't know what the look meant. Was it an am-I-dreaming-or-is-this-really-happening kind of look? Was it apologetic? Was it ashamed?

In the dark of my room, I lay on top of my comforter. Through the thin walls of our older Bay Area home, I could make out soft murmurs and kissing sounds. Fumblings. The weight of two people falling into Henri's creaking bed.

I rolled over and cried into my mattress. They weren't trying to hurt me—Jesse didn't know how I felt and I'd sworn to Henri I wasn't into him—but all the things they didn't know couldn't stop the pain from flooding the empty places in me.

She didn't even care about him. This was stupid. An impulsive *thank-you*—Henri never did anything halfway.

I heard it. The sound of his moaning. I cupped my pillow around my head and pressed until my ears burned.

Their relationship had gone past crushes, past friendship, past anything my feelings for Jesse could ever reach. No longer did I want a house by the sea with my sister.

CHAPTER 19

We chose a spot halfway up the beach, in a wide-open space, at the highest point we could build a signal fire without risking the flames spreading to the trees. The cliff top was too windy, too hard to relight, but the smoke could climb taller than the cliff, high into the sky.

"How do we even know who we're signaling?" Henri emerged from the ocean, dripping and angry. She pulled her shorts up her damp thighs. "They could be human traffickers or mercenaries. We're probably safer here."

I glanced up from filling the impression we'd made with crisp brown leaves. "It's a cargo ship. And the best chance we've ever had at getting home."

"Maybe," she said. "Doesn't mean I'm helping."

Alex spread out on his stomach, rolling the metal spark wheel until the lighter flamed, and holding it to the brown leaves. "Surprise, surprise," he said, but Henri was already gone.

The two of us piled kindling along the base of the fire, fed wood until it roared. It sparked and crackled, the dry brush and branches burning hot and clear.

"We need more smoke," I said. "Something green."

A cluster of bamboo taller than Alex had fallen against the beach. Some fibers kept it connected to the other branches. He hacked it free with his knife and tossed it over the fire.

Gray smoke spiraled toward the sky.

Time drifted by.

No rescue boats anchoring close to our shore.

No planes overhead.

Alex had said we were invisible. As the sun went down and orange firelight filled the darkness, I felt myself fading.

A scream exploded from my throat, burst my eyelids open with the force of a physical thing. Drenched in my sweat and tears, I pushed up on my mat in the darkness.

The tree branches tied to the hammock squeaked as Alex sat up. He left it swinging and crawled down to me on the shelter floor. "What is it? What?"

"I'm okay. I'm okay."

I was dreaming of swirling oceans dragging Henri from my reach as water filled her mouth. Only I wasn't dreaming—the roaring was real.

"That's a caiman, isn't it?"

Alex's knee dug into my thigh as he crossed me and peeled back the tarp. The lighter would run out of fluid if we had to keep relighting, and Henri was supposed to be watching the fire before we traded off. "Your sister, she's—"

"What?"

"Gone."

We pushed through the door. The caiman hurting me didn't

scare me nearly as much as the thought of it hurting Henri.

Flames flicked amid the red-hot coals—she hadn't been gone long enough to let the fire die. The roars grew louder.

Alex spun right past our shelter, toward the beach. "It's coming from this way."

He was wrong. It was the other way—the wild part of the jungle, the twisted brush not far from where the caiman had sprung from the water. "No, over here."

We darted in different directions, but I doubled back to the shelter for his knife. I knew where the sound had come from.

The jungle fog was thick, then thicker. It snaked damply down my throat and snatched at my oxygen. Still, I pushed through the tangles of vines.

Henri stood in a larger clearing, under the frail tree Alex had first suggested for our shelter, her skin blending into the heavy air so I couldn't tell where she ended and the air around her began.

Something darted between the trees. It was too dark to see at that distance, but I could hear its thick body turning up the underbrush.

I lifted my finger to my lips, but Henri must have not seen me, because she said, "Emma, what are you doing out here? Do you hear them? I was just—"

The caiman snapped its head and focused its glowing yellow eyes on Henri. Flying across the embankment, it charged my sister.

I threw myself between them. Pain shot from my left wrist all the way up my arm. The edges of my vision blurred. I saw my left arm, the skin ripped open. In the moonlight, thick, sticky blood coated my hand. I scrambled up on all fours as the caiman lunged again. I raised my arm as high as time allowed and drove the knife into its skull. The caiman cried out, a terrible primal sound, and went still.

"Emma! Oh God." Henri pressed her hand to my arm and blood seeped between her fingers. My bleeding arm gave out from under me, and I fell.

Holding my wrist above my heart barely slowed the bleeding. As Alex built the fire into a blaze bright enough to flood our dark clearing with light, blood still oozed from the wound.

He fed the fire with his back to us. "What were you doing out there, anyway?"

"I had to pee, if you must know," Henri said, tying a vine like a tourniquet just above my elbow. I gasped and clenched my teeth. She'd gotten the cotton out of a tampon and was using it to staunch the bleeding. "Don't act like this is my fault."

"Oh, no, Hank. Nothing's ever your fault."

Their bickering didn't interest me as much as the caiman carcass Alex carried back with us. I'd inched toward it while Alex had tried to stoke the fire for more light—I had to know if it was the same one. Alex's knife was still lodged in its skull, and its open eyes had dulled from yellow to gray. On its back was that olive-green diamond.

"Let me see." Henri untwisted my arm against her stomach and gently lifted away the soaked cotton. "It's a clean gash and narrow, but it's deep."

"How deep?" Alex asked.

I shrieked as Henri manipulated the raw skin. "It's all the way to the bone, I think. I might puke. What are we going to do?"

"We do have a sewing kit," I said, breathing hard. Even if the bleeding stopped, walking around the island with an open wound was asking for an infection. "I guess I need stitches."

Alex shook his head. "Without anesthesia? Oh, Jones. It's going to feel like your arm is burning in the fires of hell."

"I can handle it." I looked between them. My sister, she'd never do that kind of dirty work. "Alex, will you stitch me up?"

His Adam's apple bounced. "Okay."

"Do you want to bite down on something?" Henri asked.

"Like what?"

"I don't know. Like, a belt or—"

"I've got something better," Alex said. With his back to us, he rustled around in his bag and came back with a pill between his fingers. "If you crush it, you'll get the full effects of the Oxy immediately."

"You want her to snort it?" asked Henri.

"No." He held it out to me. "You could damage your nasal passages. Just chew it."

I stared at the little pink pill. "What does it feel like?"

"Euphoric. Numb. It's an opiate. I can't say for sure—I've never tried it."

"Never?"

"Never."

I tried to make eye contact with Henri, but she glanced away. She hated being wrong.

"It's highly addictive. Not worth the risk . . ." He blinked, nodded to my arm. "Unless you really need it."

"I'll be fine without it."

With my back pressed against the palm tree, I closed my eyes just as Henri doused the cut with nearly the last of her hand sanitizer. Fire shot up my arm and I screamed, muffling my voice with my other hand. *Calm*—that was the only way to get through this.

Henri pushed her forehead against mine and whispered, "You can do this," before she reached into her bag and pulled out the travel sewing kit.

"Let's see." Alex brushed over the spools of thread, fingers quivering. "Standard surgical black or blue to match your swimsuit?" He tried to smile.

"Doesn't matter."

Henri threaded the needle with black, cleaned it with a final dribble of hand sanitizer, and passed it to Alex. "Okay, she's ready. I'll hold her arm down. Shit, are you all right?"

Alex swayed. All the color drained from his face.

"You're not feeling sick again, are you?" I held the back of my hand to his forehead, but it was cool.

"Well, honestly, I'm not that good with blood. Vomit or whatever else—that's different. Blood, though, I just don't have the stomach for it."

"Here." Henri took the needle from his hand. "I can do it."

I might have thought she would have taken some sick pleasure from sticking the needle under my skin and me trying not to cry out each and every time, but my sister winced with every jerk of my arm. She made only enough stitches to do the job, sewing me up as best she could with what she had.

After it was over, I slipped to the leaves in a fetal position to let my wooziness pass.

Alex nodded at the stitches. "They'll work until you can get home."

"Home," Henri repeated. She laughed to herself before she moved toward the fire.

A log popped, sending ash and glowing embers swirling around my sister. I remembered her, standing in the Baird hallway with a flurry of loose notebook paper suspended in the air around her.

After what I'd done to her, home could never mean the same thing to Henri.

We cleaned the caiman and separated the gross, squishy fat from the tender, flaky meat. We cooked it over the fire and ate until our bellies were heavy and full, and still there was so much meat left. That's when we spread strips on hot rocks and let them cook until they were chewy as jerky. It reminded me of the one bite of frog legs I'd tasted at one of my parents' fancy New Year's parties—but better because we were famished and had killed and cleaned and cooked it ourselves.

Rain thwacked against the roof of our shelter. The biggest leaves provided some weatherproofing, but no matter how hard we tried, there were spaces water leaked between.

Before the rain became a downpour, when it was only a drizzle, we'd dragged a fresh layer of palm fronds to the floor of the shelter. They were supposed to keep things dry, but if we moved certain ways and pressed too deep into the floor, mud would bubble up between our toes and fingers.

Alex swung in the hammock above us. We were going to take turns, but Henri said the strings made weird patterns on her arms and the backs of her legs, and she didn't want to look like a ham. And Henri wouldn't dare let me sleep any-where that wasn't at her side.

Water thundered down, and I thought about the wide-open beach. Even with the dense protection of overhead leaves, the small fire outside our shelter could barely survive the storms. Out on the beach, with the fierce wind and rain, the signal fire couldn't still be burning.

"Nobody will find us now," I said, tenting my shirt to fan myself. The warm, thick air was wet and made my shirt cling to me, the back of my neck damp with sweat. "Not until we rebuild the fire."

Henri drifted toward the door and peeked out the flap. "It's a waste of lighter fluid anyway. Using up what little we have for a signal fire that's not doing us any good."

"She might be right." Alex held up the lighter. "We shouldn't have gone so long without this anyway."

"Alex," I said. "I told you it's okay."

"Here's the thing." He rolled the lighter between his fingers. "I checked that backpack really well—two or three times. I wouldn't have risked not looking. I carried it around to the other side of the beach, and I dumped the whole thing. And I put it all back in. There was no lighter in there. I swear."

"Well, you've got to be wrong," I said. "Maybe it was stuck in the lining. Really, how could it be not there one minute and then there the next?"

"I don't know. It was after the accident. Maybe I was really out of it." He didn't sound like he thought that was it, though.

Henri tossed a handful of empty crab shells out the shelter door. "If you're going to have a meltdown, could you try to do it in private?"

"Well, in case you haven't noticed, Hank, space in here is limited."

"No, I haven't. Let's see, what was I doing?" Henri tapped a finger to her lips. "For forty-seven days, I was too busy drinking parasitic water that I wouldn't have had to drink if, say, we'd had a lighter this whole time. For forty-seven days, I've been wondering how long. How long until we end up like your cousin?"

Alex jumped out of the hammock and landed on his feet. He put on his backpack. "I'll take that as my cue."

As the tarp swished behind him, Henri yelled, "We nearly died out here because of you!"

I shook my head at my sister—she wouldn't even make eye contact—and crawled out of the shelter to follow him.

Water now soaked the ground and trees, but no more rain came down. I tipped my head to the sky. Sunlight shone through the high-above treetops.

I stepped through wet tangles of underbrush and found Alex moving through the jungle in a direction I'd never gone. After the rain, everything was green and glossy, the humid, earthy smell almost overpowering.

"Alex, wait."

He glanced back. "Please don't follow me."

"I'm sorry."

"You don't have anything to be sorry about, Jones. She does."

He had no idea.

I picked up my pace but so did Alex.

He looked over his shoulder, but his feet went out from under him. He slipped and was gone. Grasping the vines overhead, I stepped to the place where he'd tumbled, a steep, muddy embankment. I took a step back. The wet ground crumbled beneath me, and the world went sideways and upside down as I spilled down the bank. My hands shot out, but I couldn't anchor myself to anything. With a thud that almost knocked the wind out of me, I came to rest at the bottom of a mossy ravine. Clusters of vines screened us into a crack of the jungle, darkened by the mud-slicked hill.

I hissed as pain shot down to my fingertips and up to my shoulder—I'd landed on my stitches.

Alex was covered in head-to-toe mud as he crouched beside me. I started laughing but gasped in pain, feeling tears cut tracks down my muddy face, then laughed again.

"You don't look so hot yourself, Jones." He smiled, his teeth whiter in all that mud. "You didn't hurt it worse, did you?" He probed along my arm and only made it ache. "I'm so sorry. You wouldn't have fallen if—"

"It's fine. Just, here—" One-handed, I couldn't peel back the muddy bandage. He wiped his hands on some wet leaves and pulled it off. The wound was clean, with the stitches intact.

In the four days since the caiman's attack, I'd waited for the stitches to burst open. They'd held strong, but the skin around them had turned a tender, flaming red.

"It's okay. Let's see what I can do for a new bandage." Loose money escaped out of his backpack as he cut away a piece of lining with his knife and tied it over my stitches. I winced. "I wish you'd taken the Oxy," he said. "Just because I won't doesn't mean you shouldn't have."

"Why do you even have it? Was it Casey's? Did he use it?"

"Sometimes. But the bags are just samples Casey would give out to drum up business."

He finished bandaging me up. "Good as new," I said.

"That's optimistic. You needed antibiotics. You still need them. A caiman claw—I don't even know. This island, I swear—it's gonna kill us if we don't do something."

I slung mud off my shorts. "We should head back."

"You go ahead, Jones."

"Don't let Henri get to you, okay? She knows how to push your buttons now. Don't give her the satisfaction of reacting."

"But she's right."

His hair hung in his eyes, and I brushed it off his face, leaving my hand there. "You didn't kill Casey. When you pulled him up, he was already gone."

"Stop."

"The gash on his head was barely even bleeding anymore. His heart stopped before he ever hit the water."

Alex blinked. "Are you sure? You can't be sure."

"I'm sure. There was barely any. He was gone."

"I was breathing into his mouth. I was . . ."

"Alex, I'm sure."

A moment passed and he cleared his throat. A few bills had come free from their paper bands and fallen into the mud. He wiped the money on his shorts to clean it.

"You know what I still don't get? What is the money *for*?"

He zipped the bills inside. "We'd just made a delivery of cocaine and Oxy. It was payment."

"I mean—since Casey's gone. Why are you carrying it around? What could it possibly be good for?"

He sighed. "Salvation."

When he didn't say more, just fiddled with the zipper, I waited, watching him.

He looked at me out of the corner of his eye.

"Fine. Okay?" He dropped the bag. "The day of the accident, I—I tried to get Casey to talk to me. It wasn't coke right away, just Oxy, and I didn't want to mess with that— with the illegals. I wanted out once that started. I thought we could roll everything we made into an investment—a commercial fishing boat. I found one that needs work, but the problems are mostly cosmetic. If I can refinish a surfboard, I thought maybe I could work on a boat too. Maybe fix it. Stupid, right?"

"No, you could," I said. "With the shelter . . . you're good at building things."

"Our money—if I was right—it would have multiplied in one season. The fishing business, it's booming down here. It would have bought me out of this drug-running bullshit. Maybe a way back to the mainland—not that I don't love Puerto Rico—but I can't stay here, stuck in neutral. And now it just sounds lonely, being there without Casey."

"And Casey didn't want the boat?"

"No, he wanted it. Casey wasn't planning on trafficking forever. He really was a good guy." The slightest trace of a smile formed on Alex's lips.

"What?"

"I was just remembering—this thing Casey did. Back in Puerto Rico."

"Tell me. I mean, if you want."

Alex moved from his knees back onto the ground, still grinning. "There was, uh, this kid—seven or eight—who terrorized us." He glanced at me. "He would ride his bike like hell up and down the dock, almost knocking tourists over, scaring off business. A total nuisance. So one day, the kid, he's pedaling like mad right for these tourists, but they don't move—I don't know, maybe they don't see him. The kid, he turns wrong, catches himself on the side of Casey's boat, but the bike goes flying right off the dock, wheels spinning in the air, and splashes into the ocean. Casey and I, we're laughing so hard, we can't breathe, doubled over, tears streaming." Alex looked at me, put up his hand. "Kind of dickish, I know. But this kid, he was the absolute worst. And really, he was fine. Not a scratch on him."

I smiled. "No judgment here."

"So, we're waiting for him to dive in for it—it's submerged in probably ten feet of water—when the kid loses it. Just starts crying—like, bawling. And he looks really young, right? This is a *little kid*. Casey goes over to him. Finds out the kid can't swim. And Casey just takes off his shirt and dives in. No hesitation. After he gets the bike up, and swims all the way around the dock dragging this thing, the kid just gets on and rides off, doesn't even say thanks." The smooth ride of Alex's voice went rough, and he exhaled. "I asked Casey, later, why he did it. He shrugged and said maybe the kid would remember it someday."

The Casey from the boat—all I saw was him throwing out beers, laughing, Henri pulling him toward her like a magnet. I didn't know him at all.

I leaned into Alex. Hoped it was enough.

Alex scrubbed his hands over his face and was quiet. At last he said, "The fishing boat—Casey said we didn't have enough to buy it. And we didn't."

"What about the backpack?"

"We only get to keep a small cut of that money. We owe the rest to the supplier. With the accident, though, everyone'll think the money's at the bottom of the Atlantic. I was thinking— I could buy that boat outright if we ever got off this place. At first, I thought it was honoring Casey or something."

"And now?"

He picked up the backpack. "I don't know. Lately it's feeling less and less like the answer." We went silent, and as Alex wiped a hand across his eyes, he glanced behind him. "Do you hear that?"

He helped me up and we walked farther along the ravine. Vegetation clustered together, forming an almost-impassable green tunnel. The sound got louder as we walked. Something about it was familiar, even though nothing out here was *really* familiar, but I couldn't place it. We reached a point where the vegetation thinned enough that Alex could yank aside a curtain of vines. And the jungle gave way.

A silt bank surrounded a pool of water that was no bigger than my bedroom back home but so clear we could see all the way to the rocky bottom. A vent of water ran off one side of it and thinned to a brook only inches deep, eventually disappearing into the ground.

I looked toward the sky, where the shifting treetops wove together, blocking out most sunlight. When I had stood on the cliff side with Alex and looked down, those trees had completely obscured this place, this cranny in the island.

This hidden-away spot—we had to be the first to ever see it.

Alex touched the water and licked his fingertip. "It's not salty. We can drink it."

I followed the pool to the other end, where an opening in the bedrock cliff streamed water off the hillside in a continuous white sheet. It was only a few feet wide, but it was an actual, literal waterfall.

We finally had water. And it was *a waterfall.*

Alex loosened the tie on his muddy cargo shorts and dropped them. I watched him strip off his shirt and wade into the water, not cutting my eyes away when he glanced back at me.

I looked to the bottom as he swam into the middle.

"No caiman," he called. "It's clear as glass. You should get in."

I paused. Then I took off my mud-caked shorts. Watching Alex looking up at me, my pulse raced, and I took my time. I pulled my T-shirt over my head and slid off my shoes until I was down to my bikini and bare feet. I'd never stood in front of someone so fully on display.

"Come in here, Jones."

I walked to the far side and slipped beneath the surface.

The cold was like Thai iced teas and honey lavender gelato. I sank down to my waist and closed my eyes, feeling cool and clean for the first time in weeks. I looked at Alex and laughed.

"I know!" he yelled back. "I didn't think anything could ever feel this good again." He grinned from the middle of the pool. "Swim out here, Jones. It feels amazing. The waterfall—it's like a cold Jacuzzi."

"I can't." I held up my arm. "I shouldn't get the stitches wet."

He swam closer. "You could . . ."

"What?"

"Well, you could hold on. I'll keep your stitches above water and take you out into the middle." He squinted up at me, water beading on his eyelashes. "Do you trust me?"

I'd asked myself this very thing so many times in recent days.

This boy, he wasn't perfect.

But neither was I.

"Yes. I trust you."

Facing him, I laced my fingers behind his neck. He wrapped his hands under the back of my thighs and pulled me close.

His voice turned husky. "How's this?"

"It's good," I whispered.

With my arms around his shoulders and my legs around his waist, we moved into deeper water.

The force of the waterfall dropping into the pool made bubbles rise up around us. They burst against my legs and back, and we laughed and shrieked—cold, clean, alive. He pressed his forehead against mine and spun in a slow circle, making a whirlpool encircle us.

"Do you want to go under?"

"Yeah."

"Your arm will get wet."

"Like it isn't already."

He laughed and hoisted me a little higher. "Hang on really tight, okay?"

I nodded, and Alex walked forward, backing me under. Water lapped against my back, my hair, my shoulder blades, my breasts, and finally my ears filled, and I held my breath.

Everything was still under the wall of water, but the sound rushed against my eardrums. It was sensory deprivation, except for two things I felt with a new kind of intensity: the cool explosion of water over me and the warm press of Alex's body against mine.

I could have stayed under for longer, but Alex whipped me out and into the shifting sunlight. The force of it almost knocked us apart and we grabbed each other, sliding closer. I blinked away drops of water and looked at him, our faces level. My heart beat fast. "Do you know what I want?"

A breath shook free from his chest. "Jones. Are you sure? Do you want me to ask?"

"You just did."

"And?"

"Yes."

Pushing a wet curl off my lips, he leaned in. He brushed his mouth softly against mine. The touch made my whole body unspool. He teased my lips apart with tongue and teeth, gently, his fingertips stroking circles on the backs of my thighs underwater. I pulled him closer and pressed my palms against his sun-warm back. His soft, rapid breaths were inside my mouth. The kiss deepened. I made a sound I didn't know was inside me, and he smiled against my mouth, working his fingers into my hair. We found a rhythm, sank into each other, dissolved until we were like liquid, part of the water.

He broke away, searched my face, and with me still wrapped around him, said, "You're the only thing keeping me sane, Jones."

My mouth inched back to his. I closed my eyes, and pulled him closer.

❖❖❖

We ran back for the beach-trash bottles and carried enough water to the shelter for the three of us. By then it was drizzling again. The leaf cover overhead kept the sprinkling rain from putting out our fire, so we poured water inside my makeshift pot and balanced it above the flames.

"We need a longer break in the rain," I said to Alex. "The signal fire—we have to relight it. Do you think it'll stop for more than a few hours?"

"It has to," he said. "First morning it happens, first thing, we'll get it going together."

I watched the water bubble, all the muscles in my body still feeling like liquid. I could still feel Alex's phantom kisses on my lips, his arms around my legs, his skin warm beneath my hands.

Nothing like Jesse.

When I was with Alex, when he touched me, everything felt easy, natural. With Jesse, every word and touch was forced.

Jesse was safe. Was that why I'd wanted him? Because he didn't have the power to destroy me? Was that why Henri had wanted all those other boys?

After the water cooled, Alex filled a fresh bottle. "Here, Hank. You take the first sip." Henri closed her eyes as she drank. Her lips still damp, she said, "That's the best water I've ever had. Where'd you get it?"

Alex started to speak but I interrupted him. "A spring. A little spring out in the jungle. After everything, we found it, finally."

CHAPTER 20

SIX WEEKS BEFORE

I padded down the stairs in the navy-and-yellow polka-dot socks Henri had slipped into my stocking last Christmas. I couldn't stay in my bedroom any longer—my room was now the room beside the room where my sister and Jesse had stripped off all their clothes and done something I didn't want to think about.

Henri didn't want Jesse for herself. I knew my sister—she was only playing with him. Now he was ruined for me, gone from me, forever.

Pots clanged in the kitchen and my heart beat a little faster. If Mom came home early and Jesse was still upstairs, a reign of terror was about to befall the Jones household.

Jesse stood in front of the stove, dealing stacks of pancakes onto three plates and slicing up strawberries. "Morning."

I never heard him leave Henri's room.

My elbow connected with his side as I reached for a water glass.

He grunted.

"Sorry. Accident."

We both knew it wasn't.

"Hey, Em, I know you're mad at me."

I held my breath and faced him.

He braced his hands on the counter behind him and looked at the tile floor. "I'm sorry."

"Don't."

"No, I have to. You didn't go to that party because you knew I'd be there." I couldn't deny it—he'd read me too well. I didn't go because I didn't want to watch him lust after Henri and have nobody lusting after me. "You knew I'd be there to look out for Henri so you didn't have to. And I did a real shitty job. So, yeah, I'm sorry."

He didn't get it at all.

"I forgive you," I said.

Jesse didn't acknowledge me, though, because Henri stepped into the kitchen.

She wore one of her oldest sweatshirts, those same yoga pants from last night, and a pair of socks with her big toe poking through. Not the kind of ensemble I'd expect for her to wear in front of a boy. Whatever spark had ignited between her and Jesse had turned to ash, or else she'd be showing a lot more skin.

"Morning." Jesse smiled in a toothy way that made me cringe. Between that grin and the breakfast, he wasn't playing this cool. I started counting down to the moment when Henri's words would kick his teeth in.

"You cooked." She smiled and smoothed her hands over

her hair before she stepped past me and dropped into a chair at the breakfast nook table.

Jesse poured us each a glass of orange juice. I shoveled forkfuls of pancakes into my mouth while I watched them shoot sly glances at each other. As Henri ate, she walked her fingers across the tabletop, right beside Jesse's place mat.

She let him take her hand.

Jesse was at our house every moment of the rest of the three-day weekend.

Under the table, between blankets on the couch, standing toe to toe on the front porch, their hands were magnets, finding their way to each other's bodies.

I thought I would die of discomfort before Mom came home. Or boredom. There was no nail painting or magazine reading, no jaunts to Chinatown; and that Sunday, no movie date. Only three long days of Henri and Jesse locked in her room.

On Monday, I pretended to take a nap because I was tired of watching them groom and pet each other and find excuses to sneak off to her bedroom together.

Upstairs was abandoned after I woke up. I headed down the stairs, wearing my Snoopy pajama bottoms and Woodstock T-shirt—the bird, not the concert.

Moaning dragged my attention to the kitchen. I stood at the bottom of the stairs, silently watching Henri and Jesse. They were both fully clothed—I wasn't some kind of pervert.

She draped her arms over his shoulders and hooked her

turquoise-painted toes against the back of his jeans to keep him close. Henri didn't know how to love anyone without making sure they couldn't get away.

She wore a top with a boat neckline that stretched wide and exposed her shoulders. She tipped her head back, and with her eyes closed, let Jesse kiss the hollow of her throat and stretch the cotton fabric so he could get to all those covered-yet-innocent parts of her—collarbone, shoulders, a strawberry-shaped birthmark she usually covered with concealer.

Henri sighed and stroked her hand up the back of Jesse's neck. I touched my fingertips to the place between my neck and my collarbone, the place where Jesse was kissing my sister. No matter how hard I concentrated, I couldn't imagine his lips feeling as good as Henri acted like they felt.

Her eyelashes fluttered open. She blinked twice. "Emma!"

She hopped off the counter. As Jesse pulled away, she adjusted her drooping neckline to no avail.

Something about Jesse had marked a change in Henri. One I'd wanted for months, but now that it was here, I'd trade in all her good behavior if it meant I could keep Jesse for myself.

Henri sat on the edge of her window seat with the phone against her ear. Out the window, Jesse was in his room, on his own phone looking in.

I paused in the hall outside her doorway.

An arrangement of lilies dwarfed the dusty printer on her desk. A mesh red ribbon wrapped around the glass vase. The lilies themselves drooped and had scattered petals over her collection of nail polish. He'd sent them the week before and she hadn't watered them once.

I knew big bouquets of flowers like that cost a lot of money because I'd heard my dad complain about sending flowers. Before our dad had chosen a different life for himself, he sent arrangements like those to my mother for every anniversary and every Valentine's Day.

Jesse was making an absolute fool of himself over a girl who could never love him back.

She popped a chocolate into her mouth from a heart-shaped box and licked her fingers—the motion was part childlike and part sex. I didn't know how to be like that.

Jesse noticed me standing behind her and waved.

She followed his wave to where I stood in the shadows. "Oh, hey." Into the phone, she said, "I'll call you back." She paused while he said something, and smiled out the window. "Ditto."

After she hung up, she tossed her phone onto the carpet and pointed to the space on the window seat beside her. "Come here, Em. Let me look at those nails."

I sank into the paisley cushions and followed the darkness to Jesse's window. He was already gone.

She buffed my fingernails to a high shine. "Your toenails are a disaster."

I curled my toes so she couldn't see my chipped polish. "What's going on, Henri? Tell me the truth."

"I don't know what you mean." She yanked a box of nail

polish remover pads off her desk and dissolved the green polish from one nail at a time.

"Jesse. You told me you thought he was boring."

"It turns out he's rather entertaining." She shrugged. "I'm having fun."

"It's not fair to him."

Henri's lips moved into the most unreadable frown and faded away as she focused on my nails again. "I'd never hurt him."

"But you will hurt him. As soon as you move on to someone else."

She threw a glance outside, into the now darkened window of Jesse's room. "He's a big boy. He'll get over it. They always do."

CHAPTER 21

Henri's bag bulged with the shape of coconuts as I pulled back the tarp and blinked against the morning light. I breathed deep, and for the first time in days, dry air hit my throat instead of humidity. Through the spaces in the leaves above, the sky wasn't gray but bluer than the ocean.

"Where's Alex?"

He and I had planned to rebuild our signal fire the first morning it wasn't raining.

She dumped the coconuts, sticking out her foot to stop one from rolling into the fire. "Tarzan was already gone when I woke up. Maybe he's at the spring getting more water."

Henri didn't know that without me, Alex wouldn't be getting water, that Alex and I had made excuses to follow each other back to the waterfall for the short breaks between storms the last two days, telling her it took both of us to carry the water back and counting on her aversion to helping.

I wondered if Alex had got up early to rebuild the signal fire himself, but the lighter sat on the driftwood beside the fire.

I put it in my pocket and headed toward the beach.

The ocean was stiller than it had been in days, silent except for the gentle crash of waves, and flat enough to see for miles. Those cargo ships, they had to be just on the other side of the faraway horizon.

With or without Alex, I had to get the fire going again.

The water-soaked branches were heavy as I hauled them out of the pit. Searching for dry leaves and brush took longer after the storm, but inside hollow logs, I found some the rain hadn't touched.

Flames rippled across the kindling. I added enough bigger branches until the fire ignited and then greens for smoke. But the trickles disappeared as they climbed toward the cloudless sky.

It wasn't enough. I needed something that wouldn't burn clear.

From the last of the boat wreckage we'd left piled on the beach, I lifted the largest piece of cracked fiberglass and threw it onto the flames.

Black clouds pumped toward the sky. As I backed away, my arm covering my mouth, bitter vapors flooded the beach. If anything would help someone see us, this was it.

Late afternoon, under the shade of the palm trees, I watched the wind whip the dark smoke into a frenzy.

"Jones." Alex dropped his fishing spear in the sand in front of me. He coughed and lifted his shirt over his chin and mouth. "What did you do?"

"Built—" My voice was hoarse after spending hours near the fire. I cleared my throat. "Built the fire back."

"No, what did you add to it?"

"Fiberglass. So it would smoke more."

He lowered his shirt and gave me a weak smile. "And suffocate us in the process?"

"It's not that bad," I said as my throat constricted. "Okay, it is. But if it means they're going to find us faster, I'm willing to burn our lungs a little."

"Fair enough." The hollows under his eyes were cut a little deeper in the sunlight. He was thinner—we all were—but that wasn't it.

"Alex, where've you been all day? We said we'd light the signal fire first thing."

"I just went for a walk." He closed his eyes and rubbed his face, looked at the sand, the sky, everything but me. "I couldn't sleep last night. I was thinking about what your sister said about the signal fire. Maybe we are just throwing away the last of our lighter fluid."

"You're listening to *Henri*?"

He snapped his attention to me then. But it only lasted a second before he grabbed his spear from the sand and backed down the beach toward the rocky peninsula. "Look, I'm not saying you did anything wrong—but if it goes out again— maybe we shouldn't relight it."

I hugged my arms around myself after Alex was out on the rocks over the ocean. The waterfall—it hadn't felt like a mistake to me. But I hadn't confessed the things Alex had.

Now, in the empty space he'd shoved between us, I could sense his regret.

❖❖❖

The next afternoon, I walked down the beach to feed more wood onto the signal fire.

A windstorm had whipped through our island the night before, thrashing through the high-up tops of the trees. Our clearing had been mostly protected from the currents, but our signal fire was out.

A few gray coals smoked at the bottom of the pit. I grabbed handfuls of dry brush and a long stick. I stoked the coals, trying to get a spark. The coals went cold.

Since Alex said we shouldn't waste the lighter restarting the fire, we hadn't discussed it more. Now our fire was dead and so was my patience.

I walked to the waterfall first. He wasn't there. I went to the north side of the beach next, the rocks jutting far across the waves where we fished, but he wasn't fishing.

The last two days had been full of his absence. The closest I could get to touching him was remembering the palms of his hands, warm as they slipped under my shirt. My lips grazing the few freckles across his cheeks and nose. The tips of my toes lifting off the rocky bottom as he pulled me against him, like he needed me closer than skin could allow.

Slowly, I climbed up through the bamboo to the top of the cliff.

Wind thrashed my curls against my eyes at the peak. I gathered my hair at my neck, and stared out.

The force of the wind made the sea rough that day, waves tall and fierce. Over the rocky western side of the ocean, the part of the island hidden from everywhere except the very top of the cliffs, a spot of orange hurtled across the surface.

I stepped toward the edge to get a better look, got dizzy at the shock of the height, moved back. I focused on the water—and I found him.

Careening across the waves, Alex was on his stomach with Casey's backpack strapped to his back.

He was inside the life raft. The one he'd told me he'd destroyed.

Rocks jutted from the water along the coastline, and he was headed right for them. I yelled out, but even if he heard me, there was nothing he could do. The raft hit the rocks just as a swell came down over him. The ocean peeled back, and the mangled raft tossed against the churn of the ocean. I couldn't see him.

Through the brush and bamboo, the jagged paths we'd carved through the jungle, I ran without thinking.

At the shore, leaking air whistled out of the plastic. The rolling waves tugged at the raft wedged into the rocks, inching it free with each swell. I grabbed the handles, dragged it farther onto land, stared into the water. If Alex was knocked out, it wouldn't take long to drown.

"Emma."

He moved from the shadows of the cliff with the backpack swinging from his hand. His shirt was open and torn. Between the white cotton, his ribs were already purple.

"I'm okay." He pressed two fingers to his split lip, pulled them back, and stared at the spot of blood. "I'm kind of beat-up, but okay."

There he was, on the beach and above water. I wanted to touch him, to feel his chest expanding and constricting and know, really know, he was fine. But when he reached for me, I jumped back. *"What are you even doing?"* I managed to choke out.

His lips moved as he processed my words. The dazed look on his face shifted into something harder. "What I'm *even doing* is trying to get us home."

"By lying? You said the raft was destroyed."

He sighed. "It wasn't a lie." The tide came in and splashed against our legs and the raft. Alex wrenched it farther up the sand, partly off the rocks. Pieces of woven-together bamboo stuck out of one side. "When I tore through it, I only ripped one air chamber. I tied some bamboo to the deflated part to make it float."

"To go where?"

He pointed to the horizon, his shoulders relaxing as if the ocean calmed him. "If the ships out there won't come to us, I thought we'd go to them. Like those guys who escaped from Alcatraz. We'd have to make it twenty miles. Twenty miles out and we'd be right in the path of those cargo ships. We'd get their attention and we'd be as good as home. But the ocean's too rough today, and what I did made the raft unbalanced. Thought I could handle it." He shrugged and reached toward me, then hissed, crushing both hands into his ribs.

I lurched forward and stepped back. He'd brought this on himself.

"Anything could have happened to you, Alex. *Anything.* You

could've cracked your head open on the rocks. Knocked your-self unconscious. Drowned."

He gritted his teeth, swallowed hard. The wetness of his eyes, I wasn't sure if it was pain or anger. "I fucking didn't."

I looked to the ocean. If I saw him wince again, I didn't know how to stay put. "All the sneaking off, I thought it was about us."

"Us?" He tossed the backpack onto the rocks.

"The waterfall. What we've been doing there." His lips, his hands, my skin. *My* lips, *my* hands, *his* skin. "You regretting it."

"That wasn't it. Not at *all*." He moved closer. "I care about you. And not just touching you, kissing you. Not just you're here, I'm here, so why not? It's not like that." He bent closer, but I put up my arms. Gently, he tried to take my hands, but I broke free.

Alex, with his logic, his problem-solving, and his ability to see past all the messy parts and focus on surviving, he'd almost fooled me into thinking he wasn't just as reckless as Henri.

"What you did today, what you've been doing in secret, makes you not only dangerous to yourself but to me and to Henri. It's reckless."

"Trying to get us home, that's not reckless." He pointed to the sea. "Relying on someone floating on a ship out there to find us by some miracle, that's reckless."

"Maybe waiting on someone is," I said. "But how we're get-ting home isn't just your call. We're supposed to talk to each other."

He swept his hand toward the raft, flat, listless on the sand. "The raft was for all of us. You and me and even your sister."

"I don't know anymore. Between the lighter and *this* and the backpack that's still practically attached to you, depending on you is feeling more and more like a gamble."

He glanced to the backpack sitting on top of the rocks, then to the sky. "I get that the money makes it hard to trust me. Sometimes it makes me not trust myself."

It was so much more than trust, even. Surviving on this island was too big a burden for any one of us alone. *We* had to get *us* home. "You have to tell me what you're doing, make me part of the plan—I need *you* to depend on *me*, not just the other way around."

He dragged his palms slow and rough down his face. "Maybe I'm not good at that, Jones. Maybe I've been on my own for so long that I don't know how to depend on anyone but myself." He focused on me, his voice building. "But being bad at depending on people isn't the worst quality a person can have. The other direction isn't all that appealing either. I'd think you would know that."

I blinked. "You're talking about Henri?"

"Hell yes, I'm talking about Henri. How's depending on her working out for you?"

Something inside me split open, and not because he was wrong. I knew when words were meant to hurt. I knew it from Henri. I expected more from Alex.

He swore under his breath. "That was harsh." Alex, with his battered ribs, red eyes, hands shaking, hauled back and kicked the raft. The plastic crunched and deflated. "The reason I didn't tell you about the raft . . . I didn't know if I could make it work. After all that rain, I knew we couldn't survive here forever. You know it too. I saw it in the way you were with the signal fire. The fiberglass. The way you obsess over it."

"It was the best chance we had. I thought you agreed."

Sunlight shone on a shadowy bruise that ran from his temple to his cheekbone as he turned to me. "At first, yeah. But not when every flick of the lighter puts us a day closer to running out of fluid. Not after days of nobody coming close. Your hopes were so high over that stupid fire. I didn't want to get you excited about this and then crash on the rocks. Like I just did."

"Alex." My exhaustion and frustration leaked into my voice. "You've been disappearing for days, hiding out on the side of the beach where I wouldn't see you. And you made a decision that should have been mine too. Are . . . are you even sorry?"

He blinked at me, his wet hair clinging. He opened his mouth, and I thought he was finally going to say something. But he shook his head to himself and bent low to the raft.

That was it. I was in rough enough waters with Henri to know that whatever I'd been doing with Alex had to stop—if I swam any deeper, I was sure to drown.

CHAPTER 22

FOUR WEEKS BEFORE

Our house was bursting with bodies by seven o'clock that Friday night. Before our mother left for the weekend again, Henri made me ask if we could have a few friends over. If it came from Henri, Mom would know we were planning a rager. I was nervous about the whole thing, but Henri said we could sleep all day Saturday and clean up Sunday morning before Mom got home.

Because I had done the asking, the party was a go.

Henri perched on our countertop beside a few jugs of orange juice and a collection of bottles everyone had pooled together from their parents' stashes. She passed out drinks while Jesse sat on the last step of the staircase, watching her. She wasn't in her usual party attire—only a pair of jeans and an off-the-shoulder white sweater.

I dropped beside Jesse.

He took a long drink from his beer and grinned at me. "Hey."

I snatched the bottle and drank. "You know she's just screwing around with you, right?"

"What?" Jesse made a face. "Why would you say that?"

"Well"—I peeled off part of the beer label—"because it's true."

"No, it's not." He wrapped his hand around the bottle and moved it beyond my reach. "You don't know what we have. I know it's hard for you being the third wheel and all, but this isn't some fling. I love her, Em."

Henri sipped from a Perrier and smiled across the room. I glared back and she cocked her head to the side, not understanding. Mick slipped a pair of keys into her palm and she was smiling again. That dark moment between us faded.

She strolled our way and, hands on hips, stopped in front of us. "Mick's wasted, so I've got to drive Ari home. She's leaving early to tour UCLA with her fam."

Jesse jumped to his feet. "You should let me drive you."

She draped her arms over his shoulders and pecked him on the cheek. "Don't be silly. You've been drinking and you need to stay here and keep your eye on Em." She winked at me and spun. Over her shoulder, she called, "Be back in twenty."

She was going to break Jesse's heart into a million tiny pieces if I didn't do something and do it fast. Henri wouldn't even really care—she'd have someone new before the week was over.

I headed up the stairs.

Henri kept a bottle of Smirnoff hidden inside a boot in her closet. It was there for sleepovers with Ari or the occasional emergency when Henri's friends couldn't find some over-twenty-one guy to do their buying.

Henri's bedroom door closed behind me and I crossed my legs on her closet floor. I took a few tiny sips. Liquid courage, Henri called it. I needed all the courage I could find, even if it was synthetic.

I needed something else too. Henri's closet held dozens of skirts—sequins, florals, gauzy chiffons, Lurex threading. None of it was me, so I settled on one swipe of her red lipstick.

Knocking back the bottle one more time, I took a final gulp.

A few steps down the hallway, I realized I'd overdone it on the vodka. Our family pictures blurred and the music pounded through my chest as I clutched the banister all the way down to the family room.

Henri wouldn't be back from dropping off Ari for at least fifteen more minutes.

Jesse choked on his beer as I made the corner. "Nice lips. Henri's signature color?"

I stepped forward and lost my balance.

His hands caught my arms and held me upright until I found my equilibrium again. "Shit. Are you loaded?"

"A little." I swallowed. "Can I talk to you alone?"

Jesse turned on the back porch lights and shut the door behind us. He shivered in the January air and ran his hands over his arms. I wasn't cold at all.

"So what's this about?"

"You," I whispered. I reached past his shoulder and flipped

the light switch, shrouding us in darkness. I stepped forward an inch but stumbled into his chest.

"What?"

Even the liquor didn't give me enough courage to do this easily. I'd always thought it was Henri's impulsiveness—her spontaneity—that drew boys her way.

I didn't lean in so much as lunge. My lips were on him, but our mouths wouldn't line up. My kiss size was so much bigger than his.

He jerked away. "What are you *doing*?"

I pushed against his chest again, but Jesse shoved me backward so hard, I tumbled into the wicker chair by the railing, scratching my thigh deep enough that blood beaded on my leg. Only I didn't feel any pain.

"You listen to me," he said. "This never happened."

"Jesse—"

"No, I don't care. No matter what happens, you forget this night existed."

Jesse crossed the porch, smoothing down his hair, wiping his mouth on the back of his sleeve as if I was disgusting.

He turned back. "What the fuck, Emma? This would kill Henri."

I leaned over the porch railing and vomited Smirnoff onto the grass.

It was five days before my sixteenth birthday.

CHAPTER 23

Henri stacked beach-trash water bottles between two rocks to keep them from rolling away. "These have been boiled. And these haven't. Two . . . four . . . six to go."

She poured one of the yet-to-be-boiled bottles into the metal pot and balanced it above the flames. Again and again, she would empty a bottle, let the water boil, cool, and funnel it back inside.

Drizzles of warm rain had fallen for a week, dampening the dark ground and brightening the emerald leaves. Feathery orange flowers sprouted from glossy foliage, their scent catching on every breeze that drifted through our clearing.

The rain didn't keep us inside, just fell lightly against our faces like the last drops from a shower tap. We stacked dry firewood inside our shelter, made our clearing more comfortable, and organized water bottles and the splintered bits of the boat we didn't know how to use yet.

"You don't have to boil all of them now."

"Might as well. While it's not raining." With a broken coconut in her lap, Henri balanced alone on the driftwood beside the popping fire. She scraped the last of the flesh from the shell and held out the other coconut half. "Hungry?"

"Thank you." I took it and sat on the driftwood while Henri slid down to the dirt and took a handful of shells from her pocket.

The distance between Alex and me had left room for her to inch closer. Still, I knew my sister. I wasn't sure if she was getting close just to bury her knife.

As I chiseled at my coconut, Henri untied the ends of her necklace and threaded a single blue shell to mark the day.

I covered my mouth as I chewed. "What month is it now?"

"April."

"It's April?" Time wasn't moving at the right speed on our island, sometimes rocketing past, sometimes slow as a crack spreading across glass.

"Late April now." She glanced up at me through her lashes. "Mom's birthday was last week. It was her fortieth. I keep thinking about what she did that day. She couldn't have celebrated."

Our mom's devastation had to be crushing. She wasn't celebrating anything. She didn't even have anyone to celebrate with. Parents sometimes banded together in a crisis, but I couldn't make up some fantasy about my dad being any real comfort.

What Alex said—the pretending—I didn't feel like doing it anymore.

"Really, what's there to celebrate?" I said. "We're gone and so is Dad. And even with us missing, he's way too selfish to be there for her."

Henri's lips parted.

My honesty wasn't meant to hurt my sister. I almost back-tracked, made up something kinder, but she reached up and hugged me.

She squeezed me, tight, then tighter, and with our faces buried in each other's hair, I felt us rewinding back, before the music store in the Haight, rooftop parties, broken bottles, and racing engines.

Maybe all Henri had needed from me was something real. But we'd left too much unsaid for this reprieve to last.

Alex—before he almost broke himself on the rocks—I thought he was like water. Healthy and good for me.

Henri's love was a drug. The highs glorious and the lows devastating.

I pulled away and carried a stack of wood into our shelter.

"Where's Mr. Missing in Action?" she asked as I came out.

"Fishing." We had to take advantage of the lulls in the rain, when the ocean went clear and the fish bright, and Alex had said he was heading down to the beach.

Henri smirked by the fire as she worked her hair into a loose bun. "Kind of hard to fish without a spear."

I froze. Our fishing spears were leaning against the shelter.

I found Alex with his sleeves rolled to his elbows, shirt unbuttoned and gusting in the wind. He balanced at the farthest-out point on the rocks where we fished. The backpack hung by its top handle from his hand, the straps dragging in the surf, rolling in and out on the sea foam.

I jogged toward the cliffs, down the beach, slowing as my

feet found the algae-slick cluster of rocks under the waterline.

"Alex," I called as I jumped rocks out to the end of the peninsula. "What are you doing?"

He squinted at me against the sun. "Putting the money back where it belongs."

The saltwater breeze scattered some bills across the water, and I caught his hand. I'd hated that bag of money, what it represented, but now that he was throwing it into the surf, I was suddenly uncertain. All I could think about was his future drifting out to sea.

"This money's too important to me—I want it gone. I want to be able to trust myself." He lifted the bag toward the water. "I want you to be able to trust me too."

"Wait—don't do this to prove something to me."

"It's not just for you." He shut his eyes and squeezed the bridge of his nose. "I want to stop feeling so damn guilty for what I did that day—I want that so much more than this money."

"What about your fishing boat?" He could do a lot with it. College, a new car, investments, a life that wasn't running drugs. "Getting rid of the money—it won't get rid of your guilt. Alex, this money could buy you a *life*."

He looked at the bag in his arms, his hair blowing around his head. "I don't— How could I even enjoy it? Knowing I sacrificed my cousin for it."

"Alex, you didn't."

"No, I *did*. There was barely any blood in the water—I get that. It doesn't mean it's not my fault. It's not just because of the backpack. Do you see? He couldn't have kept things up without me. I knew it wasn't the right thing. I'd seen what drugs did to people. My dad. My friends. And still I was like, *Sure, yeah, let's do it.* Do you see, Jones? I could have saved him from himself."

"If Casey were here, you think this is what he'd think? What he'd want?"

The bag was high in his arms, ready to drop into the ocean below. He lowered it, stared at the bundles of bills. Sighed. His whole body went limp. He zipped it closed.

"I've been meaning to tell you something," he said as he faced me. The bruises on his face were starting to fade. "What I said about you depending on your sister, after I crashed the raft . . . that was a real dick thing to say."

"It's fine."

"It's really not."

He opened his arms and even though I was still mad, even though I didn't know if he was good for me, he needed this. I wrapped my arms around his waist. He winced as I squeezed into his sore ribs, but when I tried to loosen, he pulled me tighter to him. The cool cotton of his shirt warmed against my skin.

His chin rested on the top of my head, his hands sturdy against my back. "What I told you about Casey, the kid with the bike . . . We were holy terrors just like that kid. The whole neighborhood loathed us, and for good reason. My dad's sister raised Casey. She wasn't really any better than my dad—except she didn't hit as hard. But Casey was . . . I don't know . . . easier."

I pulled back a little. "What made you different?"

"I don't know. What made you and your sister different?"

"We weren't—" I tried to think back. "We weren't always so different. I guess I want to blame my dad, and I guess I should, for what he did, how he left. But it was also the way she reacted. That's when I first noticed a change, a difference. She . . ." Hate for our dad, and now me, pumped through Henri so fast, so fully, I wondered if her heart could keep beating without it. "She despised him. And I saw what that did to her. I see it in her every day. It's like she needs it to keep going."

Alex blinked like I'd thrown a glass of ice water in his face.

I realized what I'd said and started talking fast. "But, you— your dad—you have every right to hate him. He—"

"No," he said. "That's the difference. Casey and me. He didn't hate anyone, not even that kid. With my dad . . . I guess I should work on letting it go." He smiled a little. "Here I thought maybe Casey was so chill because of all the weed he smoked." He looked up, at me. I wasn't smiling back. "Hey, Emma, I'm sorry."

"It's okay. It was just a bad joke."

"No, I mean—I'm sorry about the raft. Hiding things from you, not trusting you to know. Scaring you. Everything."

I took each side of his open shirt in my hands, waited for him to look at me, and said, "I'm too good at giving out passes."

We stood still, under a cover of dark clouds pushing down, until he smiled. "Your next life, Jones, you deserve a beautiful one after this. Being stuck here with me and your sister and all our shit."

"I'm not as saintly as you think. Just ask Henri."

He trailed the back of his hand down my arm. "I've told you everything. You know that, right? About the accident, my dad, what I was really doing in Puerto Rico—"

"Alex, I trust you. I know you were trying to do right with the raft—"

"That's not what I mean. What I'm saying is that it feels . . . it feels really . . . *free*. Telling you, I mean. Jones, what happened between you and your sister—"

Most of my anger had faded, but his apology didn't take me back to how I felt at the waterfall. The slender thread of trust that had tied me to him was still loose. I couldn't feel good about telling him everything.

"Alex."

He nodded. Wearing a small smile, he shrugged, almost sadly.

A drop of tepid rain struck my arm, then another and another.

"Again, really?" I looked up at the sky. Alex laughed—it sounded forced, but I liked the effort—and opened his mouth to the rain.

Thunder crackled and the drizzle became a downpour.

"We're getting soaked," Alex yelled over the roar. His fingers reached for mine and I took them.

Hands slipping together and apart and together again, we leaped across rocks with water ricocheting off our legs. Our clothes sucked against our skin. Rain like this—drenching, blinding—was new. An adventure.

Pelting water blurred my vision at the shore. "Back to the shelter?"

"No, this way. We'll wait it out."

Our feet sinking in wet sand, tripping and laughing a little, we ducked under a small ledge at the bottom of the cliff.

Alex threw the backpack in first, diving in behind it. I leaned back against the rock wall that had been carved smooth by higher tides. Alex settled into the sand next to me. So still under there. Sheets of rain slid off the overhead ledge and pounded a few feet past our toes as our breathing evened out. Wet, ropy curls clung to my face and I scooped them back.

"This hair—it's wild. I love it," he said, tugging gently on a strand. "Incidentally, I'm in need of a little style advice myself." He gathered his wet hair at the nape of his neck. "This. It's a pain since I lost my rubber band. My neck gets sweaty. So, my only options are I hack it off with my knife or . . . man bun."

"A *man bun?*" I smiled and squinted at him. "I was never into it back home—but then, I used to be into shaving my legs and using a blow dryer. Out here"—I nodded—"the man bun works." I threaded my fingers through his loose hair. He looked at me as if weighing something, green eyes dark. There was some warring feeling in them—wariness, I realized, and maybe hope. I took his hand and kissed his palm. His lips parted. That faint line down the center of his full bottom lip, I gently pressed it with my fingertip. I leaned in and kissed the same spot. He pulled me against him and we stayed that way a long time. "Don't cut it," I said, "your hair," and he leaned us back onto the sand and kissed me, a slow, deep kiss that tugged at my breath as he pulled away. The back of his fingers skimmed over my shirt, down my ribs. My stomach fluttered. He watched me carefully as he caught the hem, slid his warm hand against my skin. My T-shirt slipped higher, and he untied my bikini top. Raising my arms, I helped him lift both off.

Alex's breathing picked up. He looked at me. Put his hands around my rib cage. Pulled me closer. I leaned in. "Come here," I said, pushing his wet shirt off his shoulders, his skin warm and smooth beneath, my hands wanting to explore. I kissed his shoulder, the shadowy bruises that still covered his ribs. His fingers worked through my hair, cupped the back of my head, then brushed my lips. They moved soft and sure against my body, dizzying and maddening and everything and . . . too much. I drew a shaky breath. He pulled a few inches away, smiled, eyes drowsy but intent.

We sank down to the sand again as rain further darkened the beach beyond.

Alex brushed his fingers against my collarbone. "You haven't before, have you?"

"No." I held my breath.

"I wasn't asking you—"

"I want to," I said. Because I did. But wanting Alex and being ready were different. Part of me was still afraid. Boys

248

had ruined Henri. "But there's only one condom. One chance and—"

"Emma," he started. Then laughed. "Of course you saw the condom." He shook his head and kissed me, his mouth smiling against mine. "This is really nice." His hand moved to the nape of my neck, sliding down my skin, and stroking slow circles on my breasts. "Just like this."

I arched back, then pulled him closer, felt all of him against me. Not an inch of space between us, and no longer did I want to live for the days when Henri and I were little old ladies in our house by the sea. I wanted this—the here, the now.

Alex ran his hand over my calf as we kissed. He broke away, and mouth skimming mine, he stroked the crease behind my knee. Eyes asking for each inch, his fingertips traced up the inside of my leg, higher, higher, higher. He touched me, and a breath shuddered from my throat. His hand stilled, and he looked at me. "Okay?"

I nodded. "Yes."

His fingers trailed up, then down my navel, making my stomach flip. Watching me, he moved his hand lower, carefully beneath my swimsuit bottoms, slow and achingly deliberate. His lips glided across my breast, and my shoulders lifted off the sand.

After, I opened my eyes and came back to the beach, the island, the earth.

I wanted to do this for him too. I wanted to make him feel this good.

There was a tremor.

The ground shook beneath us. I sat up, holding my top against my bare chest with one hand, while with the other I tried to steady myself.

A roar filled my ears, a crashing.

Alex's eyes darted to the ledge above. "An earthquake?"

"I don't think so." I'd felt earthquakes back home in San Francisco. This felt like something else, something in the distance.

"Henri."

Not bothering with my bikini top, I yanked my T-shirt over my head. Rain beating down, slicking my steps, I dashed through the jungle. Alex's feet hammered behind me.

A river of thick mud covered half of our clearing. The hillside had crumbled, melted into our space like dropped ice cream. Rain poured down, rinsing clean and exposing gray masses—small boulders—jutting from the mud. Two of our driftwood logs were gone, consumed by the rock and mudslide. *Henri.* The place where she'd stacked the bottles—it was buried.

Henri. Henri.

Rain blurred my vision and I blinked fast over the boulders, searching for an arm, a leg, a shock of blond hair.

The shelter's tarp door crinkled. One hand holding it up, Henri peeked out.

With my hand against my heart, I stood there, the rain dripping down my hair, my face, my clothes.

Alex overturned our metal bowl over the fire, careful to

allow for airflow. It had been protected by the tree cover and hadn't been completely killed by the downpour. A few of the coals still glowed red.

He pushed at my lower back. "Go on. Get out of the rain. I'll try to stoke the fire."

I scrambled through the door. The air inside was made more humid by our breath. Other than that, our shelter was mostly dry.

"You were sitting right there when I left you," I said. "I thought . . ."

Henri's hands were folded in her lap where she sat cross-legged on the shelter floor. I almost reached for them, but she draped her sweatshirt over her legs and buried her hands in it.

"I got inside as soon as the rain started." Her blank stare shifted into suspicion. "Where were you, anyway? You could have made it back twelve times since it started raining."

"We found a place to hide out."

Henri looked from my T-shirt, glued to my chest and hiding nothing, to my hand, where my bikini top dangled from my fingers. Her face hardened, and every bit of the contempt she'd had for me settled back into place. "Sure."

The tarp lifted and Alex crouched low in the doorway. I could see our wrecked clearing beyond, the bowl set loosely over low flames. Exhaustion weighed down his eyes in a way I hadn't seen since before we'd found the waterfall. "It almost crushed the shelter," he said. "We could have all been inside."

A cold breeze slapped the tarp aside and wafted through.

My teeth chattered. I rubbed the skin around the curved red wound on my arm. It itched all the time now and the tightening of my goose-bump-covered skin only made it worse.

Those first dry days before we'd even found water, I never would have thought the rain could be anything but refreshing. Now it was a freezing, soaking torrent that left my teeth chattering so hard, I couldn't force myself still.

Alex rubbed his hands fast up and down my arms, creating friction, heat. I shivered. He caught my hands and blew warmth into them.

Henri did a double take. Lips parted, she stared him down—Alex, with my hands inside his. I pulled away from him before she said something spiteful.

He made a face. I could tell he was tired of the secrecy, tired of her having too much power over me.

Plinks of water struck the roof. We'd stretched the overhead tarps tight but they'd come loose in a couple of places, making pockets of water sink through the spaces in the palms. The rain wasn't letting up, and after only a week of drizzle and one day of heavy downpours, the ground was already saturated enough for a rock slide.

"It could happen again," I said.

Henri pulled her sweatshirt under her chin, squeezed her eyes shut.

Alex massaged his temples. "What if we moved? Somewhere safer?"

"Away from any hillside that might crumble? There's nowhere like that. Not on this island."

"The rainy season is starting. These first rains are only a preview and . . ." Alex wouldn't say more, wouldn't fill in the blank. But I knew. If we didn't find a way off this island, we were going to die.

We spent the next morning cleaning up the clearing, just Alex and me. We carried what fallen rocks we could against our chests two-handed. My nails broke down to the quick as I combed through mud, looking for our water bottles and our pieces of ship debris. Three days later and we were nowhere near finding our supplies at the bottom.

This island, with its green and waterfalls and salty-sweet stars, it almost tricked us into believing it wasn't deadly. But no amount of water or food or fire could make it safe. Or maybe it was me and Alex. Our electric skin and hushed murmurs, our wet eyelashes and secret kisses—stunning, lulling, numbing us to the fact that, just by being stuck here, we were slowly dying.

A storm was coming. We'd had more rain, the kind of rain that fell until our nails were pliable and the calluses on our feet soft and painful. This, though—the gray roaring sky and fast-moving clouds—this was something different.

I was collecting dry firewood up near the tree line when my sister yelled, "If you're not lying to me, then why won't you show me?"

The bundle of kindling dropped from my arms as I ran to the beach.

I should have known this was coming. Henri was gasoline and Alex a flame.

Alex and Henri had been trying to fish near the cliff before the sea got too choppy. She'd been digging for any sea life buried in the wet sand.

Now they stood on the high rocks that jutted from the water under the cliff, where Alex and I would spear fish at low tide. His backpack was slung over one shoulder and he had a fistful of Henri's top as he held her at arm's length.

She glanced my way fast before she made a grab for the straps of his backpack. He twisted his body and kept it out of her reach.

"He's lying to us, Em," she said, clawing at his hands, trying to break his grip.

"Stop it," Alex said, still holding her off.

"What's going on?"

"The backpack," she said to me. "We already know it had a lighter. I'd like to see what else it has."

"Henri, I saw everything he had. It's just money. Back off."

Alex let go of Henri and took a leap back, still holding tight to the backpack. Bloody scratches covered his forearms. "Listen to your sister," he said. "You're going to hurt yourself, Hank. These rocks are slick."

"Show me what's inside and I'll never mention it again."

She stretched for the dangling strap, and Alex lifted his hand to block her. When he did, his finger hooked her shell necklace. The thread broke and Henri caught the end, but not before most of the shells plinked against the rocks, scattering onto the sand, ricocheting and dropping into the waves.

"See what you did," Alex said. "Now cut it out before something worse happens."

Henri glared back. She ripped the remains of the necklace away and shoved it into her shorts pocket. "I'm not backing down."

"Maybe you should just show her," I said.

"Really?" The hurt on his face leveled me. "Thanks for the vote of confidence."

"It's not that. You know I believe you. But if you just let her look, she'll shut up about it."

"It's the principle of the thing, Jones."

Alex's upper body was turned toward me, and Henri took the opportunity, lunging for him. He spun just in time to dodge her, but when he did, his pocketknife fell out of his shorts and clattered open onto the rocks. They both reached to grab it, but the rocks were slippery and Alex's steps were more careful than Henri's—she beat him to it.

"If you won't show me"—she held the hilt of the knife in front of her, blade up—"then maybe I'll just throw your knife into the ocean."

"That would be ridiculous as fuck. You need that knife just as much as I do."

She extended her arm, dangling it over the waves crashing below. "Maybe I don't care."

Alex slid the backpack free from his shoulder. All he had to do was let her see inside, then this ridiculous thing would be over. I relaxed, ready for him to do the right thing.

But a slow grin spread across his face, and Alex said the worst thing anyone could have possibly said to my sister: "You're bluffing."

Henri's grip on the knife loosened, and Alex went for her.

Just as his arms came around her, she pulled the knife close. Their feet slipped out from under them, and their bodies slammed onto the slippery rocks.

They fell together and Alex cried out. She reached past him and grabbed for the backpack. But Alex, he didn't get up. He stayed on his stomach, gasping, his eyes streaming.

The knife, I didn't see it.

Alex rolled onto his back and I scanned his torso for blood. Sun glinted off the knife, but it wasn't jutting from his body, only lodged in a gap between the rocks.

Pressing his weight onto his hands, he tried to push himself up. But he screamed and vomited on the rocks. He held up his right hand. Two fingers were purple and jutting out at sickening angles.

Henri had unzipped the backpack, but she dropped it and walked closer to Alex with her hands covering her mouth. "I wouldn't have let it go—the knife. I swear."

Holding Alex's wrist in my hands, I looked up at my sister. *"What is wrong with you?"*

The icy water covered my body like a million sharp pinpricks as I swam over to Alex.

Since dinner, he'd been standing shoulders-deep near the cool waterfall and soaking his hand.

My toes barely touched the rocky floor and my arms had to take big strokes to keep the motion of the waterfall from pushing me toward the embankment.

"At least I'm a leftie." He lifted his hand from beneath the surface and winced. The whole thing, not just his broken middle and ring fingers, had turned blue.

"I could try to set it?"

He grunted, noncommittal. "It's not like I haven't broken bones before."

I waded closer and rested my cheek against him, my arms circling his waist. "I don't even know what to say. I'm so sorry. She went too far."

He set his chin against the top of my head and sighed. "It wasn't so different from the last time—they're both bullies. My dad and your sister."

I wondered if he'd noticed the parallel between his dad and Henri all along. Maybe that's why he'd never had any patience for her.

"He would have won if I'd stayed," he said. "That's why I left. Because I couldn't let him win."

Winning was what all bullies wanted, including Henri, but the games she played only had losers. I didn't know how to play a game nobody could win.

"Alex, if you wanted to take the Oxy now, I wouldn't judge you."

"I'd judge myself."

I lifted his wrist from the water, inspected the blue fingers. "You're losing circulation. You need a doctor. You need to get home. We all need to get home."

All we were doing was waiting, to be rescued, to die. For something, for anything. I wished we just could float away.

"Alex," I said. "The bamboo you tied to the life raft—it floated well?"

"Yeah, it's hollow. Buoyant."

"Maybe we could start from scratch. Build our own raft. Out of bamboo. You're good with your hands."

"Might have worked a few days ago, but come on." He held up his bent fingers. "Look at my jacked-up hand and think about what you're saying."

"We'd do it together."

He sank his hand back into the water, grimaced, and swam closer. "You're not worried—after the first raft—to take something we made out on the ocean?"

"Twenty miles. You told me yourself. We'd only have to make it twenty miles before we're right in the path of the cargo ships. And we'd test it in the middle of the beach, away from the rocks."

"That could actually work."

Underwater, I touched his wrist, rubbing the tendons as if I could actually soothe the pain away. "But you'd have to talk to me, include me. Really. I'm not doing this if it means I'm going to wake up to find you killing yourself."

He looked into the water, my hand around his wrist. "I can do that, Emma. I want to."

"Good," I said. "First break in the rain and you're on."

Alex turned his eyes to the canopy of trees, and the dark clouds beyond them rolling across the existing gray. "The sky looks like hell. We better get back before a storm hits."

CHAPTER 24

Henri threw her body on the middle of my bed, scattering some of my rule-lined homework papers to the floor. She barely glanced at the trig textbook that had fallen open as she grinned to herself.

She wore comfortable jeans and boots that were basically slippers. She'd traded in tops that looked like Christmas decorations for cozy cashmeres. Every time Jesse would catch her eye, her mouth would curve into a smile she'd immediately wipe away. Like that smile was something involuntary.

Mom coming home should have changed everything between Henri and Jesse. Henri should have gotten tired of him quickly, like she'd done with every boy before. Mom should have ended Jesse being at our house during every daylight hour.

Every one of my predictions was wrong.

Mom could see the change in Henri the rest of the world could see too. Mom wasn't like me; she didn't know it was temporary. She welcomed Jesse over our threshold every chance she got.

But I'd seen Henri at school that day, and I knew it wasn't just Jesse she was keeping at the end of her leash.

Midway through western civ I'd asked for a pass to the bathroom when I realized my homework was in another binder. As I turned the dial on my locker, I glanced up the staircase toward the music room, where I saw Henri and Mr. Flynn whispering by the water fountain.

He trailed his fingers down the arm of her blazer, and I bolted back to my class without even grabbing my homework.

Now I collected my textbook from my bedroom carpet. "Why so happy?"

"No reason."

"I've gotta study," I said. "Can you give me some privacy?"

As soon as Jesse would go home for the night, she'd come into my room and interrupt whatever I was doing. I despised being his substitute. Worst of all was this: Whenever she was given the choice between us, she chose him every time.

That terrified me. I could only be defined by Henri if she was defined by me too.

Henri had left my bedroom door cracked, and Mom knocked on the open door. She held the house phone in her hand, with her palm pressed over the mouthpiece. "Hey girls, your dad's on the phone. He'd like to talk to you both. He wants to invite you out for dinner this weekend."

Henri didn't even turn around. "We're busy."

Mom's arm tensed as she pressed her palm to the phone harder. "Right now? Or for dinner?"

Henri traced the floral pattern on my comforter with her fingernail. "Both."

"Emma?" Past Henri's shoulder, Mom focused on me. "Do you want to talk to him?"

I thought about who had made Henri the way she was now. All roads led back to him.

"I'm busy too."

My mom pulled the door shut behind her and padded down the hall.

"Em, is something wrong? I know things have been hectic lately, and I'm sorry. I want to do something with you soon, only me and you and a bucket of the butteriest popcorn in the city. Can we schedule another movie day for this Sunday?"

A spark of the Henri I adored hadn't shone through since she'd started dating Jesse. Now it crackled across the walls and warmed my whole room.

She sank her top teeth into her bottom lip. "Oh, wait. I've actually already got plans."

"With who?"

"Jesse. His dad got us tickets to see the game. Can we postpone it one week? Only one week, pretty please?"

"Fine."

"But there's a party on Saturday night. It's not like an Ari Deveroux–sized affair or anything like that. Just a beach thing Mick's hosting. Jesse and I are going. You should come."

I shrugged. "Maybe."

Really, I had no intention of going, especially not to a small party where Jesse and Henri would be inescapable, where he'd kiss her on the forehead as he put drinks into her hands and wrap his jacket around her shoulders when the fog rolled in.

Henri thumbed through my English lit book. "Why are you studying?"

"Because that's what juniors do."

"Junior year is supposed to be one of the fun ones."

"It's actually supposed to be the worst." I took my textbook from her and slid it into my backpack. "Sorry I didn't spend my year taking floral design and nutrition."

Her face turned serious and she sat up, cross-legged on my comforter. "You'd better be careful. You're going to turn out as bitchy as me."

"I doubt it."

Henri huffed as she touched her feet down on the carpet. She took a few steps toward the door and turned back. "On second thought, don't bother coming to the party. I mean, who would you even talk to?"

"Huh?"

"Emma, you don't have any friends."

I swiveled my chair and stared at her. "I have friends."

"Who, Em?"

"Jesse. And Mick. And . . ." My voice shook. "And Ari."

A tiny smile crept up. "Those are my friends. Not yours." On her way out the door, Henri wrapped her fist around my soul, and my sister, she knew how to pound. "Night."

She slammed my door behind her.

A sound slipped from my mouth. My nose stung, eyes hot. I pressed the back of my hand to my lips.

Henri was right. But the worst part was knowing that if my sister truly loved me, she never would have said it.

I sank my teeth into my fist and tried to feel something else, anything but what I was feeling: *I hated my sister.*

The door cracked open.

"Emma, this thing with your dad—" Mom's glasses had worked their way down the bridge of her nose. She pushed them in place and focused on me. "Oh, honey, why are you crying? What happened?"

She shut the door behind her and crossed the room.

Henri had caught Jesse in her web and now she was ready to devour him. He didn't even know. Poor, sappy Jesse would have gladly fed her his heart. And Mr. Flynn—the whole thing was wrong. He was an adult. A teacher. It was wrong on so many levels.

She didn't deserve them both. She didn't deserve either of them.

"Mom," I said as she wiped my tears away with the sleeve of her sweater. "I have something to tell you."

"Okay." Mom crouched in front of me as I sat on my bed. She took my hands in hers. "I'm listening."

Words didn't come. I almost backed down, but not because I didn't want to expose Henri—because I didn't know how.

"Emma, sweetheart, you're scaring me. What's going on?"

I said the most honest thing I knew: "Someone's hurting Henri." I looked up at the ceiling to try to make my tears reabsorb. "A teacher at school. They've been seeing each other for months."

Mom covered her mouth with her hands. She exhaled and said, "And they're sleeping together?"

"Yeah."

"You're sure?"

"Yes."

All my agony flooded out of my eyes in an ugly gush. Mom squeezed me into a hug. "I'll fix this, Emma. Nobody's going to hurt your sister."

She had no idea the person hurting Henri most was me.

CHAPTER 25

We woke up the next dry day obsessed with the idea of sailing away, Alex and I. With our grasp on hope so tenuous, it was easy to let that raft become everything.

On the title page of his success manual, Alex used Henri's pen to draw a plan. The sketch started off simple, but a few pen strokes brought it to life.

I scanned the clusters of bamboo we'd collected. "Those guys who escaped Alcatraz, what was their raft made out of?"

"Raincoats," Alex said. "All we have is bamboo. But it's useful." He inspected the tarp and bamboo pieces we'd used to splint his fingers.

"Does it still hurt?"

He let it drop to his side. "Only if I think about it."

Henri sat in the wet sand at the bottom of the beach, letting the surf crash up and down her long legs. She hadn't offered to help, and she wouldn't.

It had to be hard to live with what she'd done, forced to spend all day, every day staring at Alex's mangled hand. Henri hadn't apologized for it. But when he'd tried to crack a coconut and couldn't hold it in place, she'd opened it herself.

That small act was the most sincere kind of apology my sister could give.

Alex lifted his shirt and wiped his sweaty forehead on the hem. "If you work on cordage, I'll work on tying the bamboo together."

"How will you tie them?"

He lifted his left hand. "This one still works. And I can use my teeth." He let out a breath as he stared at the pieces.

"What?" I asked.

"Other than wind power, currents, we won't have much control. We could . . . we could just drift. Like the first day. No land. Just blue." Watching me nod, he squeezed his eyes shut. "If you didn't want to take that risk, Emma, I'd drop this. Find, I don't know, another way."

Waiting for the island to crumble, waiting for storms to sweep us out to sea—there was no other way that ended with us alive. "I'm good with the risk."

I stripped vines, one after another, until my hands were cracked and bleeding and the sun was high in the sky. I wished I could forget we couldn't stay. Then the waterfall would be swirling around us as my mouth collided with Alex's, his arms pulling me closer, my fingers in his hair. We'd almost forget to hold ourselves above water.

Henri dumped a handful of seashells on the beach mid-morning as I cracked open a coconut. She loved searching the sand for any treasures the tide kicked up. She'd already made two necklaces long enough to wrap around her neck three times over, not including the one that broke. I was glad she had something to keep her out of our way.

Henri eyed me as I dug around her bag and came to the tampons. My period was the week before, but there were still so many left.

"Henri, you haven't had another period, have you?"

She fed a shell onto her thread. "Guess not."

"But you had one right after we got here, right? It's been two months. You—"

"What are you asking, Emma? Are you asking if it's Jesse's baby or Alex's?"

I froze. "Don't even joke like that."

"Do you trust Alex? Or the better question is, do you trust me? Are you doing the math, Em? Gavin's baby, Jesse's baby, Alex's?"

Not only was I sure Alex hadn't touched her, I was sure she couldn't be pregnant. This was another of her mind games. "Henri. Be serious. You really haven't had a period?"

"Don't be stupid. It's probably malnutrition or something." Her lips twitched with a smile. "Or is it?" Her voice stayed light, teasing. Vicious.

If she thought she could make me doubt Alex, she was overestimating herself.

Alex cupped his hands around his mouth. "Let's give it a whirl," he called. He stood far off in the surf, testing the buoyancy of pieces we'd constructed.

My sister's shadow moved along behind me as I walked to the edge of the water.

"Cozy," she said.

The whole mass of it was no bigger than one of Henri's closet doors. We'd fit, but barely.

"Well, it's not big enough yet, but it looks like it's gonna float." Alex sank his knees onto the platform. Water seeped between the bamboo, but it held his weight above the surface.

He tossed his clothes on the shore. "Guess I'm the guinea pig."

"You can't do that," I said. "Not with your hand."

"Oh come on, Jones. It's just floating. Besides, my hand doesn't hurt as bad in the water."

I stripped off my T-shirt and threw it onto the dry sand above the waterline. "I'll go too. We need to know how much weight it'll carry."

The raft wobbled beneath me as I struggled to find my balance. Henri looked surprised, then chewed her lip as our eyes met. She opened her mouth—I knew she didn't want me to go, to leave her stranded on the shore. Still, something, maybe her pride, made her hold it in.

As Alex and I paddled farther from the beach, the ocean grew colder against my palms and the water a darker blue. To keep my panic in check, I imagined I was floating in a concrete-bottomed pool.

"We got this." Alex breathed deeper, paddled harder. "It's working," he said, almost like he could hardly believe the boards beneath us would be our rescue. "It's working!"

We stopped a distance from the shore. Henri was a dot

on the beach, so small, I could almost see the jungle right through her.

The bamboo cracked.

"Shit." Alex grabbed for the end of an unraveling vine. In his panic, he tried with his bandaged hand and couldn't grip.

The raft came apart and we both plummeted into the dark ocean.

I went down, down, down, where the ocean water got colder and blacker, like the day when Casey's boat exploded and I pulled up Henri. My eyes stung as I opened them, searching the water.

My hand closed around Alex's shoulder. But the ocean knocked us apart.

I reached for him again, something, anything. Water slipped through my fingers. My lungs nearly bursting as the water lightened. Gasping, I broke the surface.

Waves crashed over me, dragging me back under. I popped up again and Alex was far ahead of me already, so much closer to the shore.

The distance between us was growing fast. He was leaving me behind. But he wouldn't. That's when I knew.

The tide—it had caught me and not him. And it was pulling me out to sea.

I fought hard to stay afloat. There was only so long I could swim before my muscles would give out. Alex made it to the shore and flipped around to the ocean. He yelled something I couldn't understand. Not with waves pounding my ears.

I remembered. My arms burned through the water as I

swam parallel to the shore. That was how to get out of a rip-tide.

A clear voice cut through. Another voice: "Harder, Emma!"

Henri.

I could hear her, but I couldn't see her. A wave rolled over me, knocking me under and stealing my breath. When I broke the surface, I scanned the shoreline.

Once. Twice. No Henri.

Then finally, there she was, struggling as Alex held her back. She lunged toward the water, but Alex's arms tensed across her body.

The ocean around me stilled. I moved free of the riptide, and swam until my feet touched bottom.

Henri broke free from him. I was close enough to see the tears streaming down her face. She socked him in the chest and stormed off into the jungle. Alex ran toward me.

Dark clouds moved across the spaces in the trees above. It had to be late afternoon. With my arms above my head, I stretched out on my back beside the fire, wearing my bikini and Alex's shirt while my shorts dried.

"We'll keep trying," he said. "If you want to."

I nodded.

"We'll make it stronger next time. Tie the pieces individually, so if we lose one, the whole thing won't separate. We can do this, Jones."

What happened out there, there was a fine line between being reckless and taking chances. After his hand, the rains, the rockslide, what we were doing felt more and more like a chance worth taking. "I know."

Alex balanced a fish wrapped in wet leaves over the bowl above the fire before he lowered down beside me. He brushed my hair back, pressed his lips to my neck, and I closed my eyes.

The trees rustled.

"Did you hear that?"

His breath tickled my neck as he smiled. "You don't have to create a distraction if you want me to stop."

"No, really, I thought that was Henri." She hadn't come back since the riptide.

"What if it *was* Henri?"

I didn't say anything.

"I'm not trying to be a jerk. I just want to know." He twirled a curl of my hair around his finger. "Are you afraid she's going to tell your parents or something, when you're back home?" Alex stared over my shoulder and focused on something in the distance. "Okay, I did hear that."

I glanced around the clearing. Silence. But a heartbeat later, there it was. A thrashing and crashing of something bursting through the vegetation.

Henri appeared at the place where the clearing met the trees. Something she was dragging made a long impression in the dirt that wound into the trees behind her.

The front piece of a canoe, with the back end busted off, bumped over bulging roots.

Alex jogged to her side and ran his good hand along the

smooth curve of the wood. "That's a pretty fabulous find. I wish we knew how to fix it."

"I'm not worried about fixing it. I found it down the beach and I think it'll make a perfect ceiling to my shelter."

"Your shelter?" I said.

Henri pressed on, hauling it over a thick root. "Yep. I'm moving out of the honeymoon suite. It's all yours, Em, and so is he."

With that, she dragged the canoe deeper into the jungle.

Raindrops splattered against our rooftop as Alex and I lay awake in our shelter.

In the larger clearing with the thinner trees, Henri had lifted her canoe above stacks of driftwood and called it a shelter. She went inside after sunset and hadn't come out.

The drizzle outside had turned into a full-fledged rain—I could tell because the plinking on our roof now made a hammering sound. We'd waterproofed our shelter with every stray tarp the ocean carried us. Henri's beat-up canoe couldn't have been waterproof.

Her games were only getting nastier. First Alex's hand and now sleeping under that canoe. Willingly making herself miserable—maybe that was her way of letting me know how far she'd let this go.

"Why don't you sleep up here with me?" Alex asked.

I glanced to the tent flap.

I knew Henri wasn't sleeping. At home, she always had the worst kind of insomnia. Long after the city went silent, she'd stay up playing music or organizing love letters from stupid boys. Crackling with electricity—that was Henri.

"I'm fine here."

He crawled down beside me. "Take the hammock."

"Alex."

"Fine. I'll sleep here." He curved himself to the shape of me and laid his bandaged hand at my waist. "If you want to talk, Jones . . ."

What I'd done to Henri, it wasn't enough to deserve these games, not after everything. Still, my guilt was constant. I thought about what Alex said after he'd told me everything. How it made him feel free.

Months ago I'd locked myself in a cage that I thought could only be opened with Henri's forgiveness. But she wasn't forgiving me. Maybe not ever.

"Okay," I said.

"What?"

My chest felt like it expanded to the point of almost exploding, and I rolled over to face him. "Henri was dating a boy we both knew—our next-door neighbor. His name was Jesse. One night at a party, I threw myself at him and—"

"Really?" He smiled down at me.

I gave him a look.

"I'm sorry. Proceed."

Everything that happened back home came rushing out. Jesse and Henri. Henri and Mr. Flynn. Henri's therapy our parents forced her to attend. When I finished, I expected Alex to look at me differently.

He sighed. "Jones, I'm sorry. That wasn't exactly what I expected. I'm not going to tell you it's not bad. But is this forgiveness she may or may not give you . . . is it worth letting yourself get trampled?"

Trampled. The word stung. "I know it's different, but what if you could . . . what if you thought you could get Casey back?"

"It's *very* different. If Casey came back, he wouldn't be trying to break my girl's hand. What you did was kind of terrible. But it's not unforgivable. The fact that *she* can't forgive you— that's got nothing to do with you. That's all on her." He stayed quiet for a long time, sighed. "It's almost too hard to imagine. Casey's gone, and I don't have hope. What happened to him, it's now beyond my control."

Hours later, I listened to the breeze swishing through the palms. Alex was asleep, the bridge of his nose tucked under my chin, his breathing steady.

Henri was beyond my control. Whatever my sister was going to do—forgive me, hate me, make herself sick, hurt me, hurt Alex—there was nothing I could do to change her. I did have hope. It was a luxury. It was more than Alex had. But my hope was worthless if I let it trample me.

CHAPTER 26

THREE WEEKS BEFORE

Mom hung up the phone and disappeared into her closet while I paced around her room. She came back buttoning her trench coat over her nightgown. "Stay in your room while I'm gone. If Henri notices I'm not here, tell her I forgot I left a file at the office."

"Will you tell me where you're really going?"

She sat on the bench at the end of her bed, slipping a pair of boots over thick socks with slip protectors on the bottom. "Your dad wants to meet right now."

Dad hadn't even met us at the ER last year when my mom was having horrible stomach pains and might have needed surgery. Henri and I sat in the hospital lobby holding hands as I wondered what we would do if something terrible happened to Mom while it was just the two of us alone at San Francisco General. I called him again and he said if anything happened to call him first thing in the morning.

Maybe Dad wanting to see Mom right then should have told me about the gravity of this secret.

Mom stood and she crushed me against her. "You must be so scared. You're afraid she's going to know you were the one who told, huh?"

That made my tears turn into sobs. Henri and I could never recover from this.

Mom, blurry through my tears, said, "How could I have found out? Tell me, Emma. How?"

Henri had been careful, and she said nobody but me knew about Mr. Flynn. But those pictures—she wouldn't have deleted them. "Her phone. She texted him some pictures."

My knees dug into my chin as I pressed my back against the wall Henri and I shared, listening to Henri screaming and crying, the thud of a shoe as she hurled it against her door, our dad ripping drawers from her dresser.

"We're not angry with you, Henri," Mom said. "You are the victim, sweetheart."

"Mom," Henri said. "You don't even get it. I was the one who went after him."

Dad spoke up next. "You don't need to lie for that pervert."

He didn't really know my sister.

The sound of my parents rifling through her things masked what Henri said next. I pressed my ear against the wall until it ached. All I caught was my dad saying, "Did he make you get these?" And I knew. Henri's birth control pills—they'd found them.

Her words were hurried. "I didn't get those because of him—"

My dad's voice roared through the walls. "Then who the fuck did you get them for?"

"Steven!" yelled my mom. "I took her to get them." The house went silent for a few seconds. Next came a muffled, "What?"

I didn't know—I thought Henri had got them at Planned Parenthood, just like everyone else we knew.

My dad left Henri's room, shouting threats behind him: *Your phone isn't your property anymore.* Harsher things: *You lock this door, you lose the privilege of having a door.*

I waited until Henri's sobs faded into soft hiccups before I tiptoed down the dark stairs. The only light in the house came from the kitchen.

"She's seventeen. What did you expect? In my opinion, those pills were the most responsible thing she was doing."

"You don't think maybe you were encouraging her?"

From the family room, I peeked around the corner. I held my breath, waiting for Mom to back down.

The women in our family had a way of ignoring right and wrong when the opposite sex got involved. I had never been like them, not until that night.

"As a matter of fact, I don't, Steven. Girls have desires too— she would have done what she wanted with or without. And don't be such a sexist jackass. I know for a fact you would have bought condoms for a son."

Never had I been so proud of my mom.

I heard my dad grunt and mumble something.

"We'll keep the girls home from school tomorrow," Mom said, her voice tired. "When they go back, they can pretend they were sick."

"I'll take off work and we'll go down to Baird first thing," my dad said.

"It could be worse," she said as she carried two cups of coffee to the center island, where my dad sat with his glasses in one hand, squeezing the bridge of his nose. "We could have found drugs."

My dad stared at the mug she set down in front of him—a white mug with a green airplane. It had been his favorite when he'd lived here. "I think I would have rather found a dime bag of Mary Jane."

Mom didn't laugh. "That shirt, it's just awful," she muttered.

He laughed. "This is my best one."

"Your girlfriend may be cute, but you really shouldn't let her do your shopping."

His voice quiet, he said, "I like them. I pick them out myself."

The house seemed to go silent.

It was a punch in the stomach, knowing he'd chosen them—and her. I'd blamed her for so much.

Mom took the barstool beside him and held her head in her hands. "Oh, Steven, how did we let this happen?"

"We can't focus on that. We need to find a way to help her now."

"Janine is taking her son, Bryce, to a great therapist. I'll call her for the name tomorrow and try to make Henri an appointment." Mom exhaled. "The question becomes what we do about the teacher."

"Ten to twenty doesn't sound too bad." My dad chuckled, a dark laugh with no humor.

"No. She said she was the one who pursued him."

"She's lying for the perverted bastard."

"I wish I could believe that," Mom breathed.

Here I'd thought I was the only one who really knew Henri—maybe our mom did too. If we were honest, maybe we both knew the truth about the games Henri played.

"Besides"—my dad snatched his glasses off the island—"he's her teacher. It was his responsibility to say no." *Responsibility.* He acted like he knew something about that. "He shouldn't get away with it, Dani. Screwing around with—"

Mom covered his hand with hers.

"She's just a girl." Dad's voice was raw.

"Legally, yes." Mom sighed. "We have to think about Henri here. We need to ask the school to handle things quietly and make this Mr. Flynn situation go away. Once he's gone, Henri can move on."

CHAPTER 27

Rain had come down that morning, and no matter how many dry logs Alex added to the flames and how much I stoked the coals, the fire beside our shelter sizzled and died.

On our knees on the hard-packed earth, shoulder to shoulder, we stacked kindling over dry bark.

Alex held his shirt tight and shivered. "What would you think about relighting the signal fire, Jones? Just once more. Giving them one more chance to find us."

I didn't know where this was coming from. I brushed my fingers against the inside of his wrist, waited for him to set down the branch, look up from the ground. He didn't.

"I thought you were worried about lighter fluid," I said.

"I shouldn't have let your sister get to me."

The lighter fluid was only necessary if we stayed. If something happened on the raft and we could get back to shore without drowning, we couldn't keep surviving without it. Using it or not using it, they were both gambles.

But the worry in Alex's voice, the way he rested his teeth against his fist, he was asking about the lighter as if there was a bigger question at play.

I sat back so I could really look at him. "You're worried the raft isn't going to work."

"All day, every day." He laughed, but the sound fell off in a sad way. "That it breaks up when we're right off the shore. Like it already did. Or worse: that it breaks up fifteen miles offshore and we drown."

I believed in the raft. Now that we'd done it once wrong, we could build it stronger, better. I believed in us.

"I really think it will work, Alex. But . . . but maybe it would be better if they found us before we ever had to find out for sure."

He nodded.

I went for the lighter, only I didn't remember where we'd left it. I turned my pocket inside out. But I hadn't had it—we always kept it by the fire.

I tore through wet layers of leaves, caking my nails with dirt. "The lighter, where is it?"

"Are you serious?" asked Alex.

Henri emerged from the bamboo with her sweatshirt zipped to her chin. She rubbed her hands up and down her arms and stepped into our clearing. "It's gone? But I'm building my own fire. I need it."

I eyed the wood bundled in her arms. "Aren't we the survivalist."

She gave me a fake smile. "We learn."

Alex hauled his backpack down from the trees and dumped the money on the ground. Most bills had come free from the wrappers. He plowed a hand through his hair. "It's not here."

I bent to help him, scooping up bills and stuffing them back into the backpack. "When was the last time we used it?"

The muscles in Alex's shoulders went rigid. And I knew. Every time the rain had broken since the rockslide, we'd been able to stoke the fire back to life. Until today.

I turned to the mountain of mud and rocks and sighed.

I heaved a rock into my arms, squeezing it against my stomach to absorb some of the weight as I added it to the ones we'd already stacked at the edge of the clearing. "Only about a hundred and fifty to go."

Alex palmed one, but it was too large to pick up one-handed. Holding his damaged hand at an awkward angle, he rolled his forearm under it and wrestled it to his chest.

"Stop." I tried to take the rock, but he struggled. "Alex, you're going to hurt me if you don't let go."

He released it into my arms. "I can't just do nothing."

"Then don't. Fish. Or get bamboo for the raft. Do something you can do, something that helps us."

Not moving, he stared at the pile of boulders. Shaking his head, he finally grabbed his spear and moved in the direction of the beach.

Playing with the fraying strings on her sweatshirt's hood, Henri kept her distance. "You really think the lighter's under there?"

"I don't know. But if you want to be warm, if you want to eat and drink, you better help me look."

❖❖❖

My arms hung like weighted ropes as I carried another rock to the edge of the clearing and fanned out my shirt. Sweat dripped down and stung the raw, chafed skin of my forearms.

Henri stripped off her sweatshirt and tied it around her waist. "My back is going to snap in two. Maybe it's not even here. Maybe we're killing ourselves for nothing."

"You need a break," Alex said. "Both of you."

He'd come back with three fish and had started cleaning them even though we wouldn't have a way to cook them without the lighter.

My wrists throbbed. I struggled to lift another. "We're almost to the bottom."

Henri cried out. I snapped around in time to see her drop a boulder to the ground.

"What happened?"

She sucked her thumb and inspected it. "It's cut."

My own arms were covered in cuts. "Get over it."

Dirt smeared across Henri's cheek as she wiped away sweat. "Get over it? *Get over it?*"

I didn't know how much I'd wanted this day until right then—when Henri would be the loser of her own game. I inhaled, the moment of silence between lightning and thunder, and then I exploded. "You wouldn't even be doing this if you hadn't hurt Alex! You'd be stringing together necklaces or working on your fucking tan or doing anything other than helping us survive. What I did to you back home was awful— I know. I get it. But this—I never thought you'd go this far. I can't understand *why* you would go this far."

Her eyes wide, she stared at me and said, "You should."

The weight of everything on the island crashed down on me. The mind games, the vicious words, Alex's broken hand. "That you would do *this*?"

"You slit my throat, Em. What did you expect me to do, apologize for bleeding on you?"

Alex and I exchanged a look. Henri and I were really—and finally—doing this. He held up his hands and headed toward the beach.

"I've said I'm sorry so many times, they don't even sound like real words to me anymore. I am—I'm so sorry. But whether you decide to accept that . . . I don't care."

Saying those words and meaning them—it was liberation, a rush of blood to my head.

She took a step back, blinked. Then folded her arms and smirked. "So you're done? When did you *decide* you were done with me, Em? Today? Last week? When you told Mom about Gavin?"

"I'm not—I'm not *done with you*. But even though I love you, I can't—I won't live my life waiting for you to come back."

"You love me? Then how did you do what you did? With Gavin? With Jesse? You broke me, Emma. Everyone knew. All of our friends already knew what had happened with Jake Holt and those guys, and the embarrassment of that was the worst thing I'd ever imagined. Until that day at school. Until now."

I swallowed down the catch in my throat. I'd never tried to

explain. "The thing is, I lied to you—I did like Jesse. Back when he liked you, and you ignored him—"

"And you thought he could be with you? How practical of you. Reallocating the male attention among us Jones girls."

It still stung. Henri speaking to me like I was her enemy, and not a sister who used to be her best friend.

"No . . . yes. I thought I liked him, but I didn't. You couldn't really love him, and—"

"That's not true. I—" Henri's clear blue eyes pooled, her lips pulled back, trying to form words. "I did love him."

She'd never loved anyone but me. She told me that day in her bedroom and a hundred other times. Those words were the world. "You loved him? Jesse?"

"I know," she said. "I didn't expect it either. I was too embarrassed to tell you. But when I was with Jesse, sometimes other things didn't matter. That I'd lost Gavin. That Dad left. I never thought I could go for a guy like Jesse—I thought he would bore me. He didn't."

In an instant, she dragged me back to that B Wing hallway when I'd watched Jesse break up with her in front of everyone we knew. Whatever she felt for Jesse, it was something different. Maybe it really was love.

"Henri, I didn't know. I thought you were hung up on Mr. Flynn. I'd just seen you that day with him, outside the music room—"

"You saw that?" she said. "Gavin was apologizing for the way we'd left things. Not for one second would I have done that to Jesse."

People always said in moments like these, they wanted to be small. I actually felt my weight sinking into the mud.

"Em, I asked you if you liked Jesse and you said you didn't." She sighed. "Of all people, *I* should have picked up on it anyway."

Henri had done a million awful things, but that wasn't one of them.

"No." I tried to take her hand, but she stepped out of reach.

"You don't even care anymore, so I'm probably just wasting my breath . . ." She rolled her eyes, as if me not caring didn't even matter, but it only spilled her tears. "For everything back home, I'm sorry. And for what you did, I forgive you."

We worked quietly deep into the day. Boulders and boulders stacked high around the edge of the clearing, a fortress of rocks as if our shelter were a castle. There was peace in knowing that maybe, just maybe, we'd found our way back to each other. Still, I was terrified I was wrong.

At the hottest part of the day, with most of the rubble cleared away, there it was, silver flame guard twinkling in the sun. I found the lighter.

The muscles in my arms shook as I held it out to Henri.

She was coated in mud from the bottoms of her canvas slip-ons to the crown of her head.

"No fucking way." Henri threw her arms around my neck. Pulling back, she caught my hands. "We are disgusting," she said, lacing her fingers with mine. "Come on."

She tugged me out of the clearing, running past the line

of trees and through the winding path our travel had made through the jungle. We ran to the beach, so fast, I ran out of my shoes. The heels of my feet burned the second they hit the hot sand. Alex was a blur on the beach as Henri picked up speed.

She wasn't slowing as we neared the ocean, and the feel of her hand in mine was too good to break.

"Aren't we going to take off our clothes?"

"Nope." Henri sucked in a chest full of air and, clothes and all, crashed us into the waves. Some of my breath came loose and bubbles drifted above my head.

Mud swirled around me as I came up to the sound of my sister laughing through the saltwater sting of our cuts.

She held our hands above water, still linked together. There was a sadness in her smile, maybe for the months we'd lost, maybe something else. I couldn't think about it then. Having Henri back wasn't everything I thought it would be. It was more. Because I'd found a way out that didn't involve winning or losing—I'd stopped playing the game at all.

CHAPTER 28

On our first day back at Baird, I stopped by my locker after first period to switch out my books. Up the staircase, no light shone through the window of the music room, keeping the landing dark.

At first, I was too busy looking up the stairs to notice what was happening around me. Or maybe I had too much faith in my parents, that they could keep this contained and get rid of Mr. Flynn in a way that wouldn't break open Henri's world.

People stood alongside their lockers, mouths open, eyes bright with concern or confusion, or glee. Sareena faced her locker, like she didn't want to watch whatever was happening, but occasionally she'd glance into the hall. Ari clutched her books against her chest and kept her gaze on me as she giggled something into Jake Holt's ear. I put my back to my locker and followed everyone's stares.

Jesse and Henri were down the hall. Something about them had caught everyone's attention.

Now he slammed his locker shut and turned to her, saying words I couldn't make out. Henri closed the gap between them and whispered close to him, her mouth pointed down to his chest. She reached up and caught his face between her hands, her finger stroking a circle under his ear. He grabbed her wrists and straightened his arms, forcing her to take a step back. His words were loud now. "You can destroy yourself, but you're not taking me with you. I can't do it anymore."

Her mouth formed his name. She reached out. For a second her face was different, raw, and her next words were clear. "You have to try to understand."

"Understand?" he shouted. "*Understand?* You were fucking a teacher!"

He hurled his binder at the bank of lockers. It exploded on impact and sent a shower of rule-lined papers into the air. He left her standing alone in the hall with paper slowly falling down around her.

They were over. But I wasn't filled with relief. Only an ache I felt all the way to my bones.

A dark look came over Henri. She saw me standing there and was beside me in an instant, sinking her grip into the soft part of my upper arm. I stumbled as she dragged me into an empty classroom.

The door shut behind us and I felt along the wall for the lights, not finding them. "Henri—"

She pulled back and slapped me across the face.

My fingers went to my cheek.

Getting slapped always seemed glamorous in the movies. What they didn't show was how your teeth throbbed and your cheek felt like someone had set it on fire. And nobody talked about the shame of it, of being hit by someone you love more than anyone on this earth.

The worst part was knowing I deserved it.

"Did you think I wouldn't find out?"

Desperate, I said the thing people always say when they're caught. "What are you talking about?" Henri was a shadow in the darkness. I couldn't see her face.

"Oh, come on! Mom and Dad went to Ari's mom with this. Of course she couldn't keep her mouth shut. Ari knows everything and now so does everyone at Baird. Including Jesse."

Tears sprang to my eyes. "I'm—"

"Don't you dare say one fucking word, Emma. You didn't just blow up my whole life, but you ruined Gavin's too. The school called the police."

"What?"

None of this was what I wanted.

My sister didn't deserve it.

Neither did Mr. Flynn.

"Oh, *I'm* going to lie like hell, but if the investigators don't believe me, he's going to spend his life registering as a sex offender."

My tears leaked out. I didn't bother wiping them away. "It was one mistake. One mistake and—"

Henri laughed. "One mistake. Do you know what Jesse told me? He said you and I are both toxic—he said you threw yourself at him at our party."

I couldn't speak. I could barely breathe.

"Henri, please. I did the worst thing imaginable to you, and I'm so sorry. If there was a word bigger than *sorry,* I'd say it."

Her silence slowly ate away at my heart as we stood there in the dark.

She licked her lips and hoisted her book bag onto her shoulder. She felt around inside it until she hooked her sunglasses and, turning toward the bright window of the door, pushed them onto her mascara-streaked face before pushing past me.

In the doorway, I caught her wrist. "Where are you going?"

Henri snatched her hand away. "Home." Keeping her eyes on the door, she said in a low voice, "Out of everyone I've ever known, you were the only person I thought I'd have forever."

"You still have me."

She took off her sunglasses, and I thought I might have a chance at making things right.

But my sister ran her eyes down my whole body and shook her head. "Why didn't I see you for what you were?"

The door slammed and I stood in darkness.

CHAPTER 29

B y the light of the blazing signal fire, the three of us feasted on Alex's fish. My hands were cut, my limbs sore and bruised from digging through the boulders, but I was also clean and full and warm.

Henri craned her neck as Alex moved down the beach to get rid of the fish skins. After he disappeared, she turned to me, eyebrows raised. "So, Alex, huh? Talk to me."

"What do you want to know?"

"Everything, obviously," she said. "You could do better. But he does have good teeth and hey"—she nodded to the back-pack hanging from the trees—"he's even got money."

"That's not funny."

"But you know it is." Her smile faded. "Is it real?"

"The money?" I joked.

She elbowed me in the ribs. "Yes or no?"

I didn't know if she meant *real-real* or more real than my feelings for Jesse. Not that my answer would have been different. "Yes."

"I'm happy for you, Em."

Something about it struck me as sad, that she still wanted happiness for me after I'd ruined her relationship with the only boy she'd ever loved. "When we get home, are you going to try to fix things with Jesse?"

She took a deep breath, cradling her bruised arms in her lap. "I'd rather not think about home until I see it." She slipped on her sweatshirt and walked toward the edge of the bamboo.

"Where are you going?"

"I think I should stay in my own shelter."

"Henri, why?"

She turned back.

The firelight filtering through the palm fronds highlighted her hands as she removed her shell necklace—the one with the rarest blue shells on our island—and draped it around my neck.

She kissed me on the cheek. "Good night, Em."

Raindrops splattered against our rooftop as Alex and I lay awake in our darkened shelter. The wind whistling through caught the straps of the backpack hanging from the ceiling.

Alex leaned over the edge of the hammock with his chin in his hand. "You two are really okay now?"

"Yes. I mean, I think so. It feels like before."

"But she's sleeping under the canoe? In the rain."

I didn't say anything. I'd lived to have her back, the Henri from before. A Henri who would drag me into the ocean, clothes and all, joke about boys, drape handmade jewelry around my neck. Something was off still—maybe just from the strain of being lost—but she was her again.

Alex yawned into his hands. "Hey, Jones?" He draped his arm down over the side and brushed his fingertips over my right ankle. "You might as well sleep up here with me. It's a lot more comfortable in the hammock."

"If Henri came in, she would feel totally alienated if I was up there with you."

"Wow." He grinned down at me. "I thought all the weirdness you and your sister had, I thought it was because of this fight." He tilted his head. "But that's over. This attachment you two have, it's intense."

If someone had said that to me months before, I might have taken it as a compliment, proof that my sister and I were obviously close. Now it was kind of unsettling.

He kissed the back of my hand. "Good night, Jones."

The hammock's supports creaked until Alex nodded off.

Half of Emma and Henri—it's what I'd always been. After months apart, she was finally the same as before. Was I, though?

The hammock jarred as I rested my hips into it and pulled my legs up beside Alex.

He righted himself in the dark, breathing hard. "What are you doing? Are you okay?"

I dropped my shoulders down to the hammock, careful to avoid his broken hand, and stretched out on my back. "I just don't feel like sleeping alone."

"You're feeling okay, aren't you?" He pressed his hand to my forehead, then each of my cheeks. "You're not getting what I had?"

"No, I'm fine. I just changed my mind. I want to be up here with you."

He pushed off the branch behind us and sent the hammock swaying. Into my hair, he whispered, "Good. I like you here."

He smiled down at me, and I took his face in my hands. I traced each eyebrow, the bridge of his nose—following that small bump, the freckles I knew well enough to name.

My fingers reached his lips and he took my wrist, kissed each fingertip.

I'd been so afraid that giving into my feelings for Alex would destroy me, the way boys led to tragedy for Henri, the way Dad led to tragedy for Mom. But Alex—after everything that happened on our island—I knew him. He wasn't the kind of boy who would break me. And after all Henri had put me through, I knew me, and I wasn't a girl who could be broken.

My dolphin T-shirt and bikini top were still soaked from the ocean, so I hadn't bothered to put them back on under my jacket. I bit my lip to stifle my smile as I held eye contact, took a deep breath, and very slowly lowered the zipper.

Alex looked at me, my face and all of me, and ran the back of his hand from my throat to my navel.

"Alex, you still have that condom, right?"

"What?" He moved back and almost fell out of the hammock.

I caught his shoulders and laughed as I pulled him close. He kissed me, then broke a few inches away. "We really don't have to."

"No, but I want to. With you." I shivered, feeling his fingers move against my skin. "Do you?"

"You have no idea."

Alex's lips brushed the tip of my nose, then each cheek. His mouth found the hollow of my throat, and as he reached my belly, a warm tingling spread all the way to my fingertips and toes and settled deep in the very center of me. My toes curled. I shuddered.

The fibers of the hammock were rough against my back as I tossed my jacket to the floor, but I barely felt them. The only sensations now were the warmth of Alex's mouth, the skimming of his hair as he trailed kisses across my stomach, my skin humming.

He paused to reach across me to the backpack hanging from the ceiling.

I unbuttoned my shorts, and as Alex slipped down beside me holding the condom, I lifted up while he slid them down my legs. Then I unbuttoned his and did the same, feeling his skin against mine.

His palm glided down my ribs and his finger curled under the hip of my bikini bottoms. His cheek brushed against mine—he was trembling.

"Alex?"

That little edge of hesitation in my voice made him freeze. "You want to stop?"

"No. Do you? You seem nervous."

"It's just a lot of pressure, Jones. One chance to do this

right." He held up the single condom and hovered over me. "Ask me what I want."

"What do you want?"

"My bed. Near Luquillo Beach. And you in it. It's nothing fancy—no nice sheets, not even a headboard—but there's a white mosquito net that hangs from the ceiling and drapes around it. When I open the windows, the ocean air comes through. I wish we could be there. Right now. I could make this really good for you."

I hooked my hands together behind his neck and pulled him down to me. "It's already good for me."

Our clothing came off a piece at a time until it all mingled together on the shelter floor. He took his time and let me take mine.

I lost things that night, fear and doubt and the worst parts of myself—they vanished in ragged breaths and hungry kisses and skin that slid together like it was never supposed to be apart.

CHAPTER 30

The night before we left for Puerto Rico, I sat on my bed, beside my suitcase overflowing with bright swimsuits, comfortable jeans shorts, and rubber flip-flops, and I cried. I cried for what Henri and I had, for what I'd ruined, and for what I knew I'd never have back.

Someone knocked at my door. I wanted it to be Henri so badly, my throat closed up.

I pushed up on my elbows and wiped my cheeks. "Come in."

"It's me." My mom stood in the doorway with a set of luggage tags in her hand. She wore a pair of yoga pants and an oversized cardigan that almost reached her knees. I hadn't seen her wear anything but business clothes or a nightgown since the day my father walked out the front door. "Are you all packed?"

"I think so. I have to put my blow dryer in after I use it in the morning."

"They'll probably have one at the hotel. It's a five-star resort."

Our parents hatched a plan one night after they'd argued until their throats were sore.

Henri blamed me for their relationship reaching an all-time most volatile. They couldn't agree on anything at all, except this one thing: They thought time out of the city, away from Baird, outside the halls Mr. Flynn had walked, would do Henri some good.

We'd travel with Mom on her trip to Puerto Rico. Five days of sun and sand on Luquillo Beach. They thought it was the perfect opportunity for Henri and me to make our peace.

Mom sat on my bed beside my luggage. "About your birthday, I'm so sorry, Em, that it wasn't anything special. We'll do something fun in Puerto Rico."

My sixteenth birthday. Henri'd lived for hers since she was thirteen. My parents filled our house with everyone who was anyone on the big day. Mom and Dad ordered a pizza and a bakery cake for mine and sent me to the family room to eat while they whispered in the kitchen about splitting the cost of Henri's therapy.

Dad gave Henri a pair of sapphire earrings for hers. Me, I got a check.

I didn't care. I didn't deserve the pizza, the cake, or the check. All I'd wished for when I blew out my candles was Henri's forgiveness.

Mom forced a smile as she refolded a pair of shorts. "Are you at all excited?"

"Sure."

"What about Henri?"

The wall separating our rooms was vibrating with Henri's angriest music.

"We haven't been talking much."

She'd only spoken to me once about the trip since our parents told us we were going. She came in my room after her first therapy session and made fun of the clothes I'd set out. Every little flaw in me was game for ridicule.

If I thought Henri's silence was bad, her pure, unadulterated hatred was the worst thing imaginable.

"You'll get past this," Mom said. "Maybe it's better, even. If she didn't know, everything would be fine between the two of you, but would that have been real?"

Mom didn't know she was wrong. That if everything really had been fine between us, I wouldn't have had a reason to ruin Henri's life in the first place.

She crossed the room and wrapped her arms under mine. She gave me one tight squeeze before pulling back. "Emma, no matter what, know you did the right thing."

The adult world drew lines in the sand. Perpetrator and victim. Teacher and student. Wrong and right. Those lines had blurred for me. I was no longer sure I agreed. About one thing I was certain: What I'd done to Henri and Mr. Flynn had been horribly wrong.

Mom clutched the doorframe on her way into the hall. "Listen. You were best friends—that can't be lost forever. I know it's horrible now. She'll forgive you, Em. But Henri, she won't make it easy."

As I lay in bed in the dark, I decided I'd reach Henri in any way I could. This trip would fix everything. I made that promise to myself.

CHAPTER 31

Alex and I bound pieces of bamboo together with cordage we made from the strongest plants we could find—palm fronds with long fibrous leaves I could strip and weave into ropes. Knowing what we were doing, we put our second raft together so much faster than the first.

Henri brought three coconuts down to the water and called up to us, "Are you hungry?"

With the ocean lapping against her feet, she tugged her sweatshirt tight and stared at the pieces of the raft fitted together. She hadn't offered to help. All morning, she'd kept to herself, her intensity replaced with something else, a listlessness.

I didn't get it.

"Just a minute!" I tied together two bamboo stalks and said to Alex, "How's this?"

He came behind me and reached around. "Looks good." As he gave the cordage one last tug and cut off the loose ends, his lips brushed the side of my neck. It was all I could do not to pull him down in the sand right there. "You okay today?"

I didn't know if he meant physically or emotionally.

As if he read my mind, he whispered, "I meant, do you regret it?"

I turned around and kissed him, breathing in his sun and sand and salt smell. "Not at all."

I didn't. Touching Alex, letting him touch me didn't mean letting him save me. They were two different things.

Alex slept on his stomach with his face against his backpack beside the fire. I put on more water to boil, took a seat on the driftwood, and tilted my chin to the sky. The full moon glowed through a space in the tree canopy above the clearing, yellow in the spinning sea of white stars. If our raft worked, this full moon would be the last I'd see on our island.

The driftwood beneath me jarred as Henri sat and rested her head on my shoulder. "I've decided I'm not going."

"Where? What do you mean?"

"On the raft."

"What? No. Come on, Henri. I know it's scary. But we're using stronger vines. I'm the one tying them, double tying them. With his hand, Alex couldn't really tighten. I'm on it."

"Double tying them?" She smiled down at her naked nails. All the polish had grown out. "With an airtight plan like that, of course I'm ready to head into the middle of the ocean."

"If we stay put, Henri, we don't have a chance. Out there, we've got something."

"Don't you remember what it was like that first day, Em? Bobbing in the ocean, hoping to see land or something solid.

Anything solid. You want to give this up? You want to die clinging to Alex's bamboo raft?"

"There are ships out there. We see them every other day. Out there, we have a chance. Here we have—"

"Land." She picked up a handful of loose dirt, let it flow through her fingers. "This stuff is pretty fantastic when you think about it."

"What about the storms?"

She scooted down the driftwood. "I'm not afraid of a little rain."

I reached for her shoulder and she dodged my grip. "I'm sorry, Em. Nothing you can say could convince me."

We'd never be old ladies together—that was my first thought as she walked away. I thought I'd already let that dream go, outgrown it. It was different when the dream let *you* go. Henri had never been clairvoyant. She'd never see the age of eighty. She'd never even see the age of eighteen. Dreaming about a future with a house by the sea couldn't make it true.

"Emma! Alex!"

I woke up that morning to Henri's voice. Shoving past Alex, I scrambled out the door first.

Flames shot up the side of the shelter. I yanked the tarp off the doorway and Alex helped me spread it across the fire to smother out the flames.

"What happened?" he said.

Henri shrugged. "I guess the wind caught the fire."

I surveyed the damage. The side of our shelter was blackened but still standing—we could replace those palm fronds before nightfall.

The tarp, on the other hand, had melted in places, which meant our shelter would never be the same. Alex pulled it off the flames before it completely melted. The taste of burning plastic in the air and the smoke in my lungs made me cough into the neck of my shirt.

"You fucking did this on purpose," he said.

At the center of the smoking pile was Alex's half-charred success manual.

"What are you talking about?" Henri said. "I was trying to put out the fire. I threw on everything I could find. Why'd you leave it out here anyway?"

"That's such bullshit. You threw it on to *stop* the fire? You burned this because it was mine."

But I knew better. Henri didn't do it to hurt Alex—not after everything—our peace, her guilt over Alex's hand. I didn't think so, at least.

"Alex," I said quietly. "The plans for the raft were in there."

"Whatever," he said, glaring at Henri. "We don't need them anyway. We're far enough along."

The look of defeat that came over Henri's face told me everything I needed to know.

My sister recovered quickly, stretching her arms over her head and yawning. "It's really smoky. I'm going to take a walk."

As Alex and I began clearing the debris and patching our shelter wall with fresh palm fronds, I wondered what else Henri had done. She wasn't just planning to stay on the island; she was actually sabotaging our plans to get home.

"Henri says she's not going," I blurted. "That she's staying on this island."

"What? I thought you guys were fine."

"That makes two of us."

Alex slipped down to the driftwood and kneaded his neck. "Why in hell would she want to stay? She can't mean it." I was silent. He looked up when I didn't reply, his eyes grim. "You know it doesn't have anything to do with that sprawling ocean out there. It's all about this game with you."

Every bit of my being wanted to believe Alex was wrong, that we were past that, that deep down inside Henri, in the tucked-away corners where her love for me still hid, all of this wasn't a game.

I sat beside him, pressed my lips against the warm skin of his shoulder as he tried to clench his fist and uncurl his fingers. He was losing range of motion—he needed a doctor.

Alex didn't say a word for a long time and then squeezed me close. I relaxed into him, feeling his heartbeat against my chest, feeling his breath on my hair.

"What if we'd met in a normal way?" I said as he moved away from me to stoke the fire. "Do you think this would have happened? Us?"

"Obviously. But not the same way. I would've taken you to the movies, opened doors, dropped you off before curfew."

"So gentlemanly."

"Not always. I've done the sneaking-into-a-girl's-window thing."

"Really? That happened, like, a lot?" I tried to make my voice light.

He smiled down to the fire, swept his hair back as he met my eyes. "Not a lot. It wasn't like this—I didn't love them." Alex went back to stoking the coals, casually, as if he'd just told me he thought it was going to be sunny out today. "We'll eat soon." He put the metal pot over the flames, allowing enough air for oxygen. "I'm starving."

Henri craved those words from boys, treated their *I-love-yous* like prizes from carnivals, beautiful orange goldfish she'd let suffocate in plastic bags.

He loved me. I felt it back. But it was something more than just me. Bigger than that. Like we were greater than the sum of our parts. Is that what he felt too?

Alex tossed the lighter into the air and caught it in his shirt pocket.

Something about the trick made me sit up. "Where did you learn that?"

"Um, Casey."

On the boat before the crash—Casey had lit a cigarette for Henri and did that same trick. But Henri grabbed him by his shirt collar and pulled out the lighter.

I think I'll keep it, she'd said.

So much happened that day, I didn't remember it until right then.

Casey never had the lighter in his backpack. Henri did.

Henri from before she started hating me.

The way our hands would brush inside a bag of buttery popcorn.

My sister painting delicate flowers onto my fingernails.

Us dancing on her bed with the Christmas lights in her room twinkling along the walls.

My dreams of our house by the sea.

Maybe she'd always been this horrible, and I couldn't see it. Or maybe I'd created a monster. Or maybe she'd simply become one.

In the clearing where Henri built her shelter, she stood in a little alcove made by the trees outside her canoe. She'd strung ropes of shells the same way she draped her walls back home in Christmas tree lights. Her clothes were hung from the tree as if they were behind her mirrored closet doors. She ran her hands over the fabric. It wasn't much to hold on to, whatever she was trying to re-create, but it was something.

She turned, revealing her faint smile. It faded as soon as she saw my expression. "Em, what's up?"

"Why are you doing this? Why are you trying to ruin our chances of getting home?"

She scowled. "What makes you think going home is such a great idea?"

I tried to keep my voice level. "By stopping us from getting home, Henri, you could literally kill us. One of us is already dead."

"And you don't think we'll die for sure on that piece-of-shit raft?"

"I know we'll die *here*. What do we do when the lighter runs out? What do we do when hurricane season hits? At least we have a chance on the raft."

Henri began stringing shells. "I know what you did," I said.

She shrugged. "So I threw his book on the fire. What good was it to him here?"

"I know what you did with the lighter, Henri."

My sister smiled at me. She brought her hands together in a slow clap. "Good for you, Em. You finally figured it out."

"I haven't, though, Henri. I really haven't. Why? Why would you hide the lighter?"

She looked back at me—a cool appraisal. "That first day— you were going to use it to build a signal fire. I told you I didn't want to go home. Not yet."

All the rage I'd managed to hold back, I let it knife through me. It tore into my veins, my arteries, my helplessness, my frustration, but I didn't bleed out. I just screamed. I worked my hands into my hair and screamed and screamed and screamed. "What could possibly be worse than this island?" I shouted. *"What are you so afraid of facing?"*

Henri looked at me steadily. "You really don't know?" She dropped her head back, eyes on the fading sky. "The math? The tampons?"

A coldness settled over me, all my hairs rising. "Henri, you are not pregnant."

My sister looked at me with eyes full of tears.

CHAPTER 32

"You were on the Pill, though," I said as I paced around the outside of Henri's shelter. "I saw them in your drawer. I heard Mom and Dad talking about them."

"You have to take them right." Not making eye contact, she fidgeted with her shell necklace. "I think I missed one. Maybe two."

I cringed. "With Mr. Flynn?"

"No, Em. Jesse." She squeezed her eyes shut. "But that's what everyone would think, right?"

Jesse, who I thought I'd loved before I understood anything. But it wasn't that—it was thinking of Jesse as a father. Jesse, who couldn't eat anything without dropping it across his shirt. He was a boy. And Henri was just seventeen.

I stared at my sister's stomach. It was still lingerie-model flat. "How many periods have you missed?"

"Three. I think it's three. I missed one right after we got here—I thought it was just stress or something. But I remembered. What I did back home, the month before we left. I threw out my placebos to skip my period—my Winter Ball dress was white, for fuck's sake. And I realized. Oh my god, Em, I realized I probably wouldn't have gotten one at all. I was already pregnant by then. Then I missed the next one too, and my last one. Three periods, I'm sure, Em."

"Henri." I squeezed her shoulders and made her look at me. "If you are actually pregnant, this island is the worst place you can be. You need to see a doctor. You—"

She knocked my arms away. "I'm not going. There's nothing you can say to convince me. Stop trying."

We finished the raft after dinner. Before the sun set over the water, Alex pushed off and the two of us sailed far into the sea. The bamboo was solid and sturdy beneath me—it worked. We reached the breakers and turned the raft toward the island. I scanned the shoreline, hoping maybe Henri had a change of heart and was taking some interest in all this.

The beach was empty.

As we walked back into the jungle toward the shelter, my fingers intertwined with Alex's. I couldn't stop thinking about Henri being pregnant and not wanting to leave the island. There always seemed to be a method to Henri's madness, but there was no logic to this.

With my back to Alex, I watched our fire long after the sky turned dark. My coconut was full of my uneaten dinner. Even though only a light breeze wafted over our island, I slipped my arms inside my jacket.

Alex pressed close to my back and rested his chin on my shoulder. "I thought it would feel better, being done. Jones, aren't you excited to get off this island?"

"No, I am. Just give me a day or two. To convince Henri."

"Okay." He kissed my neck in a way that made me shiver. I turned, sliding my arms over his shoulders. "A few days is good," he said, looking down between us, at my halfway unzipped jacket, the gap where the center of my bikini top didn't quite meet my skin. "We'll need to gather supplies—as much water and food as we can carry." He slowly dragged my zipper open, the warmth of his palms slipping around my waist and pressing against the dip of my back. "Are you ready to go inside?"

"Are you tired?"

He grinned. "Not even a little."

My teeth tugged against his bottom lip. Until I remembered. "You know we can't."

He pushed his forehead against mine, smiling. "There are other things."

I wanted right then for us to lose ourselves in discovering more of each other—the sweet distances between the places that felt good, better, best. But I couldn't put off talking to Henri.

I kissed his jaw, his freckles, the small bump on his nose. "I'll come in soon."

The tarp flap closed behind Alex, and I tiptoed through the trees to Henri's shelter. She sat beside her own small fire, wearing only her bikini and the necklace made out of little blue shells. Sixty-five blue shells, if I remembered right. Henri would know exactly how many—she always did.

"What are you doing with this? You know our shelter is more comfortable."

Her hair was knotted high on her head, and she folded her sweatshirt as if she had a drawer to tuck it inside. "Maybe I just want to know what it's going to feel like. Being here. Alone."

I sat cross-legged in front of her and sighed.

"What?"

"The raft is done, Henri. Alex and I are leaving in a few days. You're coming with me. You have to."

"Wanna bet?"

"This makes zero sense. *Zero*. How would you even deliver a baby on your own? You could have complications. You could die."

"I'm—I'm not ready for home."

"But you're ready for the alternative? You have choices at home. Lots of them. And anything you choose, anything under the sun, I'll support you."

She made a sound between a huff and a laugh. "How charitable of you, Em."

To make myself small, I wrapped my arms around my knees. "Are we not okay?"

She lifted her still perfectly shaped eyebrows. I didn't have a mirror, but I knew mine had probably grown together. "We are. Really. It's just . . . I told you I wasn't going and you didn't . . ."

"I didn't what?"

"Say you'd stay with me." Henri rubbed a fingertip across her bottom lip and took my hand. "Promise me, Em. Promise you'll stay with me."

Everything I thought I wanted before we left for Puerto Rico, she was giving to me—a home with my sister by the sea. Staying meant dying, though, and I didn't know how to promise her I'd die with her. It was the one thing I couldn't do. I'd wanted her back more than anything. And now that I had her, I was losing her again. I couldn't live for my sister. I almost couldn't believe she wanted me to.

Her face fell. She understood my silence.

Henri used the heel of her hand to wipe tears from her cheeks before she closed herself inside her shelter.

A life for myself had to be built. But doing that meant leaving Henri.

I didn't know how to stay with her, and I didn't know how to leave her behind.

Alex watched me as I crawled into our shelter and never climbed up beside him. "Are you going to tell me what's up?"

I wouldn't tell him Henri was pregnant—that was her secret to tell, if she ever wanted to. "Henri wants me to stay."

He draped a long arm over the edge of the hammock and gave me a hand I wouldn't take. "Jones, if I make it to one of those ships, I don't know if I'll be able to lead them back to you. It's disorienting out there on the water."

"They'll get a search-and-rescue team going, though. They won't stop searching until they find us."

He turned away and coughed into his sleeve. "But we don't know how long that'll take. Or if you two can survive until they do, especially once storm season hits."

"The storms might not be here for weeks." I stood and swung my legs up into the hammock and stroked his stomach. He was warm and safe and we never hurt each other, only helped.

"It could be days. We just don't know."

Getting off the island meant leaving Henri all alone. If we couldn't get back to her, or we came back to the island and she hadn't survived, my world might as well quit turning. But no longer could I live for Henri. I had to live for me.

CHAPTER 33

Sparks rained down like fireworks. They stung my arms, my legs, my cheeks. I blinked myself awake to the orange-soaked walls.

Our shelter was on fire.

I gasped. Shot up. My hands were burning.

I wiped my palms on my shorts. The melting fibers of the hammock clung hot and sticky. My skin wouldn't stop stinging. The hammock creaked and collapsed. Flaming walls spun, spun, spun as we went down. We struck the ground, and Alex jolted awake.

I inhaled scorched bamboo and bubbling plastic, my own singed hair. Smoke filled my mouth and nose. The stabbing pain in my throat throbbed in my ears and teeth.

Alex's skin glowed red through his thin white shirt. We had to get out.

Blackness climbed up the frond-covered walls. I glanced to the door. It was still clear.

Before we could make it, a ribbon of fire caught on the shifting breeze. It dragged across the palm-frond floor, to the foot of our piles of firewood and kindling. So dry, so flammable, they didn't just ignite, they exploded.

The air inside the shelter crackled, and the force blew me back. Liquid heat sizzled over my skin.

Waving away the thick black smoke, I staggered. I slipped. Got my balance. Rushed through the heat. Which way—the heavy gray smoke was too thick to show.

"This way, this way!" I heard Alex shout.

Our hands, they found arms and backs and pulses that raced against our fingertips. Alex stumbled.

I squeezed him close. "I've got you."

White-hot heat shot up my bare legs. Alex and I carried each other through the sagging shelter door and into the clean air outside.

We dropped. Alex lay flat on his back, with his chest constricting and expanding. Too fast. Too hard.

Wooziness overtook me. My eyelids grew heavy, heavier. The air in my chest thick, thicker. Everything went weightless.

The world came back a second later, brighter, more vibrant.

Henri, she stood over me, shaking my shoulders, pushing water to my lips. "What happened? Are you okay? Em, open your eyes."

I choked on a gulp, which only made me cough. Breathing was a knife in my back.

"Em, your lips, they're literally blue."

I lifted up on my elbows. A wave of heat stung my cheeks as the shelter's dry palm fronds and soft grasses erupted in flames. Sweat beaded on my skin.

Alex glanced to us, then back to the blaze. "I'm going back in."

Henri whipped to face him. "Do you have a death wish?"

My heart rate climbed. I coughed and coughed. My voice refused to come. My fingers stretched toward him. He pushed himself up from the dirt and out of my grasp.

"I'm going." Without hesitation, he stepped through the fiery debris.

Why, why, why? I coughed again. Couldn't stop. But Henri, she knew. "The backpack," she whispered. "The money."

Maybe I was destined to only love people who wanted to destroy themselves.

I rolled to my side, knees to my chest. My throat stung—and not just from the fire—I'd told him he needed that money. I told him that money was *a life*. He'd been ready to let it go.

I did this.

Keeping my eyes on the shelter, never leaving the shelter, I coughed up a handful of blood. It was thick as honey and scarlet by the light of the fire. The contents of my stomach rushed up next. Vomit seared my already-burning throat.

Henri tried to tug me farther away, but I wiped my mouth and held my ground.

The burning shelter was still, no signs of movement.

I managed, "Please, Alex, please."

Squeezing my hand, Henri stared at the fire now shooting out of our tarp rooftop. Her lips, they mouthed, *Come on, Alex.*

Tears poured out of my eyes. My vision clouded. Sobs wracked my body so hard, my hands couldn't stifle the sound.

I couldn't lose Alex like this. I had grieved for Henri as if she'd died. But she was living and breathing, and I didn't know it until now, but that wasn't real grief.

I crawled to my knees. My bones ached as Henri crushed my knuckles and anchored me to the ground.

Coughing, I tried to speak.

"I'm going in." Henri jogged toward the shelter and looked back. "If you come in after us, Em, I swear I'll never forgive you. If anyone knows the strength of my will, it's you."

Before I could say anything, Henri too was gone in smoke and flames.

I held my knees to my chest and stared at the blaze.

Seconds dragged by. No movement. Alex and Henri were my world, all I had, and all I'd ever have if I didn't get off the island.

Fire crackled and popped and smoldered and took away everything. Everything.

The shelter leaned precariously. I saw a shadow inside. Movement.

Henri emerged, legs stepping through a ring of flames. She had Alex under his arms.

"He passed out inside." Henri dragged him out of the fire, through the brush, and to my side.

A crack built to a roar and the roof caved. Heat blanketed us as what was left of the shelter imploded.

Coughing and choking and rolling through the brush to extinguish her burning clothes, Henri collapsed.

My muscles heaved and screamed, straining against waves

of weakness. On my hands and knees, I pulled myself through the dirt.

I squeezed Henri so hard, our sharp, protruding bones dug into each other's flesh. I didn't care.

I pulled back. My stare asked, *Why?*

She looked into my eyes. "You said it was real."

Alex lay motionless in the dirt with his chin tipped toward the black sky. The inferno had taken the money—his backpack wasn't on his back.

Breaths shuddered between his lips—he was breathing, just unconscious.

I pressed my hands to his face. *Come on. Wake up.*

His arm had fallen across his chest when Henri had let him go. I threw it off him to give his lungs more room. It struck the ground and his hand unclenched. His fist—I hadn't even noticed. Tucked inside his palm was the lighter.

He didn't go back for the backpack. He'd gone for the one thing we needed on the island to keep going. And miraculously, it had survived. The plastic ridges were caked with dirt—it must have fallen to the ground, saving it from the rising heat.

I forced my voice into my ragged throat.

"Alex, wake up!" I slapped his cheek, then harder, and then with enough force to sting my palm.

I crawled to our water—our last boiled bottle—and even though my throat ached to guzzle every drop, I dumped it in his face. With wide eyes, he sputtered and gasped awake.

The larger tree sprouting from the roof of our shelter cracked along the trunk. It crashed into the smaller tree, downing it in a gush of heat that slapped against my exposed skin. I covered my face.

Fire spread up the finer branches—I inched backward. If the fire was going to take the whole jungle, we desperately needed to get to the beach. A deep, gutting sense of loss hit me at the thought of the island's incineration. Flames licked against the boulders around the clearing. That rock wall we'd built snuffed out the fire's edges. Unless the wind shifted, unless that tree ignited, only our shelter would burn.

Light and heat doused over us as the fire overtook what was left of the shelter. Henri wrapped herself so small, she almost looked like a child.

There was nothing left to do but watch as what was once our home—the one Henri and I had slaved over, finished with our own four hands—smoldered and burned.

Smoke still spiraled up from the debris as morning light flooded the jungle. We picked through what was left, throwing into a pile our knife that had melted shut and wouldn't pry open. Except for Henri's things, in her own shelter, it was all we'd had that survived.

Alex hadn't said anything about the money. After everything, the life I'd claimed the money would give him hadn't mattered more than the lighter, more than survival if the raft failed. More than us.

He'd been looking for redemption, and maybe he'd found it.

Henri's skin was black with soot except for the red burns that covered her legs. Her hair had singed above her shoulders. I ached for a small hint of her perfection. The island had finally wrecked my flawless sister.

She noticed me staring, and her hands went to her hair. Her fingers closed around the ends that were gone. Her lips parted.

Alex grabbed a handful of Henri's shirt and tugged her close. "You fucking started the fire, didn't you?" I couldn't blame him. We didn't know where Henri's sabotage began and ended—and he didn't know the full truth.

Tears left white lines across Henri's blackened skin. Snot leaked from her nose as she sobbed. *"I didn't. I didn't."*

"She didn't do it," I said. "The wind. It must have carried the sparks from our fire."

He shook Henri like a doll, like he didn't even hear me. "What's it going to take to satisfy you? You want to see us all dead, is that it?"

"Alex," I said. "She was the one who went in after you. Henri pulled you out."

He stared at me. His arms went slack, his mouth opened, but no sound came out. He looked back at Henri. Took a step away. He staggered toward the beach.

Henri let out a scream so shrill, the birds in the trees burst toward the sky. "You both spend all your time trying to make me feel like the terrible one, but you two are the absolute worst! What have I done that's so horribly bad?"

I didn't say anything. I didn't have to.

"Oh, Alex's hand? What part of *I'm sorry* did you not hear? Believe what you want, Em, but that was an accident.

I didn't want to hurt him—well, not badly." Henri shrugged before she snapped to me and her voice climbed higher. "Am I totally innocent? Of course not. Yeah, so I burned the raft plans because I didn't want to face home yet. And yes, when you started talking about a signal fire, I hid the lighter. When I realized we could use it to boil water, I planted it on Alex—I couldn't just pull it out of my bag after you'd searched it with me—but you took for-fucking-ever to doubt him and search his stupid backpack. Does it make me a terrible person if I enjoyed it when you found the money and didn't trust him? Am I worse than you, Emma, for leaving me behind?"

She turned to stalk off, and I brought my hands to my mouth.

At the center of the sweatshirt tied around her waist was a small spot of blood.

"Henri. I think—you just got your period."

Henri turned, eyes stark and blue in her soot-covered face. I took a small step forward, and like a wild animal, she bolted through the trees.

CHAPTER 34

Henri shivered inside her shelter with her arms looped around her knees.

"Are you okay?" I crawled under the canoe and reached out to her, but she knocked my grip away.

"I feel so stupid," she whispered.

"Why? A lot of people would have thought the same."

She looked down at her concave stomach and crossed her arms. "I tried to do everything right. It's not like I was just fucking with you the whole time. I ate the coconuts because I thought they were the only thing safe. You're not supposed to eat raw fish, you know, when you're pregnant. And I couldn't drink that disgusting raft water, Em—I needed the coconut water to stay hydrated. I thought if I could just keep us here for a few months, I'd start showing, and when they found us, me with my big belly, everybody'd feel so sorry for me, they wouldn't judge me anymore. They'd understand."

Henri wasn't relieved—and I didn't know why. She wasn't pregnant. Never was. She didn't have to worry about what to do and she didn't have a reason to avoid home.

"Henri, did you—did you *want* to be pregnant?"

"I don't know. Maybe. It's not like I wanted to be a teen

mom or anything like that. But if I was pregnant, that meant it was Jesse's."

"But what were you going to do with a baby? Did you think you were going to use it to get him back?"

"No." She smeared tears across her cheeks. "I guess I wanted it, just for me. Until a few days ago, I didn't have you anymore and I still don't have Jesse. I wanted something that was just mine."

"*A baby?*"

She looked at me.

"A baby to keep you up all night," I said. "To need you every minute of the day. To feed, and clothe and support. You would have had to explain it to every guy you dated for—for forever. I mean, if it just happened, that would be one thing. But to *want* it? At seventeen? Someday, yeah. But now?"

"No." She shook her head so hard, I felt her tears strike my arms. "It's—it's not that I want a baby."

"Then what do you want?"

She blinked as if someone had slapped her. "I just don't want to be alone. I just—I can't. I *can't* be alone."

I felt like that day when she was in my bedroom and told me I didn't have any friends. The realization knocked the breath out of me.

I'd seen the way Henri would latch on to the nearest person when I couldn't be at her side. When a boy hadn't landed her attention, she was mine, and usually I was so thrilled to have her back that I didn't notice the obsessive way she demanded I drop everything for her.

"It's why I didn't want you to leave the island," she whispered. "It's why I asked you to stay. And everything back home—all the boys, running from Jake to Gavin to Jesse. I couldn't stop."

I knew then why Henri felt differently toward Mom after Dad moved out. Those fears that had always been inside her, the way Dad left so abruptly, so casually, he only made them rise to the surface. Henri saw in Mom exactly what she didn't want to be—someone who got left.

"How Dad left," I whispered.

Henri didn't blink her tears away. She let them roll down her face. "It's why I told you I wasn't going to college. I wanted you to think I was doing something nice for you, that I was waiting for you—but that wasn't it. I just couldn't leave by myself. I needed you."

All that time, she'd made me think it was the other way around.

"The house by the sea, the dozen cats, the faded curtains— I told you that story when you were like four or five, when Mom told us we were named after Dad's aunts in Maine."

"What?" I shook my head. "No," I said. "Maybe you planted the seed, but I—I needed you just as much as you needed me. I embellished that story. I added to it. I loved it. With Jesse, I did think I liked him, but when you started dating him, it wasn't him I wanted. I think I just—I was afraid you'd love him more. More than me."

"Impossible," she said. "I've never loved anyone like you— that's why this year ripped me apart. But it's a different thing anyway—the way I feel about him, the way I feel about you."

Henri held herself as if only her arms could keep her pieced together, and I saw that behind all her fake control—throwing herself at a teacher, carving our dad out of her heart—was something fragile. I wish we'd seen it sooner—my dad and Mr. Flynn, they had a responsibility to see it, to do better. Those moments were my sister spinning out.

With the heel of her hand, she ground viciously at her tears. "We're all kinds of screwed up, aren't we?" She laughed and wiped a hand under her nose.

"How did we do this?"

"We didn't mean to hurt each other—at least I don't think you did. Or maybe a little. But I never meant to hurt you—not before. After Gavin, okay, yes . . . I was kind of out for blood. I just couldn't believe it. But even in the deep, dark pit of me being my absolute worst—I couldn't hate you. I didn't even know that about myself until I saw you with Alex. At the waterfall."

A weight built in my throat and sank through me. I stared up at her, bracing myself.

"You kept sneaking off together. It was so obvious. So one day I followed you. When I first saw the two of you, wading into that clear water, it made me so raging furious—that you'd kept it from me, lied to me. But then Alex swam close, and the way he looked at you—the way *you* looked at *him*. I couldn't ruin it. I wanted you to be happy so much more than I'd ever wanted to hurt you." She closed her eyes, pushed her forehead against mine. Then looked at me and locked her hands over my shoulders. "Even if we loved each other in the wrong ways, Em, it doesn't mean we loved each other any less."

I wrapped my arms around her, and we sank into each other, not letting go.

"So, what if this is all true?" she said into my ear. "Where do we go from here?"

"Home? Come home with me and we'll figure it out."

She pulled back and said, "Okay."

A breeze blew through Henri's shelter, taking with it our stray cats, our faded curtains, our missing marbles. I was sorry to see them go. But then again, I wasn't.

CHAPTER 35

Alex said we should get started at sunset and sail through the night. We needed our first few hours free from the sun beating down on us.

Henri cut tarps into pieces and sewed little bags using the last of her sewing kit. We filled the bags to their brims with coconut and cacao pods and caiman jerky. It felt safe having all that food—we had enough to last longer than our stamina ever could.

Alex held one end of some cordage between his teeth as his hand jerked harder at the already-tightened ties. "Is everyone ready?"

I nodded first and then Henri.

We loaded Henri's bag with every full water bottle our bags could carry and strapped it down to the raft with the strongest vines.

"Get low!" Alex yelled, and we dropped flat on our bellies. He was the only one who knew how to sail, so we did everything he said to get past the first mile of waves.

With my hands wrapped around the bamboo and my nose inches from the ocean flowing through the raft, I sealed my lips to keep from swallowing salt water.

If he said "Right," we leaned right. "Left," and we went left.

It was the first time Henri ever listened to Alex without argument.

I faced our island when we were a distance away, beyond the breakers. It looked so large and solid, my feet ached for it one last time. Out on the open water, there were predators and the beating sun and enough ocean to drown us a billion times over.

Alex rigged up a tarp to keep us from getting totally scorched when the sun rose, and then stared at the island too. He wore a wide grin I hadn't seen since before the accident, back on Luquillo Beach.

"A day," Alex said, as if he was reminding himself for extra courage. He reached between us and wove our fingers together. "Two days at most."

Two days at most until we crossed paths with those ships.

We took shifts sleeping. Alex was worn out from managing the sailing, so I insisted he take the first one.

"You can sleep too," I said to Henri. "If you want."

"I'd rather stay up with you."

My sister and I sat with our knees pulled to our chests, gazing up at a sky full of stars. The moon shone so brilliant and bright, I could see it reflected in Henri's eyes.

"Do you think everyone thinks we're dead, Em?"

"I hope not," I said. "But probably."

"It's had to be hell for Mom after this last year. After Dad."

"Yeah."

"Why don't you hate Dad? How can you not?"

I sank back against the raft. "I don't hate him. I just try to accept him for what he is—kind of an asshole. Hating him doesn't make him less of an asshole, but I don't like what it makes me."

Out of the corner of my eye, I noticed her watching me. Slowly, she nodded. "What do I do back home?" she asked. "What does a person do when her whole life has been caught up in other people?"

Eyes still on the sky, I said, "I think you have to try to do something for just you."

"Like what?"

"You could get a stupid boy to pay your way through Europe, or you could do it on your own." I glanced at her.

A small smile graced her lips. "Maybe."

Alex clambered to grab the tarp when the morning breeze caught it, but a blast of wind ripped it right out of his hands. "Son of a—"

Without thinking, I stood to get it. The raft tilted and Henri's backpack slid toward the waves. She went for it, and a side of the raft lifted out of the water. We were about to capsize.

"Whoa!" yelled Alex. *"Down!"*

Henri and I both hit the deck. We all rocked back and forth until the raft's movements slowed. We couldn't even see where the tarp landed, somewhere out there in the waves.

Henri plucked her backpack from the very edge of the raft and tied it back down. "Well, there goes not getting fried."

We bundled up with all the layers we had. Heat burned

through our clothes by the afternoon. We watched the horizon for a ship that should have saved us. A ship that never came.

"Don't worry," said Alex. "I'm sure those prisoners escaping Alcatraz went through worse than this."

I didn't have the heart to remind him that nobody knew if they'd lived or died.

We floated, not talking, barely moving that second day, except to switch off watching for boats to rest our eyes from the sun. The blue glittery waves reflected rays so bright, it hurt to stare too long.

Alex shook my arm halfway through his turn.

The glow of sunlight was orange through my closed eyelids.

"A plane," he scratched out—he wasn't drinking enough water.

Henri scrambled to her knees. "Seriously?"

The plane shot across the sky, a small passenger plane that wouldn't see us unless it was looking. Still, I lifted up and waved.

After the plane was only a white jet trail, I sprawled against the raft.

On the third day, Henri unscrewed the cap on the last bottle. "I guess this is it for the water."

She passed it to me, and I couldn't help myself from gulping three large swallows.

Henri closed her mouth around the bottle and took a small drink. Her chapped lips had cracked open and bled.

Alex was stretched out on his stomach, his temple pressed against the bamboo. His quick heartbeat was visible through his skeletal back. He'd been so careful to not drink too much that he hadn't drunk enough at all.

Henri crawled to him with a bottle of water. "Here. You need this more than us."

Careful not to put weight on his broken hand, he rolled to a sitting position. His left hand shook, and he steadied the bottle with his splinted hand. "Thank you, Henri."

Alex had been wrong about the distance, and I waited for Henri to attack him over it. But she never said a word, only wrapped her arms around her legs and rocked herself as she waited for help to come that never materialized.

We drifted at sea, and by the fourth day—with no water except salt—our motor skills were gone, our heartbeats rapid, and once Alex had blacked out.

Even though we were on fire, we wore our shirts draped over our legs, our jackets or sweatshirts on our backs, and our sleeves pulled down over our fingers. We had no protection against the sun without the tarp. The island had browned us dark, but the reflection of the ocean water was savage. The raft was like a rotisserie spit.

Henri tied her hair in a thick knot and fanned her neck. "I'm too hot with these clothes on."

Alex tossed handfuls of ocean water down the back of his shirt. "We gotta keep them on. If we get any more sunburned, we're as good as dead."

I leaned back on the raft and let the water lap against my legs between the spaces in the bamboo. It looked so delicious to my thirsty eyes.

My knees knocked together as I unzipped my jacket and dropped my shorts down my legs. We were very possibly dying, and I decided I wouldn't do it sweaty and burning up.

"Jones," Alex said.

"I don't care."

Henri stuffed my clothes in her tied-down backpack and stripped to her bikini.

The sky above blue and blistering, we all stretched flat against the raft.

The moon overhead bathed us in the brightest white light as Alex slept on his back on one side of me.

His shirt was open and I rolled onto my side to face him. My fingers traced the ribs straining against his skin. He was emaciated, but his heart kept beating inside his chest. I turned to my other side, toward Henri, whose veins popped from the thin tissue around her eyes. Still, her body refused to give up.

I wedged myself back between them and gazed up at the night sky. Out here, the stars were brighter than they'd ever been—even on the island. I remembered how so many stars we see have died long before their light reaches Earth.

I was staring up at a graveyard of stars.

Looking at the beautiful blackness, I wasn't thirsty, hungry, tired, hot, or cold. My heartbeat didn't jump through my thin, dehydrated skin. Part of me, maybe the delirious part, wished that when the sun rose in the east the next morning we wouldn't wake up.

Water ran past my cracked lips and into my mouth. My chest convulsing with hiccups, I opened my eyes. Morning sun reflected off the ocean as I looked to Alex and then Henri. I grabbed one of each of their hands and shook.

Spatters of rain fell from the sky and they both gasped awake. Henri jumped when the first cold drops struck her tanned belly. She scrambled to open the water bottles, but it took my help, and Alex's too, to make our weak fingers unscrew the caps. As they filled, we held our leathery tongues to the sky.

We relished the blissful feel of water filling our mouths and cooling our skin.

I realized how absolutely thoughtless it was to wish for anything but survival. Because if we didn't make it, one of us would have to watch the other two die.

Hours later, the storm still raged. My fingers bled from holding myself against the raft that bucked beneath me. Lightning crackled across the horizon.

Henri squeezed her eyes shut. "Tell me again about the chances of being struck by lightning."

"About as good as getting stranded on a deserted island. So for us?" Alex's voice went dry. "Odds are good."

The sea bounced us up and down, thrashing my already-black knuckles between the bamboo slats. My stomach tangled in knots that kept lurching toward my throat.

Henri hung over the edge and Alex held back her hair while she vomited into the ocean.

Before long, she was on her own, because Alex was puking too.

A tall wave rolled through the water, growing higher and higher as it neared.

I worked my fingers into the slippery bamboo. "Hang on!"

The wave crashed over us. Everything went silent. The water pulled us under. I opened my eyes to the deep dark but didn't let go. I told myself we could only go so far before the buoyancy of the raft pulled us out.

Pain hammered my ears, and the raft buckled. Any deeper and the pressure would break the bamboo apart.

The raft popped out from under us. I gasped and heaved. We were still hanging on. But everything—our water, our loose clothing—was gone.

Alex reached for my hand and looked from me to Henri and back again. Over the wind, Alex screamed, "I'm so sorry. I'm so sorry."

"*Alex,*" yelled Henri. I cringed—I didn't know what she might say next. "Shut up. Not your fault."

My sister gripped my right hand and Alex squeezed my left. We all closed our eyes as the raft bounced beneath us. Soon we'd be too weak to hang on.

"Em, look. Emma! Emma!" Tears spilled down Henri's cheeks.

Alex got down on his stomach, arms over the edge of the

raft, air rattling from his chest as he splashed and paddled. Drizzling rain stung my eyes as I blinked at the horizon.

Cutting through the waves was the hull of a cargo ship.

"They don't see us!" Henri yelled, throwing a spray of ocean behind her hands as she paddled.

We fought the walls of water, trying to put ourselves in the ship's path but also terrified we'd get too close, they wouldn't see us, and we'd collide.

We drifted close enough to see movement and waved our arms over our heads, screaming until we ran out of breath. Then gasping and screaming again.

The ship blew its horn. Three short bursts. We were found.

A pulley system lowered a smaller motorboat into the waves. It puttered toward us, and Alex jumped off the raft and splashed into the ocean. He let Henri wrap her arms around his neck as she lowered into the water. I dropped off the raft's side too fast and my weight sank.

My eyes stung as I opened them underwater, fighting toward the top. I popped above the surface, gasping.

Henri wrapped an arm around my waist, and we paddled toward the boat, clinging close.

Alex swam ahead, glancing back every few seconds to make sure we were behind him. He clung to the motorboat's edge, waiting for us, even though the driver tried to pull him up. He helped Henri into the boat first, lifting her from the water and giving a final shove.

Alex reached for me, but we were weak and fighting to hold on to each other. Legs kicking under the surface, I held his gaze.

He straightened the bikini strap that had fallen off my shoulder and hoisted me into the motorboat.

The three of us huddled together in the shade of an awning. The storm had blown through as quickly as it came, and now our sunburned bodies shivered as we took turns offering pieces of our story to the captain.

A deckhand brought us bottles of water. Alex drank his too fast and vomited it back up on the floor, letting some of the water—still cold—slosh onto my feet.

My sister cringed and patted him absently on the back, but I wasn't bothered. Alex's puke was nothing to me now.

Henri clutched at the deck's floors as if she needed them to live. Her equilibrium was off after so many days of bobbing in the sea. Someone brought granola bars, and when Henri reached up to grab one, she plunged forward and planted her hands on the deck for balance.

Ship workers walked up and down the deck, staring at our raft bobbing in the ocean below. Waves rocked it against the ship, and soon it shattered against the hull. As splintered pieces spread across the water, I wondered how it ever carried us so many miles.

The ship medic unwrapped Alex's broken hand, and he flinched when he saw the dark blue fingers tied to jagged pieces of bamboo.

He squeezed Alex's hand in different places, checking for nerve damage. "You look familiar," he said, "Alex, huh? You're not Casey Roth's cousin?"

"I was. Casey didn't make it."

The medic stared back at him, and threw a look to me and my sister. "Let's go below so I can reset this with something clean."

Alex came back a few minutes later and crumpled to my side as if his thin limbs couldn't carry him any farther. With my stare I asked what was wrong, but he looked away.

The captain glanced from our dirty bare feet to our singed hair. "How long were you on that island?"

My teeth chattered as I tried to speak. "Seventy—"

Alex's arms came around me, wrapping me tighter in a scratchy blanket the workers brought. "We've been lost for seventy-three days, sir."

"Well, we're heading back," the captain said. "We've radioed the coast guard. They'll get the three of you to a hospital. Fast as they can."

I nodded, only to find Alex shaking his head. "I don't need a doctor. Have them just take the girls."

The captain huffed. "We'll see about that."

The ship turned toward Puerto Rico and barreled through the waves as the captain led us all below deck. In the cool shade of the cabin, Henri and I wound our fingers together. Alex's breath left his chest with a shudder, and he kept his head in his hands the whole way back.

CHAPTER 36

My vision exploded with doctors and nurses the moment the paramedics wheeled us through the hospital doors in San Juan.

The fluorescent lights against the white ceilings, people shouting orders and information to each other, the monitors beeping in rhythm with our vital signs—it was all too much. With my eyes closed, images flashed of blue skies, bright nights, deep pools, sharp teeth, warm hands, wet lashes, flowers, flames, strands and strands of seashells, and ocean waves crashing on our shore.

"It's really them," someone said.

The room fell away and rushed back to me.

We were alive. Reborn into a world where everyone had thought we were dead.

"I need a phone," I told the nurse as he fastened a hospital bracelet on my wrist. "My parents—we have to call them."

"Save your strength." The nurse tightened a tourniquet around my arm. "They're in Atlanta. They got on a plane before the cargo ship even made it to the shore. They'll be here as soon as they can."

"Atlanta?" I said.

He didn't answer, and I didn't ask again.

A doctor ran her fingers over the glands in my neck while the nurse punctured my arm once, twice, three times. Finally he got my IV in. "Sorry. You're too dehydrated. I couldn't find a vein."

He lifted my other arm toward the doctor, who peered through her glasses at the puckered wound that ran the length of my arm. Henri's stitches had come loose and some trailed from my skin.

"Who stitched this?" she asked.

"My sister."

"Are you allergic to any medications? Penicillin?"

On the examination table across from me, a different doctor and nurse looked over Henri. Her knees were purple from banging against the bamboo raft for four days. I stretched out my legs—our knees matched.

They kept Alex on the other side of the room, behind a curtain that gaped open a few inches. He'd been too quiet since the coast guard transferred us into the ambulances. *Dengue fever,* I heard a doctor say. It was a mosquito-borne virus that they thought had made Alex so sick on the island. The next thing the doctors did was examine his hand—they weren't sure he could keep his fingers. If he did, he wouldn't regain full mobility again.

A couple of uniformed officers lurked outside the door.

I was sure the police wanted to talk to Henri and me—we were two teen girls missing from a vacation spot. There had to be missing-persons reports filed. Of course they had questions.

But they seemed more interested in Alex.

A doctor peeled back the curtains and one of the officers moved forward, flashing a badge. Alex kept his gaze on the floor while they spoke. Their words were muffled, but Alex nodded and followed the officer toward the doorway.

I craned my neck, hoping Alex would make eye contact and give me a sign that everything was okay, or terrible, or something. Anything.

He never turned around.

The doctors said we were all suffering the effects of smoke inhalation, and our kidneys were shutting down from dehydration. They pumped our veins full of fluids and electrolytes. Our first meal was only a few cubes of chicken breast, overcooked broccoli, and a small cup of a vanilla nutritional drink that left a powdery residue on my tongue. We'd been malnourished for so long—they didn't want to feed us too much too fast. Even though those few bites were the best I'd ever tasted, my stomach cramped and everything came back up. They increased our fluids then and gave Henri and me shots for nausea that made us so tired, we swayed on our feet.

They gave us soap, shampoo, and toothbrushes and showed us to a couple of showers. The water scalded my skin and I stayed under the hot stream until my knees were too weak to keep standing.

We were sunburned, heatstroked, exhausted, but we would survive. We *had* survived.

Sunlight streamed over the buildings and through the vertical blinds as I sat up in my hospital bed. Henri breathed softly as she slept in the next bed over. We must have been out all night—it was morning.

My bladder felt like it was going to burst. I tried to sit up, but something tugged at my arm and stung. It took me a second to figure out how to unwind the IV stand to take it with me.

The floor swayed back and forth as I moved into the bathroom.

As I washed my hands, the face staring back at me in the mirror made me gasp. My hair and eyebrows were bleached out against my tanned skin, and my cheekbones were higher under my sunken cheeks. The island made me look less like me and more like the old lady I imagined I'd become one day.

I pushed the IV stand back into the hospital room first, closing the bathroom behind me.

"Em," Henri said. Her bare arms looked unnaturally tanned against the white hospital sheets as she clutched the bedding to her chest. "I—" Her voice rose. "I woke up and thought we were still on the island."

She swung her legs off the bed before tearful hiccups wracked her whole body.

My sister wasn't okay.

Henri shut herself in the bathroom while I collapsed into my too-soft bed.

Voices trickled in from the nurses' station.

My mother's words were first: "We got here as soon as we could."

"The name?"

My father's next: "Jones. Henrietta and Emmalyn."

"Oh, you're—" Chair legs scraped against the floor. "This way."

Shoes echoed through the sterile halls, clicking louder as they neared our room.

Mom filled the doorway. Her eyes were sunken deep into her skull, and her clavicles jutted from under her skin. She'd lost so much weight—too much—and her gray trouser pants bagged around her thighs as she crossed the room.

"Mom," I croaked.

She squeezed me hard, falling against me and crushing my chest. "You're okay. You're okay. You're okay." She repeated those words until my dad cleared his throat.

He shifted his feet back and forth. With his eyes red and full of water, he covered his mouth and his short beard. His strangled words—"You look good, Em"—almost didn't slip between his fingers.

Mom pressed her palm to my forehead, the back of her hand to each of my cheeks. "My God, you're burning up."

"It's heatstroke." My hand touched hers—she'd finally stopped wearing her wedding band. "I'm okay. I'm just—"

The bathroom door opened and my parents looked to my sister.

Henri clutched the doorframe and didn't speak.

I half expected Henri to give them each a quick hello hug and ask what Mom had brought her to wear on the plane ride home. But my sister's expressionless face cracked.

My dad reached a hand out; it trembled as he patted Henri's back twice and clasped her shoulder.

Tears rolled into my mother's frown lines, and she used her hands to steady herself against my bed instead of wiping them away. Mom crossed the room and caught Henri under the arms, wrapping herself around my sister until Henri's sobs turned to soft gasps.

Henri pulled back and blotted her cheeks against her hospital gown. "Were you still looking for us?"

Mom collected Henri's hands and pulled her to my hospital bed. The bed creaked with the weight of the three of us, while my dad pulled a chair closer to the bedside.

Mom smoothed back Henri's singed hair. "We didn't know if you'd been kidnapped or killed or . . . All anyone knew was that you were missing. I saw you at breakfast that morning and then the hotel caught some footage of you leaving the property an hour later—that was all we had to go on."

My dad spoke up, shaking his head and staring out the hospital windows. "That kid with the boat, nobody even reported him missing. A fisherman's saying now that he noticed the boat was gone. But the kid was kind of a drifter and he assumed he'd just taken off for another island. I wish we could sue—"

Mom shot him a look. "Steven."

He sighed. "Search teams were canvassing Puerto Rico for six weeks before they refused to keep looking—"

"Stop," Henri said.

Both my parents looked to Henri. The room was too small to hold so much silence.

"Don't blame yourself for giving up," she said. "Anyone would have—"

Dad reached his arms around Henri and squeezed. Cradling the back of her head in his hand, he whispered, "But we didn't. Even after everyone else did, we couldn't. We never could have given up on finding our girls."

I couldn't stop my tears from coming. I wasn't crying because our parents didn't give up, but because, since the divorce, I'd never seen Henri give grace to my dad.

"We can forget all about this," he said. "As soon as the hospital says you're well enough to fly, we'll take you home." He met Henri's eyes and then mine. "We'll forget this ever happened."

Henri frowned at me. We couldn't afford to forget, didn't want to forget. She knew it—so did I.

Our parents would only remember that they'd almost lost us out there, but for my sister and me, it was the opposite. Our island was where we found so much of what we desperately needed.

"It wasn't as bad as you're thinking," I said. "We had each other. And we had Alex."

My dad's voice climbed. "That boy—"

Mom gave him a warning look and he slumped back in his chair.

She pushed my hair out of my face. "Nothing happened with him on the island, did it? He didn't do anything to either of you?"

"What are you talking about? Alex?"

"Alex," she said, "has an officer guarding his room. They're telling us that he's the reason we almost lost you."

"What? No, it wasn't like that."

"Emma, stop." She forced our eyes together. "He's in an awful lot of trouble."

That night, I lay awake in my too-soft hospital bed in my too-quiet room missing the hammock and the sound of Alex's breathing.

Henri was curled on her side with her back to me and her legs pulled to her chin when Mom cracked open the door.

My bed creaked as Mom lowered her hips onto the side. "The police questioned him all day. He wasn't cooperating. They said you can't see him."

"Why?"

"There was a raid last month on a drug house. The police found explosives. One of the dealers cut a deal—he admitted some of the others had rigged the cousin's boat to blow up when it was far from shore. Because they were rivals. Because Alex and the cousin were running drugs."

"And they're building a case based on what this dealer said? This is ridiculous."

Mom held a finger to her lips, glanced to Henri asleep in the next bed. "Emma, the way you're being about this boy, it worries me."

"Have I ever given you a reason to not trust me?"

"Oh, Em. It's just that we went through so much with your sister. We'll talk more about this when you're rested." She kissed me on the forehead. "Get some sleep, okay?"

I sat up to argue, but she was already across the room. After Mom pulled the door shut, Henri rolled over and said, "We'll fix this."

I wasn't so sure.

The humid tropical breeze of San Juan blew against my arms and tangled my hair as Henri and I sat in wheelchairs outside the hospital's electric doors. For a moment, I imagined I was on a different island—our island—and we weren't about to board a plane for San Francisco.

"It's fifty-eight degrees in the city today." Mom fanned herself with our boarding passes. "I just realized I haven't seen home in almost three months."

I hadn't remembered until then to ask—"Mom, why were you and Dad in Atlanta?"

She refolded her papers and shoved them into her tote. "Filming for CNN. Until a few days ago, we hadn't left Puerto

Rico—of course they'd find you the day we left. These trage-
dies, they only hold people's attention for so long. We thought
doing the interview was a way to keep the media interested."

I'd underestimated my mom. She'd come out of everything
not unscathed but stronger for it. Maybe I'd underestimated
all of us.

Henri pursed her lips—she loved attention, but not this
kind. "You mean we've been all over the news?"

"It'll die down soon enough. It almost had—but then you
were found. The airline made arrangements for you two
to preboard because of your condition. They expect a lot of
reporters back in SF, but your dad will have a car waiting to
get us out of there as fast as possible."

Our taxi pulled up and Mom rolled her luggage close to
the curb while the driver loaded her things and Dad's into the
trunk. The bandage they'd tied around my arm was itchy, but I
couldn't scratch hard enough through the gauze, not with my
brittle, waterlogged nails.

Henri nudged me in the ribs and pointed to a police cruiser
parked in the roundabout, with someone in the backseat.

He looked up, and I couldn't breathe.

Staring back at me were Alex's green eyes. They focused
from the other side of the glass to where I sat, and they
burned right through me.

Amputating two fingers only kept Alex at the hospital for
a little more than a week. Now they were taking him away to
face an uncertain future.

We'd tried so hard—not only me but Henri too—to make

the police understand who Alex really was. They'd grilled us for hours about the day the boat went down. Had we taken any drugs? What did the explosions sound like? It wasn't easy to know what words would help him the most.

Mom checked our flight information on her phone and glanced through the glass doors. "I wonder what's taking him so long."

Dad was inside, signing papers saying he understood it was against the doctors' recommendations for us to fly so soon.

Henri squeezed my arm and mouthed, *Go.*

I didn't understand until Henri closed her eyes and slumped forward in her wheelchair.

"Henri!" Mom got to her knees in front of my sister. "Help! Someone help us!"

A couple of nurses jogged through the hospital doors to the sidewalk. Behind me, my mom's voice was frantic. "She was fine and then she just collapsed."

Henri'd made just enough of a distraction for me to slip away and move toward the police cruiser.

In Alex's lap, his wrists were handcuffed together and he stroked his bandaged hand. He tried to smile as he saw me. With his blistered, peeling cheeks and shaggy dark hair now past his shoulders, he wore the strain of what we'd faced, of what he had yet to face, but the eyes looking back at me were those of the boy I met on Luquillo Beach.

His handcuffs scratched against the windowpane as he pressed his good hand to the glass. I held my palm against the outline of his.

The car's engine rumbled to life. My breath came fast as I tried to think of what to say before the officer put the car in drive.

"What can I do?" I said over the humming engine.

Alex's voice was muffled through the window. "Nothing, Jones."

I kept my hand against his until the car rolled forward and broke us apart.

CHAPTER 37

After everything on the island, it wasn't easy for us to slip back into double-feature movies, dim sum, buttery popcorn, and nail painting. Home wasn't the same, and neither were we.

We had doctor appointments almost every day because of severe headaches that sometimes left us so weak, we couldn't stand. The doctors ran tests for days until they could rule out dengue fever, like Alex had. We were prescribed long doses of anthelmintics to kill parasites and given MRIs to check for damage outside our digestive tracts.

We would snap back, the doctors said—we just needed time.

When we weren't being poked and prodded, we steered clear of the phone that never stopped ringing.

Our return after seventy-three days missing and the truth about our shipwreck made national news. Almost every channel showed clips of us—an overhead view of search teams canvassing Puerto Rico on foot, commentators discussing the odds of finding us, security footage of Henri and me walking out of the Luquillo Beach Resort the day we disappeared, our mom wiping her eyes while swearing she wouldn't give up hope.

Henri had to keep seeing her therapist, and Mom and Dad scheduled me with my own. Henri told me her sessions weren't like her first two. They weren't about Mr. Flynn anymore, only the drowning nightmares that made her wake up screaming.

I stood on the porch one morning before another of our many doctors' appointments, waiting for my mom and Henri, when Jesse crossed from his yard into ours.

"You look really good," he said. "For everything you've been through."

I smiled. "I don't know how to take that."

"I mean you look good. Sorry." Jesse blew a breath into his hands. "I'm sorry for everything, Em."

"Me too."

"That guy you were stranded with, what was his name?"

"Alex."

Even in the brightest spots of my days, Alex was never far from my mind. Alex, who was made of ocean water and sand and sunlight, he didn't belong in a sterile gray cell.

The first night back in San Francisco, my shaved legs had felt so slick sliding against my sheets. In my stationary bed, I'd swayed back and forth, imagining the feel of the hammock under me, Alex's arms, his warmth radiating, the sound of distant ocean waves.

"What was he like?" Jesse asked. "The media's acting like he was some kind of a drug trafficker or something."

I'd devoured the news for the first month we were home, surviving off the scraps about Alex's pending charges and the occasional pictures as if they were cacao pods and fresh rainwater. Mom would crowd around the TV beside me and Henri, waiting with just as much hope for a little good news. When we'd got some distance from Dad, when Henri and I were able to make her understand, Mom had seen that no matter what mistakes Alex had made, he was the reason she got us back.

Eventually, though, the media turned on Alex, painting him as a thuggish drug runner who led astray two sweet, innocent girls. Maybe the networks were hungry for a more sensational story, for higher ratings. That's when I stopped watching, also when I learned not to trust the news.

Now my memories were the only place Alex existed.

I wished people weren't so often known for only the smallest parts of them, their careless mistakes. "Alex was smart," I said to Jesse. "And he was brave. What you see on the news—that was only a fraction of him, and not a fraction I knew."

Jesse nodded like he understood.

The front door creaked behind us, and Henri stepped onto the porch. Her purse slipped off her shoulder when she saw Jesse. I moved to help her, but she held her hand up and hoisted it a little higher.

Jesse cast his eyes to the ground.

"Hi," she said.

Jesse looked up. "Hi."

I took several steps down the driveway to give them privacy. Maybe their relationship could never work past what had happened, but Jesse caught Henri's hand as she walked away. The way she kept her fingers intertwined with his for just a few seconds made me think someday they'd try.

My dad spent a lot more time around our house after we came home. He'd do little things like change the air filters or drag the trash cans to the curb. He thought he was helping by staying close, but all he did was tease. Because late every night, Henri, my mom, and I would walk to the door and wave as he'd climb back into his BMW and drive off. Leaving us for her all over again.

Dad was the same, but he was trying harder to show we still mattered. It made it not hurt the same way as before.

We sat around the TV that July, Mom, Henri, and me, with the air-conditioning whirring to keep the heat out of the room.

Henri's thumb was moving fast over the remote and skipped past a still of Alex. We hadn't seen his face on the news in weeks. As she clicked back, I walked to the TV.

The words *breaking news* were emblazoned across the screen as they filmed Alex leaving the courthouse. Since the hospital in San Juan, it was the first time I'd seen him in street clothes. He wore dark jeans and a crisp white button-down as he shut himself inside a taxi.

His hair was shorter than I'd ever seen it. He'd cut it since those last glimpses I'd had of him on the news. It would have been barely long enough to hold between my fingers.

"Turn it up," Mom said.

Henri fumbled with the remote. The volume surged and the newscaster said the word I'd wished for: *exonerated*.

Our shocked laughs became gasps that faded into stunned, euphoric silence.

He was free and not broken and ready to move on. My relief burned so bright, I was surprised at the shadow it cast.

I'd been so worried about wanting Alex to have his life back that it hadn't occurred to me that his life probably wouldn't include me. What we had on the island, I never questioned if it was real—it was—but maybe it wasn't something we could sustain in a landlocked world.

I was only sixteen. In a year and a half I'd have the freedom I was already starting to crave.

As the broadcast threw out theories—that Alex had information and had cut a deal, that the police didn't have probable cause for the search of Alex and Casey's apartment—Mom said, wet eyes on the screen, "You must be relieved, Em."

Tears leaked down my cheeks, and I laughed through them, gave my mom my most brilliant smile.

Henri just came up behind me, rested her chin on my shoulder, and sighed. I could feel her smile too.

One August afternoon, I was standing in the checkout line with Mom as she checked her grocery list. "Parmesan. Basil . . ." My dad was coming to dinner and Italian was his favorite. "The marinara," she said, glancing to the three carts ahead of us. "I forgot it."

"I'll get it," I said. "Stay in line."

In aisle 9, between the soda and candy, I froze.

Mr. Flynn wore a Violent Femmes T-shirt and a pair of

ripped jeans as he thumbed through a copy of *Rolling Stone*. At his feet was a bundle of bananas balanced on top of a case of Stella Artois.

If I just kept walking, he would never see me. But I stood still in the aisle, alone with my shame and his and Henri's, as his gaze drifted my way.

He did a double take and put the magazine back on the rack. His eyes were sad at first, but he gave me a faint smile as he raised his hand in a small wave. Before I could wave back, he lifted his chin and headed for the registers. Forgiveness didn't take an island for Mr. Flynn.

Then again, we weren't sisters.

CHAPTER 38

M y first day of senior year at Baird, I stepped off the BART platform and onto the train for the first time in my life alone. Lights flickered in and out as the train plunged underground.

This ride, I'd worried about making it for a full year. Now I was choosing it.

Mom gave me the option of going back to school or doing homeschooling till graduation. I chose school. My teachers had let me take my junior year finals at the end of summer so I could go right into senior year. It felt like I'd bubbled Scantron boxes haphazardly, but somehow when I logged into the Baird grading system, I saw I'd passed all my classes.

I took out my phone to check the time, and even though I had just cleaned out my in-box, a little red 1 hovered over the mail icon.

The liquid pulse of my heart filled my ears as I noticed the name of the sender. *Alex.*

The train car was less than half full, but I glanced around. This was for me and only me.

With my upper back pressed against the window, my book bag in my lap, and my feet in the seat beside me, I opened the message.

Jones,

If you're reading this, Henri wasn't just messing with me when she got in touch and told me how I could find you. I hope it's you—I don't think even the cruelest parts of your sister could joke about something as important as this.

I guess you know about the deal I cut. I've been working a lot since I got out—three (legitimate!) jobs. The rickshaw is the best of my gigs because once in a while, my tires hit the sidewalk between that resort and Luquillo Beach and I remember meeting you. I work so hard because the busier I stay, the easier it is to forget about an island that's otherwise always on my mind.

This island, it's not as sunny or warm as ours, but it's also a real nightmare to escape. I have almost enough in the bank to make it out your way. Maybe you'll consider another boat ride with me? Rumor has it the Alcatraz tour meets at Pier 33.

Alex

The train rattled to a stop and I slipped my phone into my bag. All the missing parts of me were slowly drifting back.

"Emma?"

Sareena Takhar stood in the aisle in her Baird uniform, the paper cup in her hands sending up tufts of steam, and a book bag on her shoulder.

"Hey." I hadn't seen Sareena since before the accident, and I'd never seen her on this train before. "I didn't know you lived around here."

"Oh, I didn't last year. We moved this summer. My parents want something smaller since I'm going to college next year. Less of an empty nest to cry over, I guess." She smiled.

The doors sounded the warning they were about to close, and I dropped my feet off the seat so she could sit beside me.

"I didn't know if you'd be at Baird this year," she said. "After everything. Before Mick and Ari left, we were all totally glued to CNN." She smiled as she peeled the sleeve off her drink. "Ari wasn't exactly a fan of Henri's sudden fame."

"No surprise there," I said as the train gained speed for the short trip to Baird.

"But I wasn't much of a fan of Ari's, so . . ." Sareena shrugged, and I had to laugh.

"Where did Mick and Ari go?" I asked.

"Mick took the band on the road—get ready for Ambisextrous, unsuspecting ears—and Ari moved to LA early."

"Get ready for Ari, Los Angelenos."

"For real," she said, and laughed. "What's Henri doing?"

"Prague right now. Then she's taking the train to Vienna."

Henri had thought about what I'd said that first night on the raft. Mom and Dad weren't happy, but her therapist agreed and so did I that Henri needed to do something that was hers and hers alone. Even though I'd miss her, maybe backpacking through Europe was the answer.

As the train stilled at our stop, Sareena scooped her dark hair over her shoulder and slipped on her book bag. "I'm glad you decided to come back, Emma."

Fog melted off the warming sidewalks outside Civic Center Station, and as Sareena and I moved toward Baird, I saw myself in the year ahead—dizzy and dancing, music pulsing into my chest so hard, I didn't know where the song ended and my heartbeat began. My mailbox, flowing with thick envelopes from universities, full of risk and independence and tiny towns and huge cities. Camera clicks inside a photo booth in Chinatown, striking poses between bright flashes. The boat to Alcatraz, salty air whipping tangles into my hair as I stared into the ocean, with familiar hands on my waist, anchoring me to the world. The sun rising over a San Francisco rooftop after a Saturday night that lasted so long, it bled into Sunday morning.

In stunning clarity, there it was—I didn't even have to be clairvoyant to see it—the wonder of what was soon to be my now.

ACKNOWLEDGMENTS

Bringing *A Map for Wrecked Girls* into the world involved many people coming together, each lending me their individual talents and unfailing support. This book will forever hold a small piece of all of them, and for that, I'm eternally grateful.

First, to Melissa Sarver White, my tireless agent, fiercest advocate, and kindred spirit. Without her advocacy and guidance, I'm certain this story would be just another file on my computer. I can't thank her enough for restoring my confidence in my work and changing my life.

Working with my dedicated editor, Jessica Dandino Garrison, has been a constant joy—she might be the kindest person in publishing. I have been so astoundingly lucky to benefit from her editorial skills, perfectionism, and unwavering excitement. Heartfelt gratitude to Jess for loving even the most broken parts of this story and knowing exactly how to make them whole.

Lauri Hornik, Namrata Tripathi, Dana Chidiac, and the entire brilliant team at Dial Books, for the dream come true. I have admired Penguin authors from afar for all of my life—and they've made me one of them. A special thank-you to my copyeditor, Regina Castillo, whose attention to the details and timeline has been invaluable. My gratitude also goes to Elaine Damasco and Theresa Evangelista for the gorgeous cover, and to Mina Chung for the beautiful interiors. Thanks also to Penguin's dedicated Publicity, Marketing, and Sales teams who've worked so hard for this book.

Many thanks to everyone at Folio Literary Management—I couldn't be prouder to be part of the Folio family. Lisa Mulcahy, thank you for your help in whipping the manuscript into shape.

I would be lost without these talented friends who read early versions of this story and offered advice: Julie Murphy, always the first eyes on the roughest of my words, for forcing me to push myself further, and for offering years of direction and dozens of cupcakes. My dear friend and the brightest spot of sunshine in YA, Stephanie Garber—it has been a comfort to share our lows and the delight of my life when our highs collided. Alexis Bass, the Rachel to my Monica, for early insights that improved this story greatly and gave me the confidence to pursue finding an agent. I. W. Gregorio, for extending her medical expertise to the story and for her friendship.

I'll always be indebted to Kim Culbertson for taking the time to talk to me about writing all those years ago and befriending a clueless fangirl. Authors like Kim are the best thing about the book world.

I'm lucky to call myself a friend to many gifted authors who were guiding lights through an uncertain time: Stacey Lee, Jennifer Mathieu, Sabaa Tahir, Joanna Rowland, Kelly Loy Gilbert, Valerie Tejeda, Janelle Weiner, Rose Cooper, Katie Nelson, Jenny Lundquist, Shannon Dittemore, Sarah Clift, Kristin Dwyer, and Adrienne Young.

My lifelong friends, Allison Fuller, Ardeep Johal, and Vishaal Pegany, thank you for all the nights we felt infinite.

Endless love and gratitude to my parents, who have given me more than anyone deserves. Their most incredible gift has been their limitless support and encouragement. Because of them, I have the luxury of waking up every day and doing what I love.

JESSICA TAYLOR adores atmospheric settings, dangerous girls, and characters who sneak out late at night. She lives in Northern California, not far from San Francisco, with a law degree she isn't using, one dog, and many teetering towers of books.

Connect with Jessica online:

jessicataylorwrites.com

🐦 @JessicaTaylorYA

📘 @JessicaTaylorYA

📷 @JessicaTaylorWrites

𝐭 @JessicaTaylorWrites

📌 @novelista85